D0455457

The Secret Stream

Books by Marcel Aymé

THE SECRET STREAM

THE SECOND FACE

THE WONDERFUL FARM

THE MIRACULOUS BARBER

THE BARKEEP OF BLÉMONT

THE TRANSIENT HOUR

The Secret Stream

Marcel Aymé

Translated from the French
by Norman Denny

HARPER & BROTHERS, NEW YORK

Library of Congress catalog card number: 53-11828

The Secret Stream

ONE

THE TAG FELL on Buquanant. They could have got on very well without him, but he had attached himself to the gang as they came out of school and had followed them to the blind alley which formed a part of the Rue de l'Herbe-Sèche. He started by saying that it was a very funny thing that out of seven of them he should be the one to be chosen. They replied that if he didn't like it he had only to go home, back to his own quarter, which he seemed to be so fond of, always swanking about being out every evening with street urchins and tramps and vagabonds. He might as well go straight there, like he generally did. Nobody had asked him to come with them.

'O.K.,' said Buquanant. 'I'm not saying there was anything wrong about it. I'm not saying.'

Without haste he pulled up his black overall, tying the ends behind his back. The others, already in line, showed signs of impatience; but before taking his place he made sure that he had his purse safe, and he fastened his pocket with a safety-pin. Just for the four sous that he had in it! Nobody was going to rob him. At last he bent forward so that his shoulders were level with his behind, and said as he covered his head, 'I bar squeakers and bangers,' by which he meant that no one might speak or hit him, or else they would have to take his place.

Charnotey, who was first in line and just getting ready to jump, exclaimed :

7

'You aren't allowed to bar squeakers and bangers both at once.'

'Not allowed?' said Buquanant, straightening up.

'No. Not allowed.'

'Pretty bossy, aren't you? Why aren't I allowed? Go on, you tell me!' Buquanant grinned, trying to bring the others in on his side. 'Go on! You say I'm not allowed. So I'm asking why.'

Charnotey gazed steadily at him, then shrugged his shoulders and said, turning to the others :

'Talk about an ape!'

His nostrils quivered with disdain, and there was a murmur of approval from the rest of the row. The gang really all agreed with Charnotey. With only a wretched half-hour to spare after school—and even this would have to be accounted for to their parents—they didn't want to waste time arguing. Buquanant was more afflicted by their support for Charnotey than by the insult. He turned pale, and advancing upon him with clenched fists said in a threatening voice :

'Say that again!'

The line broke up in order to form a circle. Charnotey, feeling a slight weakness at the knees, replied feebly :

'All right, I'm saying it again.'

'Well, go on, say it, instead of just saying you're saying it.'

'I tell you, I'm saying it again.'

'Just the same, you haven't said it, so you're a funk!'

Buquanant uttered an offensive laugh which made more than one of them ponder. Nevertheless, Charnotey felt that he had got out of the difficulty by sufficiently honourable means.

'I'm not climbing down,' he said in a mild voice. 'I'm only saying that no one's allowed to bar squeakers and bangers both at once. So then you say, why not? But what am I supposed to answer? That's just the way it is.'

8

'Quite right,' said Pucelet, a sturdy hanger-on more than half a head taller than the rest.

Without contradicting himself, without seeming to have given anything away, Charnotey had contrived to reinstate himself in the esteem of the party.

'If that's the way it is, well that's the way it is,' he added.

Again he received a murmur of approval. Buquanant, finding that he had been tricked out of his victory, burst again into a rage.

'And if I sock you on the jaw,' he said, 'I suppose that'll be the way it is!'

Charnotey shook his head in a manner designed to reconcile dignity with his desire not to make things worse. The others had drawn back a little to leave space for the two adversaries, and there was an interval of complete silence. All eyes were upon Buquanant's right fist, which he drew slowly back under his armpit, partly to gain impetus but also to allow Charnotey time to get ready. And that was decent of him. One could say what one liked about Buquanant, but he wasn't the sort to strike a foul blow. Meanwhile Charnotey took up his guard with a despairing slowness, knowing that he lacked the heart to do effective battle. He would get a bloody nose, and he would simply push out his two fists weakly, like a girl. His eyes besought help from his friends, especially from Pucelet, whose strength might save him. But Pucelet did not respond, and he turned to Rigault, but without seriously hoping that a boy so reserved would want to intervene in a matter of this kind. Rigault, however, understood his distress and took pity on him. As Buquanant extended his left arm he broke out of the circle and stepped between them.

'Stop it,' he said. 'You're spoiling the game for everyone.'

Charnotey dropped his arms at once, and his fists opened,

9

the five fingers spread, with a haste that made the others smile. Buquanant maintained his boxer's stance, but he gazed at Rigault without anger, rather with a shy friendliness. Antoine Rigault was a likeable boy, a bit melancholy, not given to causing any kind of disturbance, and even the boldest were inclined to be shy with him. Even at the height of the roughest sort of game, when they were on the verge of tearing each other to shreds, he was able to keep calm and a little detached. No one had ever had a grievance against him. He was good at school work, and did not mind if his neighbour copied his composition; and although he never joined in an organised rag, he accepted the penalties without complaining. A fine runner, too, however soft he might look!

Buquanant fell back into a pacific attitude, and Charnotey, regaining his confidence, called Rigault to witness that it was against the rules to bar squeakers and bangers at the same time. Antoine Rigault, forced into the role of arbiter, was for a moment embarrassed. He felt sure that Buquanant had only followed the gang in order to interfere with its arrangements. To uphold him was in a sense unjust. Nevertheless, and knowing this, Antoine felt obliged to support him, simply because he thought that in this particular matter he was right.

'You can play it any way you like,' he said. 'It all depends on what's been agreed. You have to agree to start with.'

Buquanant's face became radiant, and he gave Antoine a look of admiration which he somewhat exaggerated.

'So I was right all the time,' he said. 'We've got to decide what you can bar and what you can't. But then he went and called me an ape, and——'

'Well, let's decide,' said Antoine. 'What are we going to bar?'

The mortified Charnotey did not reply. He waited, pre-

pared to walk disdainfully off if the decision was not in
accordance with custom; but here again he was disappointed.

'Round where I live,' said Buquanant, 'you're allowed to
bar squeakers and bangers. But if you play it differently I
don't mind. We've just got to agree, like Rigault says.' He
smiled at Antoine with a warm friendliness; and before
resuming his place—just to prove that he didn't care for
either squeakers or bangers, so long as justice was done—
he added generously: 'I'm barring tails-up and left-leg-
forward.'

From then on he was all gaiety and amiability, and they
started calling him 'Buq' again, as they had done in the old
days. At half-past four Pucelet, who had a watch, warned
everyone that it was time to go home; but the game was
going so well that they decided to take an extra ten minutes.
Only Antoine seemed, not vexed but worried by the prolongation.

After playing ordinary leap-frog they played statue-
jumping. Each jumper had to stay rigidly in the position in
which he had landed. It was not so easy for the last jumpers,
because the space became narrow between the 'mule' who
was jumped over and the motionless forms of those who
had jumped. Antoine was the last of all. Buq, who was
fourth, had just jumped with a generous attempt to leave
as much room as possible for the others. Pucelet followed,
and stayed motionless with a hand between his thighs,
laughing at the top of his voice at a gesture of which the
obscenity was, to tell the truth, not very clear. Before taking
his turn Antoine looked for a vacant space between the
statues, and it seemed to him that something moved at his
feet. It was a dark shadow shaped like a head. He turned
round and saw, silhouetted against the sun in the entrance
to the blind alley, the tall form of Sergeant Maillard, of the

11

municipal police. The huge man did not seem to be aware of his surprise, or even of his presence. The gaze of his big blue eyes passed from the group of statues to a side wall where the panes were lacking from several windows. He himself had the immobility of a statue, except that on his broad torso, enwrapped in the tunic of black cloth, the row of silver buttons writhed like a lazy serpent to the deep rhythm of his breathing. Antoine lowered his eyes, uncertain what attitude to adopt. The sergeant was showing the greatest interest in the broken panes of the empty house, and his curiosity could scarcely fail to be dangerous. If he began to ask questions, which of them could be sure of keeping his head ? Antoine felt a clutching at his heart. Just because he had once joined with the other boys in breaking window-panes—just one single time ! . . . If the matter were reported at the police station, and so came to his father's ears, he would pay dearly for the fun of that riotous moment.

Charnotey, with his back bent and his hands on his thighs, was still awaiting the last jumper. Wondering at the pause, he glanced round, saw Maillard, and straightened up at once looking uncomfortable. The others felt that something was going on behind their backs, but suspecting a trap they stayed fixed in the attitudes which the game prescribed. After waiting a whole minute Buq turned, and at first forgot to be angry at the sight of the sergeant. He recovered almost at once, and said to Antoine :

' Well, what are you waiting for ? '

' I'm ready,' said Antoine with a show of unconcern.

But Charnotey was plainly reluctant to go on. Moreover, the other statues were coming to life, and seeing Maillard they forgot the game at once. Buq was sickened by the sight of them—the bunch of fools, letting the sergeant see they were frightened ! It was easy for him to be indignant. Not having taken part in the stoning of the windows, he had nothing to fear. Maillard, still unspeaking, pulled his tobacco pouch out of the pocket of his huge blue trousers cut to a hussar pattern, and began to roll a cigarette. The silver double-chevrons of his rank shone on the dark cloth of his sleeves. The state of confusion into which his mere presence had thrown the gang seemed to please him, for he wore a satisfied smile. Antoine had stayed where he was, but the others had moved so adroitly that they were now all drawn up behind Pucelet, whose tall form hid the entire row; and he, the one who always followed, half-innocent, one hand still clutching between his thighs, was gazing at the sergeant without realising that he served as a screen for the rest. The whole thing was so ridiculous that Buq couldn't stand it. He went towards Maillard, and said, throwing back his head :

' Sergeant, won't you go away ? We don't like being disturbed when we're playing.'

Maillard looked down with an air of astonishment. His forehead wrinkled under the peak of his cap. He glanced quickly at the broken windows, and it seemed that his anger must break out ; but instead he gave a great laugh which exposed his gums as far back as the molars. Turning away, he walked with long, leisurely strides into the Rue de l'Herbe-Sèche, where they could hear him still laughing.

' That's the way I treat coppers,' said Buq to the others. ' Maillard needn't think he can scare me. I've seen plenty down in the Malleboine quarter.'

However, when he learned that the gang had done some window-bashing the week before he admitted that if he had known this he might have been more cautious. The boys hurriedly picked up their books and satchels, fearing that Maillard might yet return. Soon Buq and Antoine were alone in the blind alley with big Pucelet, who said in a confidential voice :

' I've got some photos—five sous each . . .'

The son of a photographer, he sneaked photographs of the prettier clients out of his father's studio and sold them to his schoolfellows to raise pocket-money. When Buq and Antoine refused, he offered to lead them into a passage-way which was particularly dark and deserted; and being again refused he went there himself with a haste which was unaffected by their disapproval.

Turning his back on his accustomed route, Buq walked with Antoine along the Rue de l'Herbe-Sèche. They wanted to talk about their friendship, but hardly knew how to begin. Finally Buq said:

'You'd do far better to come down where I live at four o'clock, instead of wasting half an hour with that gang of idiots. Even if you did break some windows the other day, you've only done it once. In our quarter we have real fun.'

'It's too far,' said Antoine. 'I should hardly have time to stay a quarter of an hour. Even as it is I've got a mile and a half to go to get home. There's always a row when my father finds I've got back late. And I never know whether my mother's going to give me away or not. Sometimes she tells him everything, and sometimes she doesn't.'

Coming from Antoine, who so rarely departed from his attitude of extreme reserve, this was a very exceptional confidence. Buq showed by his silence that he understood its value. He tried to picture his friend's loneliness, living with censorious parents at the dividing line between the town and the plain, in a little outcropping of suburb where liveliness was rare and the countryside forbidding. Having seen him several times in company with Antoine, he thought of the elder Rigault as a tiresome, stiff-necked man with a flavour of dreary work about him. And he thought of his own mother, the Widow Buquanant, as the legend ran on the printed letter-paper of her dyeing and cleaning business: when he entered the shop on returning from school she welcomed him with a youthful smile and her face became suddenly tranquil and happy, as though she had spent all the afternoon awaiting that moment. Buq turned his head towards Antoine, and encountered a look which seemed to be an apology for bringing nothing to their friendship but constraint and melancholy. He passed an arm round the other boy's neck with an entirely feminine gesture which showed his mother's influence, and which was surprising in a boy generally so rough in his manner. Antoine, whose family life had scarcely prepared him for such effusiveness, felt the kindness all the more. It seemed to him that the simple and candid gesture instantly dissolved the shyness which on other occasions had always stifled his impulses at their birth.

'Honestly,' said Buq, 'you ought to come to my house. If it's just a matter of time, I could take you home in ten minutes on the back of my bike, so you see you'd gain by it.'

Antoine was weakening. Buq completed his seduction by describing the delights of the Malleboine quarter, which were for the most part indescribable. There were no words to convey the charm of those narrow, crowded streets—the Rue de la Clé-d'Or, the Rue du Sire-de-Roulans, the Ruelle du Rus, the Rue des Nonettes, the Rue du Papegai or the Passage du Vert-Vert. They brought a new savour to the simplest, stalest games, and one could be happy in them simply doing nothing. Despite the time he had been playing in that quarter, Buq maintained that he still did not know it thoroughly because of all the passages, the unexpected alleyways and houses with two entrances.

'And sometimes not only two, but three and even four. It's like the underground stream. I can't say I know the underground stream.'

'The underground stream?' said Antoine with a thrill of curiosity.

'Yes, the underground stream. You know the place where the Sourdine flows into the river? Yes, you do—just by the bridge. Well, before it gets there it runs between the houses for about two hundred yards; and before that it runs under the Upper Town. I've seen the place where it comes out of the rocks—a great black hole . . .' Lowering his voice, himself stirred by the evocation of these shades, Buq went on: 'It seems that in the old days there was a fortified castle near where the station is, and the *oubliettes* dropped down into the underground stream. I've even heard that they weren't all blocked up. It's quite possible, you know. And I've an idea that if one followed it to its source one might find a grotto, or perhaps catacombs . . .'

Overwhelmed by the splendour of this vision, Antoine inquired timidly:

'Hasn't anyone tried?'

'The entrance is covered by a wire grill,' said Buq, 'and it isn't easy to get even that far. Still, one might be able to find a way . . .'

'Of course,' said Antoine warmly.

They looked gravely at one another, and after a long silence Buq went on:

'You can't just *imagine* what the Malleboine is like. You've got to *know* it—the same as with girls.'

He allowed his gaze to follow a dog crossing the road, as though he thought nothing of those last words. Antoine prompted him:

'How do you mean, the same as with girls?'

'Well, girls . . . For instance, you take chaps like Charnotey. From the way they talk you'd think they'd all got girl-friends, but when one knows what really happens . . . Well, yesterday I saw a whole gang following the two Jaillet sisters and shouting things out behind their backs. Just shouting nonsense at them. And that's what they call having girl-friends ! It makes me laugh.' Buq permitted himself to laugh and repeated, shrugging his shoulders, ' Girl-friends ! . . .'

Antoine felt obliged to laugh too, but without much knowing to what he was committing himself.

' In our quarter,' Buq went on, ' we know what love is. We know what girls are. We play with them ; we talk to them just like I'm talking to you, and we say whatever we want to say. I've got a girl. Her name's Marie-Louise. I see her every day, and we play together or we go out for a walk. In the winter I mostly went out with her in the evening, round about six, when it was dark . . . You just don't know what it's like to go out for a walk with a girl after dark. It's marvellous ! '

Antoine, greatly stirred and trembling at the thought of the wonders assembled in the Malleboine quarter, felt ready to brave all perils, even, and above all, the paternal wrath. The underground stream excited him more than anything else. Not even a Marie-Louise could equal in his eyes that heroic and labyrinthine cavern where he imagined himself groping through darkness on the track of a mystery. Love, in such an adventure, could be no more than an added embellishment, a golden gleam snatched from terror and the night. He even saw himself forced to leave the enchanting captive at the mouth of the cavern after he had heroically rescued her. What else could he do ? He could not marry her, being only twelve ; and as for taking her home with him, he knew what his father would say . . .

' Girls . . .' he said dreamily aloud. ' Girls . . .'

Buq mistook the sense of this murmur, which really betrayed a celibate tendency. He thought Antoine was inviting further confidences, and taking him by the hand he asked in a rather solemn voice :

' Do you want to see something ? '

17

' What ? '

They had stopped on the pavement of the Avenue Raymond-Poincaré. Buq removed the safety-pin with which he had fastened one of the pockets of his shorts, and got out his purse. It was made of red leather, and had three compartments, in one of which there was a franc and in another a five-sous piece. He opened the middle section, murmuring :

' Look. I cut it yesterday.'

Antoine gazed, not unstirred, at a lock of fair hair tied with a white ribbon. A wisp of myosotis was attached to it, like a cornflower in a sheaf of wheat. Buq watched him with intent and rather anxious eyes.

' It's nice,' said Antoine.

' I cut it off yesterday, from the nape of her neck just by the ear. Gosh, how she jumped when she felt me cutting it ! '

Buq restored the purse to his pocket and then remarked that it must be getting late.

' My mother won't be at home all to-morrow afternoon,' said Antoine. ' I could come with you then.'

' To-morrow ? ' said Buq. ' But to-morrow's Saturday. I can't. I promised Marie-Louise we'd climb the cathedral tower. But why not come with us ? '

Antoine accepted, having never climbed the cathedral tower, and they parted on this understanding.

The Avenue Raymond-Poincaré was flanked by solid and simply-built villas as far as the edge of the town proper, but as one left the town behind the houses became skimped and tortuous in style. Jerry-building began to predominate. Amid their kitchen gardens, lacking in flowers and foliage, they had a sickly nakedness, the walls thin and rootless, porous and scrofulous. Antoine looked disdainfully at these dreary dwellings which as a rule he did not notice at all. He was angry with his father for having chosen to live in this borderland where the drab surroundings discouraged every adventurous impulse. His mind was filled with glowing thoughts of the Malleboine quarter, the warmth and humanity of that densely packed town within a town, striking down into the entrails of the earth. Absorbed with these thoughts he did not see coming towards him a man of about forty whose face and clothes were both remarkable. He wore a dark, wide damask stock on a very high collar, and under his black jacket a very light waistcoat with leather edging. Without making any concession to the current style, he was clad in a way that could disturb no one, and was not lacking in quiet elegance of a deliberately old-fashioned kind. A thin border of black beard framed his sensitive, intelligent face, and there was a great sweetness, an insistent kindness, in his gaze. As he drew near to Antoine he raised his bowler hat, disclosing a bald head.

'Excuse me, young man,' he said. 'I seem to be lost. It's a long time since I came to this part of the town, and I find that a lot of building has been done. I'm looking for the Chemin Emile-Voirot.'

Antoine, startled out of his day-dream, looked up and recognised Maître Marguet, the notary from the Rue Jacques-de-Molay. He had always been intrigued by this gentleman's old-world aspect, and he had a lively recollection of his charming house, where his father had taken him one day last year, when he had gone there on business connected with a small legacy inherited by his wife. He gave the necessary information, and the lawyer, without being able to place him, vaguely recalled having seen this child before. Fearing to offend, he did not ask his name, but took leave of him after ceremoniously thanking him. Antoine, who had never before been treated with so much consideration by a man that age, was charmed by his amiability and extreme courtesy.

Maître Marguet entered the Chemin Emile-Voirot, seeking as he did so to escape from his depressing surroundings by meditating on the hard lot of lawyers, whose fate it is to be castigated by right-minded citizens as the symbol of bourgeois tyranny and bigoted imbecility, and by wondering whether he really deserved to be so harshly judged. He considered these matters, never for an instant suspecting that he was destined on the morrow to commit an outrageous crime.

TWO

IN HIS INNERMOST heart Maître Marguet hoped for the failure of the negotiations he was entering into with old Butillat. Nevertheless he did his utmost to try and persuade the eighty-year-old gentleman to sell the two acres of land which he owned flanking the Rue Jouffroy. He used sound arguments, and his offer was enough to attract any reasonable man—three hundred thousand down, or annuity payments at the rate of forty thousand. Seated in iron chairs in the garden of the old man's cottage, the negotiators studied one another with great interest. Butillat's eye was ironical but not unkindly. Although he was firmly resolved not to sell, he was gratified by this confirmation of the value of his property. After listening to the lawyer's preliminary remarks, he said good-humouredly :

'I don't insist on knowing the name of your client, although I have a shrewd idea who it is. I might as well tell you at once that what you propose is out of the question. Considering how long the Municipality has been trying to get me out in order to build a school on my land, I'm certainly not going to let it go now, when the scheme's on the verge of being voted, at a third or a quarter the price I may expect to get later on ! '

He gave a little, excited laugh, and the eyes glittered slyly in his bony, parchmented face. As he regarded the little old man's head, dried-up in its fixed idea, Maître Marguet felt something like a shiver of pity and admiration.

It was clear that in this matter the money counted for almost nothing. For thirty years Butillat had lived in a state of poverty bordering on destitution while he nursed the hope of being expropriated by the town, and for a long time the amount of profit to be realised had been the least of his preoccupations. Rather than accept a good price from any other quarter, he was prepared to part with his plot of land to the town for a song. It was a passion as pure as that of an astronomer watching for the passing of a comet. At the beginning of their interview the lawyer had been afraid that the old man, tempted by the money, might give way and thus surrender his only reason for continuing to live. Had he done so, abandoning those two acres, that patch of waste land guarded at the cost of privation in the very heart of the town, and which invested him with an almost feudal dignity, he would have become nothing but an aged miser lacking the teeth to devour his hoard. Maître Marguet was relieved, although he was impelled by his professional conscience to go on pressing him.

At the end of an hour he had got nowhere. As he talked his eye wandered abstractedly over the confusion of small houses and kitchen gardens disposed in parallel rectangles between the Emile-Voirot road and the railway cutting. And while he was thus idly gazing he experienced a sudden, violent emotion, a shock whose succeeding waves seemed for some seconds to go on pounding against the inside of his skull. A man had appeared at the bottom of the garden, standing just beyond the wire fence with his back to the railway. He was a short and powerful figure, head and shoulders enormous, chest deep and arms very long, legs short and bowed. But his face was even more extraordinary. The bridge of the nose was sunken, forming a deep cavity between the protruding forehead and out-thrust lower jaw. All the contours were sharply defined, and any movement of the jaws brought about a strange modification of its whole aspect. Even in repose his face had a brutish ugliness that was at the same time simple and pitiful.

Maître Marguet knew the monster by sight, but had not seen him for a long time. He suddenly perceived in him an almost perfect resemblance to a stone figure carved in the lower part of one of the pillars of the cathedral. He was fond of visiting that devil starting out of the pillar and grimacing beneath the weight of the stone mass pressing on its shoulders. A poor, suffering and laughing devil, condemned, so long as cathedrals lasted, to offer nothing to the passer-by but a convulsed face : but in its tormented features there was an expression of humble warmth which touched the lawyer. He often seated himself beside the imprisoned demon, stroked it, worshipped it a little. He pitied it with all his heart for having to bear on its shoulders the humiliat-ing burden of a church ; and dreaming that he rescued it from the stony grip of the pillar, he offered it his hand that they might run together in pursuit of unbridled joys. It seemed at that moment that this fantasy was be-come fact, and that the demon of the cathedral, released by Maître Marguet's fervour, had come to bring him his reward.

The man leaned over the fence and called to its owner in a voice of such power that even he was slightly em-barrassed by it :

'Remember me, Monsieur Butillat ? It's me, Trousse-quin. I worked for you last year. I've just got back from my travels and I'm looking for more work. Is there anything I can do for you in the garden ? '

The old man shook his head, while a sudden anger dis-tended the veins on his forehead.

'Nothing for you ! ' he cried. ' All you can do is wreck everything. Clear out ! '

23

But his feeble voice did not reach the bottom of the garden. Troussequin persisted :

'I said the garden, but I'll do anything else you like. I wouldn't ask much.'

Maître Marguet, already shaken by the apparition, was overtaken with warm-hearted pity for the unhappy monster seeking a livelihood. It was at this moment that the idea came to him, an idea that seemed to burn through his whole flesh like a flame. It was even more than an idea ; it was an entire plan born of a sudden inspiration, and which he accepted without a second thought. In a dazzling vision of what was to take place he perceived the significance of certain familiar obsessions, of others more secret and less known, and felt them come purposefully together. The gesture with which he hailed Troussequin was the first step in an adventure of which even the smallest necessities were already plain to him. But he had sufficient self-control to conceal his feelings. He said to Butillat :

'Another poor devil out of work. We live in hard times, Monsieur Butillat. I'll see if I can do anything for him.'

'You're full of kindness,' sniggered the old man. 'A ne'er-do-well like this chap, who spends his whole time getting drunk and God knows what . . .'

'I know. But still . . . people have to live.'

Troussequin was climbing the wire fence with an ease which further enraged Butillat.

'Couldn't you have come round ?' he demanded.

Breathless after crossing the garden at a run, Troussequin humbly removed his cap and replied :

'I should have had to go by the road. I didn't want to keep Monsieur Marguet waiting. He might have been in a hurry ; he might have gone ; and then I'd have been out of work again. Out of work, you see, that's what I'd have been.'

The lawyer was staring at the monster with an eagerness of which he was suddenly aware. Veiling the light in his eyes, he said briskly :

'I called you because there's a small job which you might be able to do for me. I want someone to whitewash the tool shed in my garden. If you think you could do it——'

'You couldn't have found a better man,' said Troussequin. 'House-painting's the first job I ever did.'

'When can you begin ? '

'That's for you to say. I'm ready any time. To-morrow, if you like.'

'Very well then, come to-morrow. But we must fix the price. How much do you want ? '

Troussequin hesitated, swaying back and forth on his short, thick legs, while his face, torn between doubt and greed, became strained in a terrifying grimace.

'What about three francs an hour ? ' he at length asked tentatively. 'I'm a skilled man, you understand, and I wouldn't be fussy about the time. The odd quarter of an hour, or even half-hour, I wouldn't reckon that.'

Butillat silently moved his lips, hoping perhaps to make his indignation felt, while he gazed disgustedly at Troussequin. After a pretence at reflection, Maître Marguet agreed.

'All right, three francs an hour. By the way, what's your name ? '

'Troussequin. Marcel Troussequin, born in ninety-five, in the Rue du Sire-de-Roulans.' He made a movement as though to search his pockets, and went on with an air of embarrassment : 'I haven't got my papers on me, but I'll let you see them to-morrow. In any case, I know you well, and not just from the day before yesterday. I——'

'Good. Well, that's settled, Monsieur Troussequin, and I shall expect you to-morrow. You may go now.'

Troussequin thanked him warmly, and disregarding the

25

old man's protests made for the bottom of the garden and climbed the fence a second time. They saw him sit down on the path running beside the railway-line and take off one of his boots to examine the inside. He amused himself for a moment by studying a passing locomotive between his toes, and then he chatted with a worker on the line. Maître Marguet apologised to Butillat for having troubled him with the presence of Troussequin, who did not, he agreed, show a sufficient respect for other people's fences.

'You'll find that's not the only thing wrong with him,' said Butillat dryly. 'He worked for me a couple of days last year, and I don't intend to let it happen again. You'd hardly believe what a nuisance he was.'

'Let's hope he has improved,' said the lawyer. 'Otherwise, I shall feel that my visit to you has not been a very happy one. You've refused to meet me over this matter of the land, and so firmly that I must admit I have no great hopes.'

The last words, and the smile which accompanied them, placated the old man.

'At least you've given me the pleasure of a visit. I expect to return it very shortly. I have neglected to make a will, and I think I've been wrong not to do so. Supposing I die before being expropriated. My heirs wouldn't hesitate to sell the land to a private buyer—perhaps to your client, who would be clever enough not to let himself be expropriated . . . You may say that when one is dead those things don't matter, but——'

'On the contrary! Of course they matter!' protested Maître Marguet, who was obliged, like all lawyers, to believe that the dead are interested in the conduct of the living.

He gently dissuaded the old man from disinheriting the poor souls who for twenty years had been looking forward to his death ; and having taken leave of him, and regaining the Chemin Emile-Voirot, he relaxed after the effort which the last minutes of the interview had cost him. Several times, with all his thoughts elsewhere, he had let slip the opportunity of a reply, or had checked himself on the verge of speaking the words that were teeming in his bewitched mind. Now that he had escaped he could murmur them under his breath and revel in the violent images they conjured up. But prudence was still necessary. Butillat might be watching him from one of his windows. Other people might observe him from the neighbouring houses ; and the nearer he drew to the centre of the town, the greater was the danger.

So with his head seething the lawyer walked at his accustomed pace, his eye watchful for all encounters. He raised his hat, smiling with apparent unconcern ; but such was his state of inward disturbance that he trembled at the thought of being spoken to. At about half-past six he came in sight of the T.D.C. factory, whose manager was expecting him. While he was still some way off he recognised one of the office staff, a man named Rigault, who was standing in the gateway talking to another employee. Maître Marguet knew Antoine's father in his professional capacity. It seemed impossible to avoid saying a word to him, the more so since Rigault, on the threshold of the factory where he worked, was in a sense at home. In any case he did not care to wound, even slightly, a man whom he knew to hunger for other people's recognition. But the thought of entering upon a conversation in public, and at such a moment, filled him with an alarm that was almost panic. In order to gain time and recover his self-possession, he turned down a side-street and made a considerable detour which would eventually bring him back to the road he had left.

Rigault was nearly half an hour late. He had been helping

to trace an error which had crept into the monthly statement, and although the matter was not his responsibility
he had stayed in the dispatch department until half-past six.
He had done more than duty or even friendship required,
for it was he who had drawn attention to the error in the
first place, after glancing over a column of figures of which
only the total concerned him. Standing in the gateway of the
factory, Musson, the culprit, was paying tribute to Rigault's
alertness, which had saved him from serious trouble.

'If it hadn't been for you the statement would have gone
to the Paris office just as it was. It might have got me the
sack, and yet it's the sort of thing that could happen to
anyone. When the total's right one doesn't think of the
possibility of two mistakes cancelling out—or if anyone
does, it's because they've got a nose for figures, like you
have, Monsieur Rigault.'

Musson's young face was glowing with gratitude, but
Rigault responded coldly.

'If you paid more attention to what you're doing, other
people wouldn't have to waste their time clearing up after
you. I might add that you aren't paid eight hundred francs
a month just to amuse yourself.'

Musson blushed, caught out with a smile still on his lips.
He felt badly let down and angry with Rigault for not
having known how to live up to his esteem. For a moment
he was silent, half-remorsefully conscious of a renewed stir
of the antipathy he had always felt for his colleague. As
they separated he made an effort and managed to say:

'Well, thanks again. You did me a great service.'

'You may well say so,' said Rigault.

Musson flushed a little more, hesitating between a sharp
retort and a last impulse of gratitude. Finally, after shaking
hands, he made off for the centre of the town, to stare at
the women in the High Street until dinner-time. Rigault

had a moment of suspecting that he had hurt his feelings, but all things considered he did not regret it. The youth was altogether too familiar. In any case he was angry with him for having made him late, because he had been invited by the mayor to take coffee at his house after dinner.

On the death of his father-in-law, who had been vice-president of the Freethinkers and an influential member of the Radical Party, Rigault, rather in his own despite, had inherited his political opinions and certain trifling obligations. On the day of the funeral itself, Philippon, the mayor of the town, had talked to him at the cemetery as to a pillar of the Party, and had thus made sure of his political support. Small tasks were entrusted to him of the kind in which dutiful spirits excel, such as that of influencing the mood of a meeting by cries of approval or protest delivered in unison at appropriate moments. The mayor's invitation had undoubtedly been prompted by something of this kind, and Rigault expected to meet other devotees of the cause at his house.

His way home took him across the New Town and along the extension of the Avenue Raymond-Poincaré, before he reached his house on the Route Nationale. Once again he debated the thorny problem of acquiring a bicycle. It was not the cost that worried him, but the fact that no senior member of the staff of the T.D.C. factory had ever possessed one. Only the workmen and a few very young clerks rode home on bicycles. This was purely fortuitous, and Rigault knew perfectly well that there was no reason in principle why a senior employee should not do so. But although reason might convince him of the necessity of using a bicycle, the fact remained that the best people did not. Rigault sought to excuse his childishness by telling himself that he was modestly trying to behave like everyone else, but he knew in his heart that he was swayed by a tyrannous vanity.

As he entered the Rue Gustave-le-Bon he saw Maître Marguet at the far end, walking on the opposite pavement. He never encountered him without a twinge of anxiety. The fact was that sometimes the lawyer recognised him, and returned his greeting or even anticipated it, and sometimes he passed by without noticing him. The thing might be accidental, or it might be capricious (he himself never failed to recognise the town's leading figures, some instinct warning him, even when his thoughts were elsewhere, to raise a hand to his hat). Rigault kept his head carefully rigid, glancing furtively sideways to see what the other did. The lawyer was walking with his eyes lowered, seeming very preoccupied. Deciding that the raising of his hat would probably go unnoticed, Rigault resolved to begin this gesture only at the last moment, which left him the possibility of completing it or abolishing it by pretending to scratch his ear. But then a reasonless, almost religious apprehension caused him to hurry his movements. They were still four paces removed from the orthodox, level position when his hand went to his head. Maître Marguet, on the opposite pavement, looked up and replied with an ample gesture; and Rigault, instantly relaxed, felt a wave of well-being pass through him. It was more than gratified vanity : it was the sweetness of a response, the fulfilment of a social instinct. He was suddenly conscious of the tenderness of the season. Like a slice of lemon, the spring made his mouth water.

He walked under the chestnuts bordering the Avenue Poincaré with a lightness of heart that he did not remember ever feeling before. He thought lovingly of the wife and son awaiting him. The delicate green of the young shoots brought to his lips a snatch of a street song which he had not known he knew. He rebuked himself for childishness, but with an indulgence which in itself was strange.

When he reached the railway bridge he leaned over the parapet to watch a train pass through the cutting. And suddenly his heart froze. Down below, on the path beside the railway-line, he saw Troussequin. The monster was rolling along on his bow-legs, his head wagging, as though he too were preoccupied with a song. Rigault started back, but not quickly enough to avoid being seen. He heard Troussequin cry :

'Fabien! Hey, Fabien! Wait for me, you old rascal! It's me, Troussequin!'

Fortunately one could only get from the pathway to the road by means of a long detour. Rigault bolted for his home, which was only a few hundred yards off. He had forgotten his happiness, and did not even regret its passing. He was appalled merely by the abrupt reappearance of a man from whom he had nothing serious to fear. It was like the sudden, acute return of an old illness which one had thought forgotten, a hand of torment pointing towards death. When he reached his house he looked round. Five hundred yards behind him Troussequin was approaching with great strides, and signalling with his hand—or with his fist.

THREE

MAITRE MARGUET ENTERED the yard of the T.D.C. factory with a sense of relief. He felt that he could not have managed to get all the way home without betraying the fever that consumed him. His forthcoming business talk with the factory manager would restore his confidence, and being reabsorbed in professional matters he would be able to forget the strange crisis that had overtaken him. As he crossed the empty yard accompanied by the caretaker, he tried to recall the details of his interview with old Butillat, so as to be able to render the manager a full account. But his memory was not working well. He was still distracted by the picture of Troussequin at the edge of the railway cutting.

Devard, the manager, received him with a deferent courtesy, and waited for him to take his time in coming to business. Maître Marguet was conscious of the civility, but unmoved by it. He had a lively dislike of the people in the higher ranks of industry, who owed their position to aptitudes of an over-specialised kind which could be detected at a glance. Devard, despite his good manners and his sensitive hands, seemed to him to be without light or shade. His alert, youthful figure, his precise, intelligent gaze and economy of word and gesture, placed him in the lawyer's eyes in a certain category of lucid, limited beings lacking in the refinements of ignorance and the prudent, slowly-shaped passions of the ruminative bourgeois, who wishes to discard nothing but seeks to live in the present moment through all the ages of his life. Secretly Maître Marguet refused to allow him the quality of a bourgeois, and rather disdained his activities.

' As I expected,' he said, ' M. Butillat is not at all disposed to sell. Ever since there was first talk of his being expropriated by the town he has clung to the idea of getting a huge sum in compensation, and he's more determined than ever to hang on. I'm bound to confess that if my offer has had any effect at all, it has been simply to make him more obstinate. Perhaps I should have taken a different line. If you hadn't been so anxious for a quick decision I might have gone to work more gradually, and . . .'

The manager's faint smile made him feel that it was unnecessary to continue. Devard seemed to be implying that to him matters of buying and selling had long ceased to be psychological problems, and had been raised above the level of horse-trading.

' You offered him three hundred thousand cash. That's a tidy sum for this M. Butillat, and more than the town would ever give him. The fact of getting a firm offer ought to induce him to make up his mind.'

' Undoubtedly it's in his interest to sell,' Maître Marguet agreed.

' Well then ? '

' Well, it's very simple. Butillat is convinced that the compensation will be far higher than any reasoned valuation might lead one to suppose. In short, he's an old man who has been waiting too long for the chance of doing a deal with the town. His imagination has run away with him. He——'

' All the same, he's not a fool or a half-wit,' the manager interrupted. ' Figures must mean something to him.'

Maître Marguet stayed silent for some moments, not in order to consider his reply but to reflect on what Devard had said. He seemed to see clearly in his attitude a definite need *not* to understand which was no doubt favourable to the exercise of authority.

'You're quite right,' he said at length.

'Well?'

'As you say, Butillat is neither a fool nor a half-wit, and yet nothing will make him sell his land. I don't know if I can make you understand. Butillat derives no pleasure from the mere thought of selling. Yes, that's it—no pleasure whatever . . . Although, mark you, he listened to my arguments with great interest. He even made a very shrewd remark. "Why the devil," he asked, "should your client want to buy a plot of land from which he will be expropriated in a few months? It can only be because he expects to make a large profit." I naturally assured him that we were certain the town would never buy that particular plot. But it was a defeat. I could see my reply hadn't convinced him.'

'Any more than you were convinced yourself,' said Devard. 'And yet you were telling him the truth. If we were to buy that land the town would never turn us off it. It's in the town's own interest that the factory should grow and overflow on to that plot. We should employ more workers, and under better conditions than we can create for them with our present limited space.'

'Precisely,' said the lawyer. 'It's a pity M. Butillat should be so obstinate. But at least it is some consolation to me to feel that the economic crisis hasn't affected you. I'm glad I can congratulate you on that.'

'Don't deceive yourself, Maître Marguet, we're affected like everyone else. This plan to expand is really part of a larger scheme for regrouping our factories because the company can no longer carry the overheads of some of the smaller and less productive units. In short, it's a matter of increased centralisation. There's no secret about it.'

'Then if I follow you correctly,' said Maître Marguet,

34

'it depends on M. Butillat and the town whether this particular unit will continue to function at all? That is more serious than I thought.'

Devard appeared irritated at hearing the matter stated in these categorical terms, the more so since he seemed to catch a note of irony in the lawyer's voice.

'Things aren't really as simple as all that,' he said. 'At present we're simply a little apprehensive. In any case, that's between ourselves.'

Maître Marguet noted that it was nearly seven and began to think of taking his leave. He replied absentmindedly when the manager went on to talk about the forthcoming election to fill the vacancy caused by the death of the local Deputy. Parliamentary elections interested him scarcely at all. He was one of the two hundred electors who voted communist. He did it from perversity, simply for the pleasure of being opposed to the people of his own world. Devard tried to get a little information out of him concerning the Radical candidate, but he was less well-informed than most people and replied that it didn't matter anyway, because the Radical was sure to be elected no matter what he was like. He knew quite well that this was beside the point, and that the manager was chiefly interested in the personality of the candidate and the petty intrigues which had led to his being adopted by the Party.

'There's no one in the town who knows less about these things than I do,' Maître Marguet said. 'My business as a lawyer doesn't inspire confidence among the left-wingers, even when they're my clients. You've no idea how isolated I am. I have often heard it said that a lawyer's office is another kind of confessional, but personally I have never found it to be so. There's no more fantasy or freedom or abandon in the behaviour of a property-owner than there is in the contractions of his stomach. When a man comes to consult you about a legacy, for example, you may think that he's going to reveal the depths of his soul. But what he really shows you, although it's a shameful and secret aspect of his soul, is only what anyone else will show you in the same circumstances. What's more, doctors are in the same position as we are. The fact that their patients show them their physical weaknesses doesn't mean that they really get to know them. And I would be inclined to say that all this applies equally to priests. A confession is not a confidence.'

Seeing astonishment in Devard's eyes, Maître Marguet realised that he was beginning to let his tongue run away with him, and he hastened to take his leave. The state of exaltation which he had suppressed throughout this interview now took entire possession of him. As he passed through the factory gates he was alarmed by the feeling of sombre, impatient joy that perhaps showed itself on his face. He wanted to run, to chatter, to break out. Never had he felt so light-hearted, so brimming with life and bursting with eloquence. He found it hard to keep pace with the leaping flights of his imagination and the richness of his thoughts, which embraced a whole universe and yet dwelt upon its smallest details. Every movement of his mind conjured up a new image, a new sensation; and amid this tumult and abundance the figure of Troussequin traced a sure and secret path.

The passers-by became more numerous as he approached the centre of the town. He had to pay attention, return greetings, measure with care the extent of the gesture as he raised his hat, and modulate his smiles—behave, in short, so that people when they got home would say that they had seen nothing noteworthy in the town. After crossing the Rue des Rencontres, congested with the seven o'clock throng, he followed an alleyway which brought him to the cathedral, opposite one of the side doors. His house was on the other side, in the quiet Rue Jacques-de-Molay. Quite often he used the cathedral transept as a short cut, saluting the main altar with a rapid genuflexion as he passed.

He entered softly, seeking amid the shadowy zones for the pillar where he sometimes communed with the demon of stone ; but then he reflected that at that hour, and in that part of the church, the faithful would be awaiting their turn to confess. He went and knelt in the shadow of the pulpit, and clasped his hands. In front of him, in the first row of chairs and at the edge of the central aisle, a young woman in black was praying, her head resting on her shoulder and her eyes raised to the altar ; but her prayer was less ardent than the prayer of Maître Marguet. It was still light outside, but in the interior of the cathedral the approach of evening was beginning to extinguish the bright higher shafts of illumination, to veil the heavy and vivid glow of the stained-glass windows and to plunge the corners into darkness. Between the daylight and the light of the candles the shadows were already gathering, and the gilt of the altar shone upon the darkness of the apse. The lawyer summoned up a remnant of religious fervour, very catholic in its nature ; he played with words, with liturgical airs, with the odours of wax and incense, and aiding himself with ejaculatory prayers, called forth phantoms in the rich shadow and silence of the cathedral.

' Dear God, my heart goes out to you, my confidant, my beloved father, my outward seeming, my watching eye, my sweet habit and all my Sundays . . .

' Dear God, I am unworthy of your compassion, so unworthy that I do not ask it. I ask only for your indifference, I wish only to be forgotten . . .

' Dear God, my very dear God, my heart goes out to you. I writhe and crouch at your feet, in my filth and vileness, calling upon myself the spittle of your disdain . . .

'Dear God, could I achieve such happiness except by disgusting you ? You turn away your head, and my prayer falls at my feet. Dear God, I feel much better. How strong and terrible you are when you turn your back, but how much nicer you are ! . . .

'Dear God, my heart goes out to you from the mire of my infamy. I come to you accompanied by the creatures who fill my nights and my solitude. You look over your shoulder, and I will tell you who they are . . .

'This one is the baker in the Rue des Rencontres. I learned the other day that her name is Roberte Boulier. She's my sturdy one, Dear God, the surest, the one I see first in my dreams because of her wide hips and full breasts . . .

'This pale girl with the yellow scarf who walks with a clicking of sandals I saw one evening when I was passing through the Malleboine quarter. The autumn wind moulded her poor, thin skirt about her, making a deep, dark fold between her thighs—a picture for my nights, dear God . . .

'And here in a white apron is the little cheeky maid at the Frainels'. One evening when I was dining with them I trod on her foot as though by accident, and the cry she gave and her look of pain have brought life to the creatures of my sleeping and my waking dreams . . .

'Here are the three Janet sisters, my Sunday Mass. I cannot separate them . . .

'Dear God, dear God, how I love you ! Let me sweat on your feet ! . . .

'Then there is a graceful schoolgirl with fair hair on her calves, and the concierge at the Mairie, and the two Misses Vatard, the one chestnut, the other red-haired, and so puny, so humble, that they trouble me at times even when I am working. And so many others . . .

'You can see them all, dear God, startled and servile in the light of the candles ; and among them the one I have not named, the one you have chosen for me. Flesh and clothing tremble with horror in your divine light which draws a gleam from the metal of suspenders; and the dampness of their bodies steams on the altar-steps . . .

' Dear God, I have sniffed for so long at these feminine mysteries, I have suffered so much in daring from afar and in daring all things; now, from the depth of my despair, I see the dawning of the day of bounty. Dear God, you have told me that I am free, that the matter does not concern you. You have said so because you are kind, and because you want to make me love you more. Our Father Which art in Heaven . . .'

Maître Marguet unclasped his damp hands, tightly locked in invocation, and made the sign of the cross. He was deeply moved. Far more so than he had hoped. He closed his eyes for a minute to allow his fever to abate. Behind him, from the shadow of a side aisle, he heard a soft sound of footsteps and the scraping of chairs. He reflected that his wife was probably in the confessional, letting fall into the hairy ear of the Abbé Duperron the soft snow of her trifling sins. He would have liked to be able to hear, not from curiosity, but in order to marvel at the glowing whiteness of that child's soul against the heady obscurity of the cathedral. He uttered another prayer, addressing it to the Holy Virgin and beseeching her blessing upon his wife. Although he believed no more in the Virgin than in God the Father, he prayed with a fervour no less sincere than his feeling when he played the piano. He even thought, without precisely formulating the thought, of a chronic ulcer on his thigh which had troubled him for many years, in the hope that the Virgin's heart would be touched by his discretion. Finally, on the fourth level of his conscious-ness, he laughed at himself—telling himself, for example, that he would be a very bad catholic if he attributed to the divinity a taste for modesty and temperance. And so on.

Brushing as he passed against the young woman in black, who was still praying, he made a genuflexion before the main altar and went out by the little doorway on the right. At the entrance to the Rue Jacques-de-Molay, Sergeant Maillard, propped against his bicycle, was talking to Rebuchat, the process-server from the Place Aubert. To be exact, Maillard was doing more listening than talking. While he rolled a cigarette he swept the crossing with the stern, abstracted gaze that was customary with him. At the sight of him Maître Marguet felt a slight twinge of disquiet. His house was so near at hand that he had not troubled to compose his features when he left the church, and he feared that his face might be red and beaded with sweat. He prudently went off at an angle, in the direction of the pre-cinct, but when he had gone a few paces reflected that the nearness of his house made this an unnatural route to follow. So he resumed his original course, then veered again to the right, then to the left, and finally decided to go straight ahead. Agitated at the thought of this zigzagging carried out in full view of the sergeant, he forced himself to walk steadily ; but the pavement danced under his feet, and the whole crossing seemed to swing to and fro. Rebuchat raised his hat as he passed, thrusting his chest out. The sergeant, who would not, if he had been alone, have taken the liberty of saluting a gentleman of so much importance, raised a hand to his cap.

The danger past, Maître Marguet smiled at his own timidity. This childish fear of the policeman seemed to him charming. 'Danger is youth,' he reflected. 'Nothing else can enliven our feelings with the freshness of our early days.'

He had the presence of mind to avoid his neighbour, Crepel, the cathedral organist, who was probably in his cellar watching the passers-by through a periscope. This apparatus had been installed by Crepel for no unworthy purpose. It was not at all a matter of studying women's legs, but simply a way, at once scientific and original, of watching people pass. Whenever the lawyer appeared within his field of vision, he called him through a loud-speaker to come down and join him. Maître Marguet could not always refuse ; but although he counted him among his friends, he fought shy of the company of that impassioned music-lover, who firmly believed in his own genius and played the organ like a man exercising with dumb-bells. He passed close to the wall so as to defeat the periscope, and seemed to catch a murmur of disappointment from the loudspeaker.

Finally he reached his home. Tendrils of ivy and virginia-creeper made a thick curtain over the outer wall. Pushing open the door he entered a spacious courtyard flanked with a double row of trees and ornamented with flower-beds. The three-storey house was simple in its lines and well-proportioned, with a steep, sloping roof surmounted by tall, slender chimneys. It had been built in 1720. A few years before the war, Maître Marguet's father, while con-structing three attics for the accommodation of servants, had adorned it with a Renaissance pediment to frame the extra windows giving on to the façade. This embellishment was rendered the more unfortunate by the fact that when one entered the courtyard one was sufficiently far away to be able to take in the whole house at a glance.

Glancing at his watch, Maître Marguet saw that it was just seven o'clock, at which time the maids might be expected to be in the kitchen. He thought with a sudden surprise of how much he had done in half an hour, and ran over the items in his mind : a quarter of an hour with Devard, seven or eight minutes from the factory to the house, and about as long in the cathedral. The thought that a very considerable event might be confined within the space of a few minutes occurred to him as he walked up to the first floor, and it led him to certain conclusions of such significance that he had a feeling near to giddiness. He stood listening when he reached the landing, and heard sounds of activity from the end of the hall. His heart beat more slowly and his hands were ice-cold. He detached his gold watch from the heavy chain across his waistcoat and held it clutched in the hollow of his left hand. The minute-hand was midway between the first and second minutes after seven. He silently opened the door of the wooden stairway leading to the attics, and climbed the stairs two at a time. A round window looking over the big garden at the back of the house gave enough light to ensure that he would not be taken by surprise. The attic landing was darker, but the three doors were indicated by faint streaks of light at the floor level. With a quick, silent movement he opened one of these and then closed it behind him no less silently. The attic room, clean and bright, was furnished with a narrow bed, a wardrobe with double doors, a chair and a dressing-table. He went first to the window, and with a pretence of shutting it gave a quick glance outside. The house was so hidden by its trees and outer wall that there was scarcely anything to be seen beyond the courtyard—nothing of the town but its rooftops and, very close, the belfry-tower of the cathedral. Maître Marguet looked again at his watch. A half-minute had passed since he had left the first floor. On the other side of the courtyard the door opened and Mme. Marguet appeared. He had drawn back from the window, and he stood gazing with veneration at the badly-dressed figure, thin but heavy, which now crossed the courtyard with long, ungainly strides. Her clothes, her bearing, seemed those of an old woman, but there was a childlike grace in her face and clear eyes and in the carriage of her head. He hurried down to meet her on the first-floor landing.

FOUR

THE TABLE WAS laid in the middle of the kitchen, and
Antoine was doing his homework with a book lying
open on his plate. Now and then he gave a covert, apprehensive glance at his mother, who was sitting opposite him,
sewing. His disquiet amused her, and she mocked him with
a fragment of a song picked up at the time of the Armistice,
when she was still a young girl in a small town crowded with
greenish uniforms :

> ' I am sorry, I am sorry,
> *Dit-il, monsieur le curé.*
> I am sorry
> *C'est elle que j'épouserai.*'

Her thin voice, growing arch as she repeated the lines,
lent a small, tart hint of mystery to the refrain. Antoine
had a feeling of acute filial revulsion. His eyes grew hard,
and he said angrily, more accusing than questioning :
' So you're going to tell him I got home late ? You're
going to tell him ! '
Juliette Rigault smiled at him affectionately and did not
answer.
' *I am sorry* . . . *I am sorry* . . . You weren't born when
they were singing that song—not for another five years or
more. If you'd seen the town as it was then . . .'
With her needle poised she let her gaze stray out of
the window towards the ill-finished houses and the wire-

43

enclosed gardens that marked the last encroachment of the suburb upon the waste land surrounding the town. The song had revived her memories of the last year of the war. The Rue des Rencontres at six in the evening, under an autumn rain lending a bluish tinge to the gas lamps, had been a sea of soldiers taking their leisure—women pursued and children pursuing—washing back and forth in the light of the shop windows. Juliette had strayed amid the crowd with other sixteen-year-old girls, thrilled by the glances of the men and the rough cloth of the uniforms that brushed against her. She had ' dates.' Her mother searched for her everywhere. The neighbours may perhaps have noticed her in the back streets, sighing in the arms of some young man with family connections and a safe job in the commissariat, who wore expensive spectacles and pigskin gaiters. There had not been time enough for all the terror and all the fun.

Her husband's figure, passing in front of the window, brought her back to the present. Antoine tried in vain to catch her eye as she rose to get the dinner. Rigault greeted them in a chilly voice and went to wash his hands at the sink. He had decided long ago, after giving the matter consideration, not to embrace his wife or son upon his return from work; he never failed to adopt a manly and austere attitude towards problems that were not worth raising. He sat down at the table with the preoccupied, withdrawn air from which he seldom departed, and which was an oppressive enigma to his wife. Nothing in his demeanour betrayed the state of anxious apprehension which he felt was almost causing his heart to stop.

The Rigaults began to eat their soup in silence, while Juliette racked her brain for some remark which would enable her to make contact with her husband. Antoine sat huddled in his chair, seeing his mother's nervousness, and noting also a gleam of wifely self-assertion in her eye which made him uneasy. Rigault seemed to see nothing. Juliette raised her bosom, smoothing a lock of hair on her forehead, but without apparently succeeding in drawing his attention to herself. So she leaned across the table and said to her son in a voice made sharp by self-consciousness :

'I've already told you that you make too much noise eating your soup. Look at the way your father eats.'

She glanced at him for approval, and Rigault said after a pause :

'Quite right. You're nearly thirteen, and you still don't know how to use a spoon properly. Do you ever hear me make a noise ? '

Antoine conceded, with a movement of his head, that his father ate his soup without a sound ; and this recognition of his merit moved Rigault to indulgence, so that he stopped on the verge of the further rebukes and homilies he had been about to deliver. In any case, he had other things to worry about.

'Your father's only telling you for your own good,' said Juliette with a treacherous sweetness.

'Naturally it's for your own good,' said Rigault.

'And for the sake of your future.'

Despite his gnawing anxiety, Rigault seemed to rouse himself at this. His eye grew brighter. The subject of his son's future, almost painful though it was, never failed to draw a response from him. He was accustomed to talk of it with an angry solicitude, harrowed by his paternal ambitions and at the same time mortified by the thought that a day might come when his son would be his superior in the price of his suits, which caused him to wonder, growing irritated at the very prospect, whether he would dare to invest his money without consulting him. But as he opened his mouth to deliver a set speech with which his family was only too familiar, a powerful, brassy voice, coming from the garden fence, bore a flow of invective into the kitchen. Troussequin

like a frenetic gnome, was hopping up and down beyond the
wooden barrier flanking the waste land.

'Monsieur Rigault! Are you there? Hey, Monsieur
Rigault, come on out and talk to me man to man! Come
on out you shit! Where are your manners? You thought
I wasn't coming back, didn't you? Or you thought I'd
forgotten. Not likely, Monsieur Rigault! You've insulted
an old friend by pretending not to recognise him. I'll never
forget that. Who do you think you are, to go round insulting
people? You ought to think of your father, the old sod
that he was! Remember the time he was strolling down the
Rue de la Clé-d'Or with a couple of tarts, and we peed on
his head from the parapet of the Rond-Point? . . .'

His delight at this recollection caused Troussequin to
suspend his remarks for a few moments. When he had
finished laughing he shouted :

'You dirty bastard! Peeing on your own father's head!
I bet you've never boasted about that to your wife! It's
all very well for you to turn up your nose at me, but you
weren't so proud when your old man threw you out of the
house to get your living any way you could, and you came
begging to my mother. And when I mended my old pants
for you, you didn't mind that, did you, Fabien?'

Moved by the thought of his own generosity, Troussequin
drew a deep breath and did his best to see inside the kitchen,
but he could not see Rigault. That gentleman, seated rigidly
upright on his chair, was making a supreme effort to conceal
his alarm and despondency from his family. He stayed quite
silent, as though he had heard nothing of Troussequin's
bellowings. Juliette, who was not lacking in a sense of
drama, waited for him to burst forth in stupendous rage
after struggling to control himself. She was the only one
who could see the monster, and she reported his movements
to Rigault with a tendentious eloquence well calculated to

goad him to fury; but he merely studied the back of his hand, holding it close to his eyes and then farther away, as though nothing at all were happening outside.

Antoine understood his father's distress, and felt for him. He too was humiliated by Troussequin's description of a youthful prank which sounded like a biblical nightmare; but at the same time he was fighting desperately against an uncontrollable desire to laugh. Bent double and holding his breath, he hung on the verge of an explosion and finally could contain himself no longer. The thought of his father standing on the parapet of the Rond-Point, in the shameful posture depicted by Troussequin, brought the laughter bursting out of his mouth and nose. Hiccuping, with his face red and his shoulders shaking, he made futile efforts to hide his effrontery in his plate.

Troussequin, at the fence, resumed his flow of abuse. He called Rigault a mangy mule, a four-flusher, a pig like his father, a twerp, an imperialist, a turd, a dying duck and—several times—a pauper's child.

'You think you're somebody because you work in an office, but I'm just spitting in your eye, see? I don't give a fish's tit if you work in an office, see? I only got back the day before yesterday, and I've got a job already. You can have your bloody offices. You can put them you-know-where, and your penholders and your blotting-paper and your celluloid collars and your inkpots! Cowpat! Common fellow! Pauper's child!'

Juliette had managed to resist the contagion of her son's laughter, concealing her mirth behind a smile that was at least decorous. Rigault, although he remained fixed in his impassive attitude, was annoyed with her for not realising the true extent of his suffering. Finally, and with a great effort, he got up from his chair, resolved himself to perform the simple act of shutting the window. The sight of him

47

roused Trousequin to a state of delirious excitement. With his head and shoulders thrust forward and his feet suspended, he very nearly got himself impaled on the fence while he poured out insults with such rapidity that they became no more than a stream of incoherent bellowings. He soon went away, however, revenged and greatly soothed. Rigault was somewhat relieved by his departure, but he still felt profoundly despondent. He was never able to think of that early friendship, which from considerations of respectability he had repudiated long ago, without a sense of bourgeois shame which froze the marrow in his bones. It seemed to him that the town only needed to hear Trousequin's abominable revelation to thrust him back to the level of his squalid origin. The fact was that his fellow-townsmen had never forgotten his father, the china repairer known as Rigault Rigodon, concerning whom a number of vinous and bawdy anecdotes were still in circulation : but the son's state was considered so modest that no one felt any need to humble him. Whenever Rigault thought of it, which happened several times a day, he marvelled at so much tolerance.

'Well, he had to stop in the end,' said Juliette, with an air of giving her husband the credit for Trousequin's withdrawal. This embarrassed Rigault, who made no reply. Antoine seemed to have regained his self-control ; but when his mother looked at him, not quite innocently, he was convulsed with another spasm of laughter. He was afraid to apologise, but hoped his father would not have understood the cause or perhaps had not noticed it at all. Certainly Rigault did not appear to have seen anything. He had his usual preoccupied and withdrawn expression. But he was none the less wounded and struggling with an impulse to feel sorry for himself. He turned over various maxims in his mind, unearthing from the recesses of his memory a little fable learnt at school which illustrated the saw, 'Like father, like son.' It was very affecting, and led him to an examination of the filial conscience. The incident of the Rue de la Clé-d'Or weighed heavily upon him. He felt a need to justify himself, but could not bring himself to make the attempt, and fell back upon imagining the things he might have said to his son. But then he thought that it would be better still if he were addressing an audience of men of his own age. As follows :

'My friends . . . It is not without emotion that I rise to reply to an accusation that has been levelled at me in public. It is perfectly true that, obeying what I believed to be the prompting of my conscience, I failed in my duty as a son. As you see, I am not contesting the facts ; but I think, and you will think so too, that before you judge me too severely the circumstances must be recalled. I will tell you exactly what happened. You must understand to begin with that I was not alone, but that five of us were concerned in the episode. There was Troussequin Marcel, his brother, Emile, who has since died, a boy called Michon from the Rue Gorgerin, Lemontier Victor, who was killed in Champagne, and finally myself, then aged about thirteen. I must explain that in the winter evenings, after coming out of the communal school in the Rue des Visitandines, it was customary for the boys living in that quarter to climb on to the parapet of the Rond-Point and see who could make it go farthest. I am not saying that this was a very intelligent pas-time, or a well-mannered one, but perhaps the blame should be attributed in the first place to our parents, who allowed us too much freedom. I say this as much of my own father as of Troussequin's mother or Michon's parents. There are some of you here to-night who knew my father. He was not a bad man, but from the moment he became a widower he also became an idler. He worked only one day in two, and lounged about the streets and in the cafés. It must also be admitted that he had a tendency towards women. You may tell me that this applies to most men, and that it is no bar to correct behaviour ; but you must bear in mind that my father was a widower, and that his indolence was bound to drive him to bad habits. However this may be, one afternoon when we were at play the Troussequin brothers came and told me that they had overheard my father talking to Tetère's daughters, and that he had arranged to meet them in the Rue de la Clé-d'Or. Tetère's daughters . . .' (At this point Rigault began to travesty the truth, and almost everything he subsequently said was adapted to suit the argument.) '. . . Tetère's daughters were not the mere children Troussequin would have us believe, and in any case my father was not the man to take advantage of youthful innocence. I can assure you, having watched them from the parapet, that scarcely anything wrong took place, and those who know Tetère's daughters will be obliged to concede that very little of it can have been my father's doing. Nevertheless, when I heard about it I was profoundly shocked, so much so that at first I would not believe it. That is what the Troussequins counted on. You know what children are—always teasing and playing jokes on one another, and it's always the nicest children who get caught out. So when we came out of school we went and perched on the parapet of the Rond-Point, and we waited . . . I had too much respect for my father ever to say anything to him, nor would he have tolerated it if I had done so. But when I saw him in the Rue de la Clé-d'Or with Tetère's daughters I felt that I had at least the right to convey to him how grieved I was by his behaviour. So I imitated the Troussequins and the others without fully grasping the significance of the gesture. After all, I was only a child . . .'

But as he came to the summing-up Rigault realised the pointlessness of what he was doing, and with his fork in the air gazed uneasily about him. He was suddenly brought to confusion by the curiosity that he seemed to read in the eyes of his wife and son, and his face, which had unconsciously become animated, lapsed into its stubborn immobility. Their meal was nearly over, and Antoine had been beginning to hope that what he feared would not happen. But the general discomfort, rendered oppressive by the silence, grew still more acute after Rigault had caught them watching him. Juliette felt slightly to blame, and her lively eyes and expressive face became as eloquent as caressing hands. Antoine caught a certain look in her eye—a fluttering of servile joy and perfidiousness—which he feared even more than paternal scoldings. He stared hard at her in an effort to restrain her, but she pretended not to see and said in a tone of humorous indulgence :

'We haven't been very good to-day. We got back very late from school.'

The words were enough to revive all Rigault's austere passion. He was instantly seized with the thought that Antoine was eating him out of house and home, and allying himself with Troussequin to destroy his cherished nest-egg of respectability. But above all he saw a chance of revenge, a way of regaining face with a show of parental firmness. Growing angry at once, he said in a harsh voice :

'What time?'

Antoine answered, with a glance at his mother to tell her that he would spare her the need to complete her treachery.

'Ten past five.'

'Perhaps not *quite* as late as that,' his mother said. 'I don't think it had struck five.'

'It was ten past,' repeated Antoine. 'You told me so yourself.'

Rigault drank a full glass of wine, knowing that this was

going to be a lengthy business, and pushed his plate towards the middle of the table.

'Do you mean to say you weren't home before ten past five? So now it takes you an hour and ten minutes to get back from school! In an hour and ten minutes an infantry-man, with a full pack and rifle and cartridges, can do the better part of five miles in any weather; and we're only a mile and a half from the school, and you've nothing but a few books to carry! You'll kindly tell me exactly what you were doing.'

'I don't know,' murmured Antoine.

'You don't know? It takes me a quarter of an hour to get to my office, and if I'm as long as twenty minutes I know why. Where were you dawdling about?'

'I came the same way as usual—the Rue de l'Herbe-Sèche, the Rue d'Arbois and the Avenue Poincaré.'

'Well then, what did you do? I insist on knowing what you did!'

Antoine conveyed with a shrug of his shoulders that he had no idea. Rigault gazed cruelly at him.

'So you're sticking to it, are you? You're determined to stick to it. I suppose you think you aren't in trouble enough already! It's not enough to have missed being top with your last two compositions—you want to go down a few more places. Instead of working you'd sooner waste your time dawdling about the streets. When I think of all the sacrifices we've made for you, all the help we've given you, and the way you repay us, I'm ashamed of you, do you hear? You're old enough now to know that you won't always have your parents behind you, and that a day will come when you'll have to earn your living. You'll be sorry then that you didn't profit by our sacrifices; but then it'll be too late! When your mother and I are both old, and when we've ruined our health through going without things in order to give you a good education, you'll perhaps realise . . .'

Although he felt the untruth of all this, Antoine began to cry. Rigault himself, thinking of his white hair and fruitless sacrifices, heaved a long sigh, but this moment of weakness did not last. Another look at Antoine—that small, capricious head in which all the promise of the future was being corrupted—was enough to restore him to a state of wrath.

'Who were you with?'

'With Buquanant,' said Antoine in a small, defeated voice.

'Buquanant from the cleaner's? Well, he certainly isn't at the top of the form! A young lout, isn't he? A young lout!'

Antoine protested with a shake of his head, and Rigault's anger broke suddenly into despair.

'A lout! I might have known you'd go playing in the gutter with that sort of boy! I couldn't have a decent son— he has to be a guttersnipe! I couldn't—I couldn't——'

Rigault let himself fall forward over the table, hiding his head between his hands and groaning with fury and shame. Antoine and his mother gazed at him trembling, stupefied by this explosion which was so unlike his customary behaviour. Unable to meet their eyes, Rigault stayed there for some time without raising his head. Finally he went upstairs to get into his Sunday clothes for his visit to the mayor, where he was expected at nine, and his wife helped him to dress.

Antoine remained by himself in the kitchen, thinking of his arrangement with Buquanant to climb the cathedral tower to-morrow, but feeling that he lacked the courage to risk his father's wrath for so small a matter. The mysteries of the Malleboine quarter no longer interested him. Merely to evoke them, in the atmosphere of the family, was to rob them of all attraction. Still dismayed, but filled with resentment and disgust, he found some consolation in recalling Troussequin's insults and his father's confusion. Then he began to think about the belfry tower again.

FIVE

PHILIPPON HAD NOT been able to bring himself to offer
dinner to the half-dozen incorruptibles of whom he
wished to make use. He felt that liqueurs, coffee and conversation were enough. To ensure success in the business of
whipping up the enthusiasm of Rigault and the others, he
had enlisted the aid of Dr. Coinchot, whose authority in
matters of electoral politics carried great weight. He had not
been able to avoid asking him to dinner, but he was a regular
visitor to the house in any case. After they had dined the
mayor's wife withdrew, pleading a headache, so as to leave
the two men alone. Philippon and Coinchot went into the
drawing-room to await the incorruptibles. The doctor
seemed put out, and Philippon rather anxiously remarked
upon the fact.

'Frankly,' said Coinchot, ' it's not what I hoped for.'

'Why, you told me only yesterday evening that you agreed.'

' I'm not going back on that. I still agree. But all the same
I hoped for something better.'

Philippon made a gesture of helpless sympathy; but
Coinchot, who knew what his host's regrets were worth,
remained gloomy. A lifelong friendship, a distant relation-
ship, and habit, above all, kept them closely united in
political matters. The doctor, who had no official position
in the Party, was known in the constituency as a Radical
Cerberus, a sort of watch-dog of the law, and Philippon was
remarkably skilful in taking advantage of the esteem in

which he was held. Coinchot was by no means unaware of
the fact that his friend made use of him; and that night,
not for the first time, he had the disagreeable impression
that he was there less in the interests of the Party than in
those of Philippon. That gentleman, knowing him only too
well, guessed what was in his mind, and the atmosphere was
slightly strained in consequence. When the doctor helped
himself to a cigar, Philippon was afraid to ask him to await
the arrival of the others before lighting it. ' No hope of his
having finished it before they get here,' he thought with
annoyance. ' He'll still have an inch or two left, and they'll
guess he's been dining with me and that they've been asked
like poor relations, for the sake of what I want to get out of
them. I shall be lucky if he doesn't go on looking like a
funeral mute.' He passed Coinchot an ash-tray and tried to
enliven him, but without succeeding.

Coinchot was having one of those bad days when life
felt to him like an attack of influenza. He had no use for
Philippon, and the whole town disgusted him. The place
seemed to him moribund, dreary and apathetic. While the
Paris papers were bursting with stories of communism and
Fascism, meetings, riots, appeals and counter-appeals, you
might search the length and breadth of this constituency
without finding anything of the kind. Although it was a
town of working people, the communists were a mere
handful without even a red flag. The Croix de Feu boasted
perhaps fifteen members, and the Royalists consisted of four
or five twenty-year-old youths. The poor acquiesced in the
riches of the rich and submitted meekly to the threat of
unemployment. The rich only hated the poor when they
happened to think about it. Malice and rage and jealousy,
instead of gloriously exploding in public, festered in the
bosoms of families and were silently stifled. And it was the
same with politics. Excepting the people directly concerned,

no one paid much attention to them. When the café proprietor or the cobbler or the notary or the priest or the captain of Gendarmerie or even the workers at the T.D.C. factory wondered whether there was going to be a war, or ruin and death in some other form, the question had no connection in their minds with politics. Yet it had not always been so. Coinchot could recall happy moments. Only just before the war he had done battle in the streets three weeks before the elections—and in his white coat, too—he, a doctor ! Yes, he had had a stand-up fight with that chap— what was his name ?—the chap who sold bicycles—well, the name didn't matter . . . It was the same with strikes. In the old days, and it wasn't so long ago either—after the war, anyway—the workers from the T.D.C. factory and other places had gone on strike. Towards the end, when they were getting hungry in the Malleboine quarter and the eastern suburbs, the town had got so red that a priest daren't show his nose out of doors. And he, Coinchot, bourgeois that he was, with a well-paid calling and money in the bank, at those times he'd have been ready to give his last breath for the cause ; he'd have chucked up all his richest patients if Philippon, a disgusting fellow even then, hadn't had him tied hand and foot. Yes, the town had changed. Even the illnesses were not the same. In the old days there had been epidemics of one sort and another that had kept the clergy and the grave-diggers busy ; and the doctor pursued his strategy, sometimes driving back the enemy with a single stroke, sometimes giving ground— ' I've let fifty peg out, but I know what I'm doing . . .' That was real medicine, whereas nowadays it seemed to be nothing but chronic cases and the minor ailments of old families. Even the weather was different, no proper seasons . . . and so on, and so on, and whose fault was it ? . . . Or take war. In the old days . . .

Coinchot was deliberately working himself up while he looked sourly at Philippon. Thinking that he caught him smiling, he said dryly :

' That reminds me, you ought to come and see me. It's a long time since we did anything about your pox.'

' There's nothing urgent,' said Philippon, blushing and glancing apprehensively towards the door.

' I'm warning you for your own sake. At your age, and with your complexion, you may get a nasty surprise if you neglect it.'

Philippon looked alarmed, and the doctor relented. Old friendship softened his heart, and he said more gently :

' I'm exaggerating a bit, to scare you ; but you've got to be careful.'

' Don't worry,' said Philippon, relieved. ' I'll come and see you. I should have come before now, but I've had this business so much on my mind . . .'

' What business ? '

' Why, the election, of course ! Anyone would think you weren't interested.'

' Of course I'm interested,' said Coinchot. ' Very much so. But frankly I think it's a bad choice, and so do you. For eighteen years that old limpet Carmagnet was a burden on the constituency, and now that he's dead at last they can find nothing better to put in his place than a sort of political errand-boy, who writes for the police rags with one hand while he's cleaning up for his pals in the Ministry of the Interior with the other. And he's over forty-five into the bargain ! '

' Now really ! ' said Philippon laughing. ' You can't say that he's too old at forty-five. Don't forget that we're sixty.'

' I certainly do think he's too old. As we've got to have a new broom, let's do the thing properly. I don't care how clever and cunning this chap Leboissel may be, he's not the man I want.'

'Let's get the facts right,' said Philippon. 'Leboissel isn't at all what you seem to think. He was recommended to me by the secretary-general of the Grand Orient, and we had a long correspondence about him. I also made inquiries in Paris, and finally I met him. He's a man of experience but an honest one, who offers us all the guarantees we can expect. What you say about his work as a journalist is quite unfair. He has always stood for reasonable opinions in the left-wing papers.'

Coinchot conceded that he might have been unjust to Leboissel, and that in any case he knew nothing about the 'police rags' or his 'pals' in the Ministry of the Interior. But he stuck to what he had said, whether it was true or not. He stuck to it because he stuck to it, and because he was fed-up with everything—the Party, and doctoring, and Leboissel and politics and men of forty-five. For two pins he'd give everything he possessed to the revolution, it wouldn't take much to drive him to it. Anyway, what he wanted to see in the Party was young men—he wasn't afraid of their being only twenty-five—intelligent, bold, educated youngsters—and good-looking too, there was no harm in that—men whom the electors would vote into power for love of them, and not simply from calculation or force of habit. You could say what you liked, but love was the source of everything . . . Philippon hurriedly brought the discussion back to more favourable ground, and laid a well-tried trap for Coinchot.

'And now I suppose you're going to remind me that Fouchard is only thirty-nine. I know that, but . . .'

Fouchard, a well-to-do barrister and a Municipal Councillor, was angling for adoption by the Party. Philippon was not at all anxious to see him elected to the Chamber of Deputies because he was already an important figure in the town, and his influence on the Council would prejudice his own.

58

For Coinchot it was an article of faith that their Deputy must either be a man from outside or a man of modest means—otherwise there was a danger that his position in the town would become so strong that the Party would no longer be able to control him. But he had a particular reason for hating the Fouchard family. The father had seduced two of his cousins, putting one in the family way and driving the other into a convent—and a liar into the bargain, and a damned, insolent fellow—when the parents of the pregnant girl had called him to account he simply said that a person sitting on an ant-heap is going a bit far when they pretend to know which particular ant has bitten them. And the son was no better if he wasn't worse—an excitable, ambitious type, a political careerist.

' Let's leave Fouchard out of it,' he said.

' That's all very well,' said Philippon, ' but he's in a strong position—a damned strong position.'

Coinchot shifted in his chair and grunted. He was undoubtedly beginning to shake off his apathy. The mayor went on thoughtfully :

' Things have been going his way for the last year or more. Don't forget he's president of the Rugby Club, which has had an unbroken series of wins this season, or almost. They won again last Sunday—Belfort or Montpellier, I forget which.'

The doctor, his eyes blazing, plucked at his moustache above his cigar. Philippon rubbed it in a little more.

' And an ex-service man as well. That doesn't do him any harm.'

Coinchot got up from his chair crying hell and damnation, and planted himself in front of Philippon.

' An ex-service man ! Well, what about our chap ? Isn't he an ex-service man ? Come on, did you or did you not tell me he'd been in the war ? '

'Of course I told you. He was in the Air Force. He got the Croix de Guerre and a bar. But the Air Force sounds a bit remote to most people—it doesn't rate as high as the infantry. It doesn't seem to have much connection with the misery of life on the ground—the lice, the mud of the trenches . . . When an infantryman talks of fifteen hundred thousand dead, it's as though he'd given them himself. The Air Force is different. And then, as I said, his rugby team has had a lot of wins. Things of that sort count more than you think. Every time the town does something to help sport it looks as though it was Fouchard who had done it, because he's on the Council. Oh, he's a clever devil!'

Philippon smiled as though in unwilling tribute to the adversary. And Coinchot exploded. He was damned if there was anything clever about Fouchard. He knew the Fouchards inside out. The old man, who had died of bladder trouble, had been nothing but an old sod, and this young one was another sod, and the two of them, living and dead, were a pair of sods. Call Fouchard a barrister! He was nothing but a small-time pleader who made you wince to listen to him. And as for larger views, he hadn't got any.

'Our man's a bit different from that anyway. He's a man who's seen the world, he's thought about things, he's studied the problems of—of—well, anyway, he's studied the problems. Although I haven't met him, I can quite easily picture Leboissel—a frank, straightforward chap who can put people at their ease and knows how to make a speech. In short, a man of policy, and a man like anyone else. Fouchard may follow the Party line, but he'll always look like one of the rich.'

Philippon agreed cordially with these last words, which he had special reasons for appreciating. Himself a large owner of real estate, who had retained a considerable interest in certain concerns purveying raw materials which he had handed over to his son-in-law a few years ago, he flattered himself that he, too, did not look like one of the rich, even in a morning-coat and top hat.

Dr. Coinchot laid his cigar against the edge of the ash-tray and moved towards the passage.

'I needn't come with you,' said Philippon. 'You know where it is.'

He looked at his watch after the doctor had gone, and saw that the time was five-and-twenty to nine. In ten minutes, because none of them would dare to come early, his guests would start arriving. Coinchot's cigar was burning away gently, a thin, straight thread of smoke rising towards the chandelier. Philippon studied it anxiously, wondering how much longer it would last. It was more than half-smoked, and perhaps another ten minutes would be enough to finish it. But Coinchot's absence was wasting time. Philippon bent towards the ash-tray. The cigar, with its chewed end flattened and sodden with saliva, was beginning to burn more slowly, the smoke curling into small spirals. Philippon reached out his hand, hesitated, drew back and then reached out again. After all, it was the cigar of an old friend. He took it resolutely between his teeth and began to draw at it furiously, releasing the smoke in great puffs and instantly drawing again. The cigar reddened, crackled, grew hot and caused a bitter juice to flow in his mouth. The tide of combustion crept steadily up it, forming a long, glowing ash of which he felt the heat on his face. When the doctor's footsteps sounded again in the passage he put it back in the ash-tray and waved his hands to disperse the thick cloud of smoke that hung in the centre of the room.

'My God, no!' exclaimed Coinchot from the door. 'I can't fancy Fouchard's chances. Look at the line he took in the Council about the question of expropriating Butillat's land. He doesn't want the town to buy——'

'Everyone is entitled to his own views,' said Philippon hypocritically.

'Everyone can think what he likes, certainly,' said Coinchot, grinning, 'but that doesn't alter the fact that only the reactionaries are going to support him. He can say and do what he likes—he can even prove he's right—but still he's going over to the other side.'

Coinchot chuckled maliciously and picked up his cigar; but the first bitter puff of over-heated, damp tobacco caused him to pull a face of disgust.

'Isn't it good?' asked Philippon.

Coinchot tried another puff without answering, and then, defeated, crushed out the cigar in the ash-tray.

'I must say, it smells nasty,' said Philippon. 'I'll take it away.'

He removed the ash-tray to the dining-room, but without ceasing to goad Coinchot, so that finally the two friends reached full agreement on the detailed methods to be adopted to prevent Fouchard's nomination. They had already agreed in principle upon a well-worn procedure—to lull the lawyer into unwariness until the last moment, to canvass the delegates from the country districts, and thus quietly to get together a solid majority when the matter came up for decision at the general assembly. The difficulty lay in ensuring that their agents would go to work discreetly, because any too-evident manœuvre might lead to discord within the Party.

Rigault was the first to arrive as the quarter sounded, in striped trousers and a black coat, his Adam's apple thrusting over the points of his high collar. He had not known how to get rid of his bowler hat in the lobby, and Philippon took it from him as he showed him to a chair. Rigault had never met the mayor except at meetings and banquets, and he was entering his house for the first time. He gazed furtively at the armchairs, the marble consoles, the green plant tied with a pink ribbon, the spinning-wheel, the moulded walls, the bronze statue whose mythological buttocks were reflected in the tall glass over the fireplace. He had little time to reflect upon all this because he was obliged to take part in the conversation, and in his eagerness was inclined to anticipate the mayor's affable questions. Coinchot, who had treated his son the year before, inquired after his health and his progress at school. Philippon, who did not want to come to business until the rest of the party had arrived, took advantage of this to talk about education in general. Rigault listened to him somewhat anxiously. Although the conversation was on simple lines, the setting and the importance of the company caused him to feel that he was being privileged to attend the gathering of a secret cult, and it was somewhat disconcerting to find that he could follow the talk so easily. Coinchot watched him with sympathy and with a twinge of conscience. A part of his medical practice, the ones that paid on the nail, lay among the class of small bourgeois to which Rigault belonged. He knew the difficulties and the cares of their laborious lives, and the limitations imposed upon them by their ingenuous sense of gratitude towards a state of society which allowed them to walk out on a Sunday with a cane and a bowler hat. He reflected that in this case, at least, Philippon had chosen well. Here was a poor devil quite without defence against him. To Rigault, the well-to-do bourgeois of Philippon's kind seemed the arbiters of conscience, midway between the white-collar workers and the Deity of the left wing . . . ' He must believe us to be possessed of a wisdom which he has not known how to deserve, and he does what he can to conceal his unworthiness. What a disgusting fellow I really am ! It's the same as when I find myself at a loss with the patient in front of me ; and so I look profound and scribble

63

down an illegible prescription . . . (one might as well admit it, if my handwriting is filthy it's because I've wanted it to be—just a trick of the trade, like the process-server's formula, or the gangster's slang, or the priest's Latin).'

The other incorruptibles arrived one by one. Boncresson, the harness-maker, who tried to maintain an air of rugged independence but was in fact blindly subservient, was the last of them. And with the party complete and the coffee steaming in the cups, Philippon by way of preliminary indulged in a series of roguish glances, snorts, grunts and slappings of his hand upon his thigh.

'If I've brought you here in this rather intimate and informal sort of way,' he said, 'it's as much to ask your advice as to let you in on a few facts which you may not have heard. I thought of you gentlemen in particular because no one in the town understands the real interests of the Party better than you do. All the same, at first I was inclined to hesitate——'

'Why?' demanded Coinchot. 'One should never hesitate.'

'Of course not. But I couldn't help asking myself whether I'd any right to bother busy men with plenty of troubles of their own. Was it fair? However, in the end I decided that it had to be done. The whole thing's too serious. I felt that it was my duty to warn and consult the people who seemed to me most capable of looking the facts in the face. You must tell me if you think I was wrong.'

'Certainly not. You were quite right,' said the harness-maker, and the other incorruptibles agreed.

'Poor old Carmagnet, with all his political experience, said to me during the last stages of his illness—"You'll see, Philippon. There's going to be trouble. Those people are stronger than you think." He had his wits about him, the old man; he saw things clearly right up to the last minute ! . . .'

The mayor paused to allow the company to sigh, and then resumed :

'But the position is serious in other ways than one might have expected. Naturally one knew that the other side would try to take advantage of poor Carmagnet's death. It was too good a chance to miss, what with the economic crisis and the difficulties of the small shopkeeper and the small farmer, and the threat of general impoverishment . . .'

Coinchot endorsed all this, his eyes half closed, with a gentle nodding of his head. The incorruptibles were stirred, visibly stirred. Things were going nicely. Philippon was about to press home the attack when the telephone sounded in the lobby. The maidservant came in to say that the doctor had been rung up from his home. The mayor was obliged vexedly to await his return before he could continue. The incorruptibles gazed awkwardly at one another, not venturing to break the silence but on the other hand fearing to be suspected of listening to what Coinchot was saying in the lobby.

'We're out of luck,' said Coinchot, returning. 'I'm wanted on an urgent case.'

'Will it take long ?'

'Perhaps not. I've got to go to the Impasse de la Sourdine. One of Tetère's daughters has been taken ill.'

Rigault, suddenly uneasy, shrank into his armchair with a feeling that Troussequin had followed him even into the mayor's drawing-room.

'Tetère's daughters ?' repeated Philippon.

Coinchot gave him an impatient glance and said irritably :

'What do you want me to tell you ? Tetère's daughters are Tetère's daughters. Everybody knows about them.'

And indeed Philippon was the only one present who did not know of them. Not one of the incorruptibles but was well-informed on the subject. Turning casually to

Rigault, the doctor called him to witness that this was the case.

'You know Tetère's daughters, don't you?' he said.

Rigault would have welcomed death. Feeling the eyes of the other incorruptibles upon him, he blushed to his collar and said, shaking his head:

'No. I can't say I do.'

SIX

SEEN FROM THE top of the long flight of stone steps, the Malleboine quarter appeared to Coinchot like a separate town, black and deeply huddled at the foot of a cliff. From the wall encircling the Rond-Point a dense shadow fell upon the lower part of the stairway and the Rue de la Clé-d'Or. Further off, at the Carrefour des Cinq, an electric street-lamp lighted the corner houses and showed up the black silhouette of a watch-tower. The Rue Gorgerin, the Rue du Sire-de-Roulans and the Rue aux Oiseaux vanished into darkness and the mist rising from the river, furnishing some indication of their winding course by the dim glow of lights filtering through lampshades or window-curtains or dirty window-panes; and beyond these corridors of darkness lay patches of diffused light, not easy to place, which revealed the existence of cafés.

As he reached the foot of the stairway Coinchot saw two men cross the Carrefour des Cinq at a run, and concluded that he was witnessing the end of a quarrel. He recalled the streets of the Malleboine in the days of his youth—an average of a death a week, and the police afraid to enter them after dark. Things had greatly changed since then, and nowadays they had practically given up killing one another. There had been some fear after the war that the irruption of Poles and Arabs would lead to a return of the old state of affairs, but the police had been firm and later the economic crisis had driven all the foreigners away.

67

In the Rue de la Clé-d'Or a man came towards the doctor, emerging from the shadow of a doorway. He was twenty-five, with a slight stringy body, taller than average. He had a very long nose, big ears that stuck out widely, a pimply skin, the generally unhealthy look of the under-nourished and ill-housed, and with all this an air of friendly and easy confidence.

'Why, it's Trésor!' exclaimed Coinchot. 'Have you come to meet me?'

'Yes, doctor,' said Trésor. 'I thought you'd come this way. My girl Minie thought you'd come by the Rampe du Blaireau, but I knew better. It was easier for you to come this way, wasn't it?'

Passing over the cross-roads, they entered the Rue aux Oiseaux. Trésor kept a little ahead because of the darkness, and warned the doctor of pitfalls in the street.

'What exactly is the trouble?' asked Coinchot.

'It's my girl Marion who's ill,' said Trésor. 'By the way, you mustn't scold her . . . Look out, doctor, there's a hole—keep more over to the right . . . My girls have had a lot of trouble lately. Last year they went to live with Billotey—did you know? For six months it was fine, but then another chap came to live with us, a chap called Manaques, who was out of a job. Billotey couldn't be pleased about it, and nor could anyone. And then, you know, four in a room, without counting me, it's not comfortable. My girls couldn't have visitors like they used to. It's really for their sake I'm complaining. With all the trouble they have——'

'And what are you doing?'

'Nothing,' said Trésor.

'You might at least do a bit of work, at your age!'

'Yes, I know,' said Trésor. 'I know.'

After following the Rue aux Oiseaux for a hundred yards

they turned to the right into the Impasse de la Sourdine. Coinchot felt a fresh, damp current of air, and he thought he caught the murmur of the subterranean stream which surfaced just beyond the blind alley after passing beneath the Upper Town.

' Look out, doctor. It's very dark. Last year they put in an electric lamp, but people always took the bulbs.'

The centre of the alley was thickly coated in slime from the household slops that flowed down it ; the sides were moss-covered and scarcely less dangerous. The doctor walked gingerly, grateful for Trésor's warnings. At the end of the alley, from the threshold of the building which closed it, shone a small paraffin lamp whose beam was constantly intercepted by the movement of figures across it. A number of people seemed to have been gathered at the bedside of the sufferer, but they vanished into the shadows when the doctor appeared, so that by the time he entered the ground-floor room, the only habitation which the building afforded, the two sisters were alone. The doctor recognised the room, where twenty years before he had attended Tetère on his deathbed. It was big and lofty, but the walls were black and sticky, the woodwork spongy and rotted. There were no windows, but in the far corner a door with glass panes gave on to the stream at the point where it flowed out of the earth. The place was wretchedly furnished—a worm-eaten cottage bed, a camp-bed derived from American army stocks, an iron cooking stove with two apertures and a kitchen table. The chairs were so dilapidated that it had been thought proper, for decency's sake, to remove them from the eye of the visitor and substitute two borrowed from a neighbour. Minie took up the oil lamp from beside the bed and came to meet the doctor. Her slight form, her pale, haggard but almost unwrinkled face, and the fringe of scarcely greying hair cut short

69

just above her eyebrows, made her look like an old little girl. Her sister Marion, rather more sturdily built, had the same appearance of a hungry and exhausted child. Although both were in their forties they were still known in the quarter as Tetère's girls.

'Well, my dear,' said Coinchot, 'tell me what's wrong.'

'I don't feel well,' said the sick woman in a frightened voice.

Minie and Trésor were making signs to one another behind the doctor's back, their argument none the less vigorous for being silent.

'Where's the pain?' asked Coinchot, feeling Marion's pulse.

'I don't know. It seems to be everywhere. I can't say . . .'

He continued to question her, and the vagueness of her replies, the hesitation and reticence, seemed to him suspicious. When he made a move to sound her chest she had a hunted look and clutched the bedclothes under her chin.

'I'm feeling better,' she said. 'The pain's gone. It can't have been anything.'

'Well, upon my word!' said Coinchot, turning to Minie. 'What does all this mean? I can't imagine you brought me here for nothing at all!'

'Of course not,' murmured Trésor.

Minie gazed apprehensively at the doctor and prodded her left breast with the point of her finger. Meanwhile Trésor leaned over the bed and smiled down at the sufferer.

'Little one,' he said, 'watch what I'm going to do.'

First he took his chin between both hands and pretended to pull it out, as though it were a drawer, but without achieving anything despite his efforts. So then he took a trouser button out of his pocket and set it on the point of

70

his chin, where it stayed as though it were fastened. This simple device enabled him to open the drawer without any apparent effort. He had only to take the button between his finger and thumb, and pull. The drawer slid forward nearly half an inch, and he was able to take from it two metal coffee-spoons, a cork, a cotton-reel, a drill from a brace-and-bit and two sardine openers. The movement with which he closed the drawer left one feeling that it must contain yet other objects. Marion, whose eyes had never left him, laughed cautiously and her tightly-clasped hands relaxed. Minie laughed too, looking embarrassed ; and a great laugh from Trésor himself caused the doctor to chuckle. This burst of gaiety restored the sufferer's confidence, and she resisted no longer. Coinchot drew back the sheet that covered the chemise of pale blue artificial silk, and at once saw a fresh blood-stain on the left side.

' So that's it ! ' he exclaimed. ' You'd better warm up a basin of water for a start.'

Taking the surgical case from his pocket he got out a pair of scissors, but then paused. Instead of cutting the chemise, he took the time to roll it up under the armpits. A pad made of face towels was held in place by two stockings tied round her body. When he came to examine the wound, the doctor found two holes a couple of inches apart. One, scarcely visible beneath the left breast, was not bleeding. The other, round towards the back at the same level, was somewhat larger, and a thin trickle of blood escaped from it.

' Have you coughed any blood ? ' he asked.

' No, doctor.'

' No taste of blood in your mouth ? '

Marion was not aware of any. Rather uncertain, Coinchot asked Trésor what had happened. The question met with a reproachful silence. He said :

'I'm not interested in your private affairs. I simply want to know how many shots were fired, and at what distance.'

'Well, it's like this,' said Trésor. 'We didn't start anything, and we scarcely know what happened. We'd been out for a drink, and it happened in the Rue des Nonettes just when we were passing the gents. Someone who was in there, about six yards away, fired a shot, and my girl Marion collapsed in my arms and said she'd been hit in the left side.'

'You're sure only one shot was fired? That surprises me. Once one has pressed the trigger of those things one generally fires two at least.'

Trésor, who seemed to have had a close view of the weapon, explained that it was an old revolver, not an automatic. The pull had probably been heavy, and it was likely enough that the attacker had fired only once. Coinchot returned to his examination and now had no difficulty in deciding that it was a simple flesh wound. The bullet had glanced off a rib and emerged without touching any organ. It was scarcely more than a graze, which in a few days would clear up completely. While he applied the dressing, the doctor listened to a dull, heavy sound which recurred at regular intervals, and seemed like a vibration of the floor. Finally he asked what it was.

'It's the mill,' said Trésor.

'The mill? What mill? I know this quarter pretty well, but I've never heard of a mill on the Sourdine '—and he turned to Minie for enlightenment.

'Why, of course. It's the mill!' confirmed Minie.

'But what mill?' asked the doctor, irritated.

Minie and Trésor glanced at one another, plainly surprised at his insistence. They found the question absurd, to say the least, since for them the term 'the mill' had an obvious meaning. Coinchot realised that this meaning was in some way peculiar to the family, and that he would gain nothing by pressing his inquiry. Just as he was finishing dressing the wound the door was discreetly pushed ajar, and a woman's voice said through the opening :

' Here's Maillard. He's in the alley with another copper.'

Minie, who was pouring water into an enamel basin, ceased doing so while she conferred in a low voice with Trésor. They were still talking when the police entered. Maillard, followed by another policeman who was hidden behind his broad shoulders, had to bend in order to pass under the doorway. He was flushed with fury to the back of his neck, and his eyes were bloodshot. He deliberately stamped on an earthenware dish lying on the floor, and kicked a saucepan and a stool to the other end of the room. At this shindy the doctor drew himself upright and said calmly :

' It's you, is it, sergeant ? I didn't hear you knock.'

Considerably taken aback, Maillard grew redder still and raised a hand to his cap.

' Pardon,' he said. ' I didn't know you were here. I wouldn't have disturbed you.'

' You aren't disturbing me. I've finished. I've put on a dressing.'

' Is it serious ? ' asked Maillard, jerking his chin towards the bed.

' No—a very small wound. You needn't upset yourself, it's nothing.'

Coinchot drew up the bedclothes and went to wash his hands in the enamel basin. The sergeant, diffidently followed by the other policeman, Charlasse, advanced to the centre of the room. He thought, quite wrongly, that he caught an expression of assurance and mockery upon the faces of Tetère's girls, and this further enraged him. Consumed by repressed fury, he began to mutter under his breath as he strode towards the bed. Finally it was too much for him, and forgetting Coinchot's presence he burst out :

'What I want to know is when you two sluts are going to stop your nonsense ! Do you think the police have got nothing better to do than to run round after you ? Are you always going on like this ? The Malleboine had become a decent quarter, and then you two bitches have to start rousing things up again. Whores at two francs a time ! Arab meat ! A disgrace to the whole quarter—the worst knock-shop in the Malleboine ! Well, I'm going to keep you in order, d'you understand ? I'll treat you the way you deserve to be treated. I'll make you lick my boots, I'll stamp on your faces, and then I'll send you to rot in prison like the filthy bags you are ! '

Maillard had a powerful and impressively resonant voice which he accompanied with an occasional forward thrust of his chest, as though to devour all the descendants of Tetère. Minie and Trésor bowed their heads to the storm, but without seeming excessively dismayed. Now and then they exchanged a glance which seemed to say that things were turning out better than they had expected. The other policeman, Charlasse, remained a few paces off dutifully admiring the power and eloquence of his superior, but nevertheless unable to resist a certain feeling of sympathy for the Tetère girls. He was a young constable who had only been accepted into the service a few months previously, thanks to the good offices of a gentleman of influence who employed his sister as a maid-of-all-work and had thereby ensured her lifelong devotion. He had been born in the quarter, and had played with Trésor as a child. Only the previous year, when he had come out of the army without work and almost without prospects, he had come to him for shelter and assistance. As he now stood in the room which he had known so well as a friend, Constable Charlasse was not greatly disposed to congratulate himself on his good fortune. He stood meditating confusedly on the nature of authority, which seemed to enjoy causing a man to be divided against himself, while at the same time he listened glumly to the thudding of the mill.

Coinchot, while he dried his hands, contemplated the parties to the dispute, whose huge, distorted shadows were thrown on the walls by the light of the oil lamp. Maillard's attitude and the torrent of abuse and threats which he continued to pour out, in contrast to the humble acquiescence of the two women, filled him with warm-blooded indignation. Crossing the room, he returned to the bedside and took Marion's wrist. There ensued a period of silence which he deliberately prolonged. Then as he crossed in front of Maillard he said to him coldly :

' My patient's tired. It might be better, for this evening, if you'd confine yourself to asking questions and work off your bad temper on someone else—on her attacker, for instance.'

Maillard started in sheer stupefaction, and very nearly exploded. Never in all his long career had he been made so vividly aware of the injustice and imbecility of the people in high places. Time and again he had resisted the temptation to resign in order that he might crush them with their own sanctimonious truths. The blasted fools ! With all their slyness they were still more stupid than the stupidest tart in the Malleboine. And dangerous, at that ! A fine gang of nit-wits and hogs and blood-suckers ! He knew them ! Yes, by God, he could certainly say he knew them, from the Prefect and the Mayor down to the little half-rich men—all of them glad enough to have a police force and a commissioner at their beck and call to fix up their shabby affairs and leave them free to wallow in their family muck. And now this one was making a virtue of being big-hearted

75

about a couple of tarts and preventing him, Maillard, from doing his job ! Perhaps they'd like to take over the job of patrolling the Malleboine quarter. That would be rich ! This bloody doctor ! Silly old woman ! Old ass ! He got sentimental about a scratch on a street-walker's skin, but what did he care about Sergeant Maillard, who after spending thirty years of his life bringing a little order into the Malleboine quarter, and making himself feared and respected, was chipped and scarred from head to foot, and thought no more of it than he did of an April shower. Nobody heard him moaning about his two knife wounds in the shoulder, or about the bullet the doctors hadn't been able to extract, which was still wandering about somewhere in his stomach. But of course Coinchot hadn't suffered for that, or any of the others. It was Maillard who had suffered ; Maillard in the Rue de la Clé-d'Or, in the Carrefour des Cinq, in the café, in the bistro ; Maillard anywhere and everywhere where his job required him to be. The blasted idiots ! If it upset them so much to see whores and hoodlums being pushed around a bit, all they had to do was to give them a chance to live a different sort of life. But the truth was that they didn't give a damn about the Malleboine quarter. Their big-heartedness was never more than a passing whim . . . Thus did Maillard reflect, and he drew a breath almost deep enough to cause all the buttons to burst off his tunic. Because it was no use saying anything. Once again he would just have to take it. This would blow over like everything else, and it was he who would have the last word in the end.

Coinchot, restored to good-humour, replaced his instruments in his case with a deliberate slowness, while he sternly regarded the sergeant from the corner of his eye. He felt happy and light of heart, like a man who has been good to the very limits of goodness. Not only had he allowed his evening to be interrupted and bestowed his professional services without thought of payment, but he had defended the wretched and oppressed against the monstrous tyranny of the police. Minie and Trésor saw the matter differently, and would, if they had dared, have given him a hint to say no more. They knew quite well that the doctor's act of generosity amounted to nothing more than a rich man's self-indulgence for which they would undoubtedly have to pay sooner or later. If he had not intervened the sergeant would probably have been satisfied with merely abusing them—not for the first time.

Maillard had no need to turn his head to know that the doctor had his eye on him. He decided to cut the formalities short, and asked in a calm, almost indifferent voice :

'Where did it happen ? '

'In the Rue des Nonettes,' said Trésor. 'But if it was Madame from Number Fifteen who rang you up, you'd better make inquiries in her neighbourhood, because we don't know the first thing about it.'

'Where were you coming from ? '

'We'd been having coffee at Jules's.'

'Who with ? '

'With Manaques and Billotey.'

Maillard smiled without otherwise commenting upon the absence of the two men who ordinarily slept in the room. Pulling a tobacco pouch out of his pocket, he began to roll a cigarette while he gazed steadily at the two sisters.

'Here,' he said to Charlasse, passing behind him, 'you go on questioning these people. I'm not interested any more. I'll wait for you outside.'

He had finished rolling the cigarette, which he put behind his ear. Before turning away he said to the Tetère girls :

'Assuming you're in the clear this time——'

'In the clear ? ' exploded the doctor. 'Well, I should hope so ! They're the ones who were attacked ! '

Maillard turned slowly towards Coinchot, and drawing back his head so as to survey him from the greatest possible height, he replied :

' I let you do your job, didn't I ? '

Coinchot went very red, but before he could answer Maillard had turned his back on him and was saying to the sisters :

' We'll assume you're in the clear this time . . . But next time I pick you up for anything there'll be no let-off. Don't say I didn't warn you.'

As he crossed the room on his way out he gave the doctor a formal salute without looking at him.

SEVEN

THE CIRCULAR STAIRCASE which led to the top of the cathedral tower was dark and so narrow that two people could not go up it side by side. Buq went first, and in the darker places reached out a hand to Marie-Louise to stop her being frightened. He had made his companions promise not to look down through the slit windows, so as not to spoil the surprise that awaited them when they reached the top ; and in order to avoid temptation Marie-Louise and Antoine kept their eyes fixed on the central pillar of the stairway. This made the climb all the more monotonous, and Buq, as the promoter of the enterprise, sought to sustain their enthusiasm with glowing promises into which crept a note of anxiety, as though he feared an outbreak of mutiny behind his back. When finally they emerged into the sunshine they were dazzled by the light and space.

While Marie-Louise adjusted her cap, Antoine ventured to examine her. She was a thin little girl, with a dark, tanned skin, but with pale, lustreless blonde hair, and her bold eyes were very light. Anyone in the town would have recognised her at a glance as an Artevel. The boys and girls of this Malleboine family, whose poverty had been proverbial for a hundred years, all possessed the peculiarity, among others, of having dark skins and light hair. It was a type which was to be found under other names in that particular quarter, but not in the Upper Town. Antoine decided that Marie-Louise was pretty, and that he might have loved her if she had not belonged to Buq. He noted that she was rather poorly dressed, but did not on that account feel any greater self-confidence in approaching her.

The square platform on which they stood carried at its centre the heptagonal tower from the top of which rose the cathedral spire. It was surrounded by a stone parapet, so high that its flat top reached to the children's shoulders, obliging them to stand on tip-toe in order to see over it. Buq, rendered tyrannical by his anxiety to please them, insisted that they should look first at the view to the north, which he considered the least attractive. In this direction lay the Upper Town, with its new girdle of suburbs, the roads leading to them narrowing away into the distance like the points of a star. Nearer at hand, and directly in front of them, lay the old town, at which Antoine gazed with astonishment, scarcely recognising it. When he walked through its streets, if he happened to pay attention to the look of that urban landscape, the impression he got was quite different. It was dark, with the houses so tightly packed together, seeming to jostle and crowd one another, that the whole thing was like a dense mass to which nothing could be added. But from this vantage point he could see big gardens, spacious court-yards planted with trees, squares of greenery enclosed within the rows of sharply sloping roofs from which the afternoon sun drew soft, clear splashes of colour. Buq explained the geography of the town, starting from the Rue des Rencontres, the principal artery and shopping street. He pointed out the school, the Prefecture, the railway station, the Blue Chapel, the convents; and he pretended not to notice the Malleboine quarter, at his left hand, which he proposed to come to later. After a few moments, since girls notoriously have no sense of direction, he made a show of speaking only to Antoine. Marie-Louise gave him several hurt glances, but without causing him to pay her any attention. It must be

said that Buq was genuinely absorbed in his exploration of
the Upper Town. Growing vexed, she tried to interrupt him
by whistling close to his ear ; but without pausing he merely
made a movement of his hand, as though to brush away a
persistent fly.

'If I'm boring you,' said Marie-Louise, ' I'm not boring
you half as much as you're boring me.'

'Did I say you'd got to listen ? ' demanded Buq, and he
said to Antoine : ' The trouble with girls is, they aren't
interested in anything that matters.'

Marie-Louise looked at him with her face close to his, and
then laughed. Spinning on the points of her sandals, she
made a double turn in the sunshine, her skirt flying above
her knees, and then went dancing and singing to gaze at
other views. After giving a quick glance at the four points of
the compass, she disappeared behind the belfry and was no
longer to be heard. Buq did his best to hide his disquiet, but
he was now talking with less assurance. At last he could bear
it no longer, and said to Antoine :

' Look round without seeming to, and tell me what she's
doing.'

' I can't see her,' replied Antoine.

Buq looked round anxiously.

' So long as she hasn't gone down again . . . She's so
obstinate . . . Wait a second, I'll go and see.'

She had not gone down—Antoine heard a hot exchange of
words between her and Buq. Troubled by these delicate com-
plexities, he was now only remotely interested in the view.
He was thinking a great deal about Buq, the anxiety he had
seen in his eyes, the splendid life he lived. Buq seemed to do
nothing except for love—love of his mother, love of Marie-
Louise, love of adventure. Even when he was talking about
a Latin prose or a problem in algebra, he did so with a
passionate fervour. Antoine thought with an angry disdain

of his own life, which was already no more than a career. An obsession with useful, sensible things, the paternal heritage, would always hold him back from adventure ; he was dedicated already to the sober path that had been chosen for him. Whatever he did, his father's eyes would follow him. For example, he imagined himself penetrating to the depths of the underground stream, brandishing a sword above his head, or a tattered flag, or anything a bit heroic. And then his father arrived, and crossed his arms and said : ' Do you think I've sacrificed myself for this ? Idiot ! . . .' So the air of the underground passage became unbreathable, and there was nothing to do but to go home and work out a square root. Antoine gazed towards the extreme point of the suburb where he could just discern his own house among the most distant. It seemed to be almost separated from the town, lost on the arid plain where meagre plots of cultivated land fought against gorse and bramble, and where quarried patches gaped with the colour of rust. He gazed with an equal disgust at the several villages occupying that expanse to the north. Sometimes on a Sunday he went for a walk there with his family. The houses and the people had a suburban look, because some of the peasants came on bicycles to work in the factory. Proud of their new status, they affected city manners. In sandals and soft shirts, with their stomachs hanging over their belts, they dribbled down a cigarette end while they gazed mockingly at Rigault's cane and Sunday bowler hat. The girls, in bright silk dresses, chattered at the roadside, smacking each other on the behind, or danced together behind the windows of some small drinking place. The villages smelt of eau-de-Cologne and factory squalor. But all that northern part, graceless as it was, gave the town its real character.

The voices of Buq and Marie-Louise now sounded softer as they came from behind the belfry. Antoine caught a murmur with a hint of laughter which only served to heighten his distress. He made a movement to join them, but then thought it better not to do so and went and gazed at the view to the south. The beauty of the countryside caused him to forget his unhappiness. Beyond the river which flowed across the threshold of the town were meadows of brilliant green, patches of shade, farms and smiling villages, and in the distance deep and mossy woods. Further still, enclosing the sky-line, the mountains rose up into the sky like an exhalation of the earth. The town itself, descending steeply towards the river, was more pleasant here than elsewhere. There were numerous gardens, even in the steepest places, where they were terraced between great sustaining walls, thick as ramparts. And in the immediate neighbourhood of the cathedral the houses were handsome and well-built, for the most part two or three centuries old. That part of the town housed the established bourgeoisie, the large invested fortunes—the 'clique,' as Philippon said. Antoine spent a moment trying to distinguish the house of Maître Marguet, whose façade he vividly recalled. He recognised it by the Renaissance pediment which showed up almost opposite him, on a level with the tops of the highest trees in the house's courtyard. Although he had only a partial view of it, the lawyer's dwelling seemed to him no less attractive than it had done the year before.

Leaving the parapet, Antoine at last rejoined his companions. Marie-Louise had Buq by the chin, and was wiping off a splash of ink near his ear with the moistened corner of her handkerchief. Having done so, she hung on to his neck for fun. Buq walked a few steps with her and said to Antoine :

' She's quite heavy to carry that way. You try.'

Marie-Louise turned to Antoine and without coyness put her arms round his neck. She looked up at him laughing, with her head thrown back, and he was troubled. He did not know what to do with his hands or with his gaze, and he was alarmed at the heavy beating of his heart against Marie-Louise. He took a clumsy pace forward, and stumbled at the next step. She put her foot to the ground and said as she unlocked her arms :

' You aren't as strong as he is.'

Antoine felt very unhappy. He would have liked to be as strong as big Pucelet, so that Marie-Louise might admire him. He went and leaned against the western parapet, and the two others came on either side of him. Buq pointed down to the Malleboine quarter. It was a deep, fan-shaped gulf that seemed to have been carved out by the river, which at that point wound in towards the town. From the height at which they stood they could see, foreshortened, at their right hand, a descent of high walls which marked the sudden breaching of the plateau. The houses aligned at the edge of this breach found their first resting-place half-way up the escarpment, on an outcropping of rock, and others were situated at its foot. The wall of the Rond-Point, at the point of the fan, was considerably the lowest. On the other side, over to the left, the Malleboine quarter mounted steeply to the plateau, but on a slope which at a pinch a car could negotiate. Seeing it thus one could understand why that enclosed town, isolated by its own depth, should lead a life apart. Unless they followed the winding road that flanked the river, its inhabitants had no access to the Upper Town except by steeply mounting alleyways or flights of steps. Their valley had no gardens, since space was too much in demand. In order that all the houses might see daylight, passages, alleyways, blind alleys, all the vents of communication had had to be multiplied. The dense crowding, the large number and narrowness of the streets, must be an invitation to neighbourliness.

Antoine was little the wiser for Buq's commentary. It was impossible to distinguish anything amid that huddle of roofs and chimneys. Buq himself was not very sure of the place where the Sourdine emerged from the earth, and he was searching for landmarks at the edge of the Upper Town.

'There, where I'm pointing, that's the prison, near the bell-tower of the Blue Chapel . . .'

'Is that the prison?' exclaimed Marie-Louise. 'Perhaps my Uncle Louis can see us!'

She reached out her arm to its full extent, affectionately waving her handkerchief. Buq was slightly embarrassed on account of Antoine. It was a matter that might appear disconcerting to anyone not of the quarter. The young men of the Artevel family were all hot-heads. Most of them served at least one prison sentence of from six months to a year. Assault and battery, abuse of the police, contempt of court, were the usual reasons. In the criminal court the name of Artevel was almost synonymous with prison, and the judges treated them severely. Being restored to civil life, they generally married and settled down in an exemplary fashion. In the quarter their terms of imprisonment were discussed with perfect openness as a tiresome necessity, not unlike the period of military service but on the whole more acceptable, since they paid for the rapture of a moment of freedom. The Artevels were neither ashamed nor proud of them, nor did they bear any resentment. Antoine did not venture to ask about Marie-Louise's uncle, but since this wrongdoer had evidently not been repudiated by his family he supposed that he had been guilty of a political offence. Uncle Louis had probably been something like a communist, and very possibly had been caught oiling his machine-gun in the family circle. Antoine gazed at Marie-Louise with envy and admiration. There was no risk of any such thing happening in his own home. He had a momentary vision of barricades set up in the heart of the Malleboine. Guns thundered from the Rond-Point, the soldiery attacked, all the insurgents were dead; Buq had been killed in the last ditch, laughing defiantly, and he, Antoine, the only survivor, black with powder, dauntless and terrible, spurting machine-gun bullets and curses, was retreating step by step to the underground passage of the Sourdine, by means of which he escaped the fury of the pursuit, because he could not go so far as to imagine himself dead.

Buq, meanwhile, was very peacefully staring down at the river and thinking of a boating party he had been on the year before. Antoine looked at him with a slight reproach and asked :

' What are you ? '

' How do you mean, what am I ? '

' I mean, what are you in politics ? '

' I don't know,' said Buq, rather taken aback. ' What are you, anyway ? '

' I'm a communist,' said Antoine, with a glow of revolutionary ardour in his eyes which, however, appeared to make no impression on Marie-Louise.

' A communist . . .' said Buq reflectively. ' Well, I'm not. I'm all for the army—or if you'd rather, for liberty . . .'

Marie-Louise yawned as she gazed over the town. She asked if they weren't going to play anything, and Buq devised a game of catch which was quite amusing. But it palled after a quarter of an hour, and they tried to think of another.

' What would be fun,' said Buq, joking, ' would be to play follow-my-leader along the top of the parapet. Anyone who fell off would be out.'

' Aren't you clever ! ' said Marie-Louise.

The almost mechanical response was not meant to offend, nor did it trouble Buq. Without any thought of vexing Marie-Louise, he went on to consider, purely in theory, the possibilities offered by this idea of running round on the edge of the abyss.

' There wouldn't really be anything difficult about walking along the top,' he said. ' It would be all right if you didn't get giddy.'

Marie-Louise shrugged her shoulders with the patient, exasperated expression she might have worn in listening to someone who was drunk. This time Buq's feelings were hurt.

' I wouldn't mind getting up,' he said. ' Perhaps I'd be the first who's ever done it.'

He went up to the parapet on the side where it overlooked the plain beyond the river. He stood stroking the top, which was not more than eight inches wide, and said that there was really nothing in it. Antoine tried to head him off with a friendly protest which secured him an honourable retreat. Buq had rather been counting on this, but Marie-Louise said defiantly :

' Don't worry. He'd be much too scared to get up there.'

Buq did not so much as look round, but grasped the outer part of the parapet with both hands. With one foot upon the swelling of a pillar, he drew himself effortlessly upwards. He was half-way on to the parapet when Marie-Louise grasped the tail of his overall and said in a breathless voice :

' Get down ! You're to get down at once ! '

The blood had left her face, and her brown skin had turned grey. Antoine saw a light in her clear eyes which he found almost terrifying.

' You're to get down ! ' she said again.

' Leave me alone ! ' said Buq.

He raised one leg to get his knee on to the parapet, but she grabbed the other and pulled him back with so much strength that he could not resist. When he had recovered his balance on firm ground, Marie-Louise slapped his face twice without saying a word. The sound of the two slaps rang out sharply in the perfect silence of their lofty retreat. Antoine was moved to admiration, and Buq himself stayed for an instant as though dazed. Marie-Louise, her arms hanging, stood gazing in the dawn of consternation at the marks of her furious hands on his cheeks. Then in a rage he flung himself upon her and rolled her on the ground, without her making any attempt to resist. He held her with her back pressed to the stone floor, digging his nails into her thin shoulders. Marie-Louise gave a little moan. He released her at once to lie alongside her, their faces close, their looks and breath intermingled.

Antoine had had no chance to intervene. Seeing the quarrel over and his friends reconciled, he scarcely knew what to do. Finally he went and sat on the ground by the parapet, and tried to take an interest in the view. With his head half-way through the gap between two pillars, he looked again for the lawyer's house, and found it easily. He saw the figure of a man appear at the attic window in the middle of the Renaissance pediment, and recognised Maître Marguet by his light-coloured waistcoat, his fringe of dark beard and his bald head. The distance separating them was not great, a little more than a hundred yards, and he could distinguish his features. The lawyer leaned out as though to examine the window-frame, and seemed to address a remark to someone behind him. After which he stepped back a pace, and without hurrying closed the window. At the same moment the cathedral clock struck five. Antoine turned and said urgently to the others :

' Five o'clock ! It's late. We ought to be going.'

He saw tears roll down the brown cheeks of Marie-Louise. Buq, also red-eyed, was holding her by the hand and saying that he loved her.

EIGHT

ALTHOUGH THE CRIME had been common knowledge in the town for over twelve hours, Rigault still had not heard about it. He had spent the Sunday morning weeding his garden paths, and about an hour before midday he sent his son to buy a paper at the nearest *bureau de tabac*, by the railway bridge. Antoine's head was so full of Buq and Marie-Louise and their love affair, and of the Malleboine quarter, which he had entered for the first time after coming down from the cathedral tower, that he had not bothered to look at the paper, but had handed it, still folded, to his father. After doing this he took a book and went and sat behind a bush on the waste land, where he was hidden from the sun and his parents.

Rigault, after putting away his tools, sat down to read the paper on a heap of weeds at the bottom of the garden. The moment he opened it he learned that a murder had taken place in the town, and was somewhat annoyed that the news should have come from Paris. 'HIDEOUS CRIME OF A SADIST,' ran the headline. The story was as follows :

'(From our special correspondent.) A revolting crime, as shameful as it was barbarous, has horrified the citizens of our peaceful town. The scene of the appalling drama is a charming period house, with a delightful Renaissance pediment, situated not far from the cathedral, where it is hidden amid the greenery and cool shade of the trees. The owner of the house is none other than Maître Marguet, the well-known lawyer, who enjoys a well-deserved reputation throughout the district for probity and benevolence. And the victim? A girl of nineteen, a simple, innocent creature who had been employed as a maidservant in the house for less than six months. An unhappy child, brimming with all the hopes of youth, who was destined by a lamentable chain of circumstances to fall prey to the vile instincts of a human fiend! The mind recoils, shuddering, from the very thought of this horror, and indeed would refuse to credit it were it not compelled by the evidence to do so.

'Here are the facts:

'At about seven o'clock this evening Maître Marguet's wife began to wonder at the prolonged absence of Charlotte Richon, the young maid—without, however, being unduly disturbed by it. Since she had been in the lawyer's service, Charlotte had been in the habit of going out every evening, between five and a quarter past, to take his letters to the post; and before doing so she was accustomed to spend a few minutes attending to her toilet in her little room on the second floor, overlooking the courtyard. This innocent vanity was destined to prove fatal. At a quarter past seven Mme. Marguet mentioned her astonishment at the girl's continued absence to her husband, who had just returned from his usual evening stroll. He, so he tells us, was less anxious than annoyed, imagining that some flirtation was keeping the girl out of doors. But after waiting another half-hour they both became seriously alarmed, the more so since in general she was most regular, and never stayed away longer than the time needed to go to the Post Office and back. The cook, who had already been questioned by Mme. Marguet, declared herself no less astonished, since Charlotte had said and done nothing to lead anyone to suppose that she would stay out so long. Acting on the lawyer's advice, she went up to the second floor to make sure that the girl was not in her room, either because she had fallen asleep or because she was feeling unwell. She returned instantly uttering cries of horror, and in a voice broken with emotion told her employers that Charlotte Richon had been murdered.

'Without wasting a moment Maître Marguet telephoned the police, and Sergeant Maillard, accompanied by a constable, hurried to the spot. Up in the attic bedroom an appalling spectacle met their eyes. The wretched Charlotte Richon was lying in the middle of the room in a pool of blood. The clothes had been torn off her, and her body had been hideously mutilated, especially in the region of the abdomen. Decency imposes limitations upon the pen of a newspaper reporter, even when it is for the purpose of enlightening those who read in good faith, and in order to stigmatise the crime of a sadistic monster. We may mention, however, that the weapon used, a large pruning-knife, a detail which was to be of material assistance to the inquiry, was found close to the body of the victim. The wounds . . . (a full description followed.)

'The Commissioner of Police, M. Crudet, being also sent for, arrived and proceeded to make a preliminary investigation. The truth was not long in becoming known, and perhaps it was the cook who had the first inkling. Upon being questioned by the commissioner, she cried :

'"It was the workman! The man who was working in the shed! He tried to pinch me only this morning!"

'This workman, of whom no one had thought in the confusion of the first minutes, is a man named Trousseguin, well known to the townspeople, and, not to put too fine a point on it, well known to the police, who have had dealings with him on more than one occasion. His monstrous, ape-like physique has, indeed, made him something of a celebrity. He had only just returned to the district, which he left last year, and he was tramping round in search of work when on Friday evening Maître Marguet charitably offered him the job of whitewashing a shed in his garden. Tragic benevolence ! . . . but who can claim to read the sombre book of Destiny ? Our best deeds, once accomplished, are no longer our own and may betray our purpose. Who can say whether the truest charity is not that which remains potential, fulfilling itself with the will rather than the deed ? Certainly this is the form of charity that prudence most often recommends, as to-day's event bears witness . . . The name of Troussequin was almost enough in itself to convince the Commissioner, the more so since the weapon came from the shed where he had been working. Maître Marguet was the only one, with Sergeant Maillard, to retain any doubt as to the wretched creature's guilt. He could not believe that the man, whom he had paid for his day's work at six o'clock that evening, and who had then seemed perfectly quiet and normal, could have committed a hideous crime only a few minutes before. As for Sergeant Maillard, his last doubts vanished when he learned, on calling at Troussequin's lodging in the Rue du Papegai, that he had borrowed a bicycle and made off. Now, while the poor, tortured body of the little servant lies in the hospital morgue, the police are actively searching for the murderer, whose arrest cannot be long delayed.'

This news, that Troussequin had become an outlaw doomed to speedy arrest, came to Rigault as a miraculous deliverance from a threat which had left him not an instant's peace during the past two days. The vice had suddenly relaxed its grip, and life and dignity were restored to him. A childlike joy, of spring and holidays, filled his being, and kindness welled up in his heart. As a fair-minded man, he did his best to feel ashamed of a burst of happiness which he felt to be inappropriate to the event, but the mere effort sufficed to appease his conscience. In any case, his joy was unsullied by any thought of vengeance. The happening meant nothing to him but the ending of a nightmare. He had a wild desire to laugh, to romp. Coming upon his son in the doorway of the house, he lifted him up by the shoulders and pressed him tenderly to himself. The action was so unusual that Antoine was dumbfounded. Rigault, too, felt that he had gone rather far, and hastened to don a more respectable countenance.

'You didn't work very long this morning,' he said. 'Have you done all your homework?'

'I did it yesterday,' said Antoine, become suddenly sulky in his disappointment.

'Yesterday afternoon?'

'Yes.'

On Sundays they had lunch in the dining-room, a ceremony of indescribable boredom. And Rigault continued to behave strangely. Arranging the newspaper beside his plate, with the account of the crime uppermost, he was shaken by a long fit of silent laughter, causing his wife and son to regard him in some apprehension. He managed for a time to contain his mirth, but his eyes danced with a wild hilarity, and finally he exploded into his napkin.

'I'm being stupid,' he said in apology. 'But you don't know what happened yesterday evening? I've just read it in the paper. Maître Marguet's maid was murdered at his house . . .'

He then sobered down and told them the story of the crime, quoting from the paper. Antoine listened with a mounting intensity which kept him rigid, his face growing pale and his eyes staring. Although he was not yet clear about the exact time, he seemed, as he listened to his father, to be witnessing the drama from the cathedral tower, while behind him Buq and Marie-Louise gazed at one another with tears in their eyes.

93

'And who do you think the murderer is ? ' demanded Rigault. ' Who do you think was in that attic at five o'clock ? You can have as many guesses as you like. You'll never get it ! '

He paused and waited. Antoine opened his mouth to cry out. He wanted to protect himself with his two hands, but his limbs seemed to be made of lead, his tongue to be immovable.

' The man was Troussequin,' said his father. ' What do you think of that ? Troussequin ! '

Antoine was now in a state of extreme pallor. His nostrils contracted and he fainted, falling forward with his head on the table. His parents started up. While his father held him in his arms, his mother laid a damp towel on his forehead and fanned him with the newspaper. When he came to, Antoine seemed to see a look of accusing suspicion mingled with their anxiety. He wriggled in his father's arms as though to escape from an unwanted embrace, and said in a sulky voice that he felt better and was hungry. Rigault set him back in his chair, wounded at having his solicitude rebuffed. Antoine's colour returned, but he seemed greatly upset. They decided that he must not have too much to eat, and must lie down for an hour or two after lunch. Then in the evening they would take him out for a walk, and he would be all right. Rigault remarked that this indisposition was not surprising.

' He was sitting in the sun all the morning without a hat. What more do you want ? You'd have done far better to go on with your homework.'

His wife's eye warned him to be careful, and he said no more. When their meal was over Antoine went and lay on his bed, but could not sleep.

He was crushed beneath the burden of his secret. He could only rid himself of it by confessing his misdeed, by letting his father know that an hour after coming out of school he had been on the cathedral tower. At first sight it seemed

94

perfectly simple : nothing mattered except to save an innocent man. But Antoine could still hear his father's terrible
voice when, on Friday, he had given way to rage and despair
because he had been three-quarters of an hour late. Must
he now tell him that the very next day his son had again
fallen from grace ?—his perverse, heartless child, steeped in
wrongdoing, defying the parental ban and mocking his
wrath ! It was not merely the scolding and the lecturing
that Antoine feared, but that cruel self-gratification of the
family tyrant whose victim offered him the pretext for
tyranny and persecution. 'It's what I've always said,' he
could hear his father exclaim. 'I've been too good to you.'
And he would wallow in hypocritical remorse for his own
generosity, delighted at the chance to humiliate and abase
under a show of justice. Antoine's heart hardened, and he
began to make up a story. He imagined his father, after
having abused and beaten him with inconceivable violence
(in fact, Rigault had never beaten his son) going with him to
the school to ask the headmaster to treat him with the utmost
severity. On the way they encountered an enormous mad
dog, or better still, a wild beast escaped from a menagerie.
His father drew back trembling with fright and waited for
the end with eyes closed and teeth chattering. But Antoine
bravely attacked the ravening monster, and (after considering various alternatives) hung it from the branch of
a tree by its tail, which he tied in a double knot. He then
said over his shoulder, in a quiet, calm voice :
'It's all right now. You're quite safe.'
His father, still white and trembling, now only wanted
to go home and recover from the shock . . . Well, perhaps he thanked his son for having saved his life . . . But
no, one might as well skip that—the words would have
burnt his lips.
But this fable did not alter things. It could not make

Antoine forget the crime in the attic. He was acutely conscious of the weakness of his age, and he wept into his pillow at the injustice which had laid so heavy a burden upon his child's shoulders.

At five that afternoon the Rigault family reached the centre of the town. Juliette, anxious to go and see her mother, whose state of health was worrying her, left her husband and son in the Rue des Rencontres. The pavements were somewhat more crowded than was customary on a Sunday. People were walking slowly, noting each other's clothes and exchanging remarks as they passed. Small clusters formed at the street corners. It was said that Troussequin had managed to get on a train and escape to Switzerland. A few lively spirits tried to spread false reports, but without succeeding. The sober crowd, steeped in its week-end lethargy, was not greatly excited by the crime at the lawyer's house. Their Sunday clothes had a damping effect on pity and indignation, which called for week-day sweat and the stress of labour. Rigault had expected to find an excitement corresponding to his own, and was disappointed. Even the news of Troussequin's arrest would scarcely have aroused them from their torpor. After all, there was no mystery about the business, and not much food for conversation. The victim was almost unknown in the town, and as for the murderer, his act surprised no one. That the little serving-maid should have chanced to encounter the lowest kind of human beast was a happening so fortuitous as to be scarcely interesting. In any case, people were rather anxiously waiting to hear the result of the rugby match between the town and Dijon.

In the heart of that placid crowd, Antoine was terrified to think that he possessed a secret which might shake them out of their apathy. At moments it seemed to him inconceivable that he alone, of all those people, should know the truth. The sluggish, monotonous tide of Sunday clothes that pressed in upon him, airing an unassailable conviction of security, caused him to doubt his own knowledge. There was something miraculous and unbelievable in the truth— the real and only truth, so terrible that it could let loose the fury of the crowd, and yet so fragile, since it had taken refuge with a child. Antoine had a sense of danger amid that soft flow of Sunday families up and down the pavements of the Rue des Rencontres. He was afraid lest their massive certainty should quite wipe out of his mind the picture of the lawyer closing the attic window, and he hated them for brushing up against him.

Rigault led the way to the Place de l'Hotel-de-Ville, where they mingled with a few sightseers who had gathered in front of the police station. Behind the unwashed windows of the guard room they could see the short, tubby figure of Commissioner Crudet, who was gesticulating freely but whose words could not be heard. Constable Charlasse, who was just going on duty, answered the questioners with a gesture proclaiming his ignorance, and went inside.

Maillard, seated at the telephone, was listening to his chief with a surly, abstracted air.

' It's perfectly simple,' Commissioner Crudet was saying. ' He left the town at seven yesterday evening, and a warning was sent out to every railway station at half-past eight. Even if he had managed to get on a train we should have known by now. A chap like that doesn't get by without being noticed. Well? . . .'

Maillard did not answer. Crudet bent forward to glare at him.

' Should the gendarmerie have arrested him this morning, or should they not? '

' Sunday isn't like a weekday,' said Maillard. ' People are less involved with one another. News doesn't get about so quickly. There are small places in the country that are as good as cut off.'

Crudet, who was now stamping up and down the room, raised his arms to heaven.

' Are you trying to tell me a bed-time story ? ' he shouted.

The sergeant stood up, very red in the face. He leaned across the table with his jaw thrust out towards the commissioner, and exploded :

' I've never let anyone treat me with a lack of respect— not even a commissioner ! Understand ? You're too small to try ! '

Crudet retreated, protesting that there had been nothing in his attitude or his words to warrant this outburst. Nothing more came of the incident for the time being. Their state of nervous impatience was enough to account for a sudden spurt of anger, without its being taken too seriously. After a brief pause Maillard said to Charlasse :

' The thing that would make me laugh, and I'm not the only one, is if it turned out that Troussequin wasn't guilty.'

' I suppose,' said the commissioner sweetly, ' you think the victim committed suicide ? '

The honeyed gibe nearly caused Maillard to lose his self-control again. He managed not to do so, however, and said as though speaking to himself :

' I've known Troussequin for over thirty years.'

' And so ? ' said the commissioner.

Receiving no reply, he jeered :

' You mean that his unimpeachable record puts him beyond suspicion ? The fact that he has already served a sentence for attempted rape was no doubt due to an error ! '

The sergeant's face relaxed a little, and he laughed quite genuinely as he recalled this heroic exploit.

' It was a pretty stiff sentence,' he said, ' —two months in prison for trying to rape the Madame of Number Fifteen! Poor Troussequin! If I'd never had anyone worse than him to deal with, I'd have had an easy time of it.'

He glanced towards Charlasse who, born and bred in the Malleboine quarter, was better able than the commissioner to appreciate the epic gusto, the riotous hopefulness of that attempt at rape. They exchanged reminiscent smiles, and the sergeant said lightly:

'One runs into some queer things. When you start thinking . . . For instance, that business of the Sourdine sluice-gates, three years ago.'

'The sluice-gates . . .' murmured Charlasse, looking slightly embarrassed.

'But you were in on that, weren't you?' said Maillard, winking. 'You were one of the gang!'

'It was before I joined the service,' said Charlasse apologetically. 'I was only a kid.'

'Go along with you! But the best of all was the evening of the Carnival, last year.'

'I wasn't mixed up in that,' said Charlasse.

'But I was,' said the sergeant. 'It's not often anything happens without my being mixed up in it. But I'm always on the same side—one of the kill-joys.'

The commissioner, disapproving of this nostalgic interlude, said in a slightly acid voice:

'Upon my word, sergeant, anyone would think you regretted it!'

'It's not a question of regrets,' said Maillard gently. 'It's just a way of looking at things.'

With his head resting on his hand he allowed his thoughts to stray over the life of constant vigilance he had lived for thirty years, wondering how it had come about that he should have devoted himself so unsparingly to the maintenance of order. Without any sense of shame he recalled the

99

days of his youth, when in blue cotton tights he had displayed himself on the platform outside a fair booth, raised above the dust and racket of the crowd, and sought by the eyes of countless women who singled him out from among other athletes who had grown pot-bellied. His life had taken a very different course!

While he was thus meditating on the past, Philippon came in. The commissioner rose to meet him, indicating with a gesture that there was no news. The mayor seemed to be more than disappointed; he uttered an exclamation of rage. This was the fourth time he had called in for news, his impatience being such that he could not wait to get it by telephone. Commissioner Crudet found this zeal peculiar. The truth was that Philippon took no interest in the crime as such, but was most anxious to have the murderer arrested as soon as possible. As luck would have it, the barrister, Fouchard, had left on a short trip to Italy two days before. If they were slow in finding Troussequin, he might be back by the time they had done so; in which case there was every likelihood that he would be chosen to defend him. A fine chance to gain prestige in the town and in the constituency! The Party would adopt him as their candidate in spite of all manœuvres.

' A creature as conspicuous as that! ' stormed Philippon. ' I simply don't understand how they haven't got him.'

' The day's not over yet. I'm sure the gendarmerie will get him,' said the commissioner, putting the responsibility on the rural police as opposed to the town force.

' The gendarmerie . . .' the mayor grumbled. ' Well, of course, the gendarmerie . . . but suppose he's hidden in the town ? '

' He left it yesterday evening. There's clear evidence of that.'

' But suppose he came back during the night ? '

The question was received in hostile silence.

'The police seem a lot more ready to badger a couple of half-starved prostitutes than they are to arrest a murderer,' said Philippon, with his eyes on Maillard.

'The prostitutes have nothing to complain of,' said the sergeant. 'Particularly when they've got highly-placed clients to take care of them.'

Philippon did not venture to pursue the matter, since the sergeant was looking dangerous. He shook hands with the commissioner, who had not understood this last exchange, and went out without being able to refrain from slamming the door. Shortly afterwards Constable Guilbon, a little swarthy man with an unprepossessing face, came into the guard room and saluted Crudet. The sergeant rose and buckled on his belt.

'I'm going out for a stroll to give myself an appetite,' he said. 'I shall be back at half-past seven.' He went out, saying to the group of sensation-mongers round the entrance, 'No, there's nothing new. Why don't you follow my example and have a walk while the weather's fine?'

Rigault, who had been standing there with Antoine for a quarter of an hour, thought the advice sensible and decided that they would go down to the river. As they crossed the Place de l'Hotel-de-Ville they met big Pucelet, with his father, the photographer. Although he was in low spirits, Antoine was forced to smile at the sight of his schoolfellow in a lace collar tied with a broad blue ribbon. His father possessed a large stock of these collars, which he had used before the war when photographing school groups : they were now quite out of date, so he was trying to use them up on his son. While the two men fell into conversation the boys moved a few paces away, and big Pucelet said :

'I've got some new photographs—jolly good—I'll let you have them for four sous each. Or if you'd like to come to our place I'll give them to you. Would you like me to ask your father if you can come round ? '

Antoine refused, and Pucelet went on to talk about something else. He broke off to stare at a young woman who passed by, turning his head to follow her in spite of the lace collar. His eyes gleamed, and he made a sort of neighing sound through his nose.

' Victor ! ' exclaimed his father. ' Do you want to feel my boot in your backside ? '

Big Pucelet buried his face in the blue ribbon and neighed under his breath.

' The boy's impossible,' said the photographer to Rigault. ' I can't tell you what a pest he is. What about yours ? How do you punish him ? '

Rigault murmured a confused reply, somewhat ashamed of the fact that he had never dealt his son the smallest blow.

' I've given up playing the martinet,' said the photographer. ' I'm not saying there isn't something to be said for treating them rough, but children soon get used to it, and then you can't catch them out any more. Setting traps isn't a bad thing. I worked on those lines for a long time with Victor and managed pretty well, but now that he's getting big I've got a new system. I just go for him with nothing but my hands, and he's allowed to hit back. To play fair, and so as not to overdo it, I only use one hand.' He smiled and concluded with a wink : ' I manage to get in a few hefty whacks just the same.'

Rigault, who had at first been disposed to wonder whether he was not absurdly over-indulgent in his treatment of Antoine, now burst into protest. The unhappy young Pucelet, whose mother had died a few months after he was born, seemed to him deserving of the utmost compassion.

' One doesn't always get the best results by beating children,' he said.

'It's all a question of method,' agreed the photographer. 'I've brought him up like that, and I've never had any reason to complain. By the way, has Troussequin been arrested yet? I expect you've just come from the police station. I was on my way there to find out.'

'There's no news yet,' said Rigault. 'If you ask me, he's got across the frontier.'

Since there seemed to be no point in going on to the police station, the photographer accompanied the Rigaults on their walk. The Rue Jacques-de-Molay, in which the crime had been committed, was a convenient way of getting down to the river embankment, and they followed it automatically. A few groups of people were strolling slowly up and down it, pausing in front of the ivy-covered wall which hid the lawyer's house. At the entrance to the street stood Maître Marguet, receiving the condolences of an importunate acquaintance who had button-holed him in passing. He was like a cat on hot bricks, his greatest anxiety being lest the cathedral organist, who was probably on the look-out in his cellar, should notice that he had come within range of his periscope.

At the sight of the lawyer Antoine stopped dead, and his father was alarmed to see him turn as pale as he had done before his fainting fit.

'What's the matter? Are you tired?'

'I want to sit down,' muttered Antoine.

'Let's go to a café and have an aperitif,' said the photographer. 'He can rest for a bit.'

Big Pucelet, of his own accord, picked up his friend and carried him in his arms with a gentleness that touched Rigault. Antoine, his head against the lace collar, felt his thoughts grow muddled and wanted to go to sleep. Behind him he heard a hearty voice say:

'The way I treat mine, I tie his hands behind his back before he goes to bed . . .'

Maître Marguet, having managed to get rid of the client who had so determinedly thrust sympathy upon him, was lucky enough to be able to reach his door without being seen by the organist. The closed attic window in the middle of the Renaissance pediment was glittering in the light of the setting sun, whose rays now only reached the upper part of the house. The lawyer paused a moment in the courtyard to gaze up at that glowing reflection, while he wondered whether yesterday evening, at the time of the crime, the sun had been low enough to light up the victim's body. It was a detail to which he attached great importance on account of the two rolls of films he had exposed in the room. That he should have been too preoccupied to notice—a lamentable oversight in an experienced photographer—caused him a sense of melancholy regret (which he admired himself for feeling, and therefore felt the more). 'What splendid circumstances escape us in the most exalted moments,' he reflected, continuing on his way into the house. 'Even, and indeed above all, in the everyday business of life ! . . .'

Mme. Marguet the younger was alone on the first floor with her mother-in-law. Her husband realised directly he entered that the old lady had been picking a quarrel with her. The pretext was ready to hand : if the household had been better conducted, if laxness and self-indulgence had not been the rule, if the mistress of the house had kept a sharper eye on her domestic staff, the maids would not have received lovers in their rooms, and so would not have run the risk of being disembowelled. It was a fine scandal that this disgusting butchery should have taken place in a house where three generations of Marguets had lived honourable lives ! Not that she was in the least surprised. She had always said, and this was a good time for repeating it, that her son had been guilty of the greatest folly in marrying the sixth daughter of a commissariat colonel, with nothing in the way of dowry except a pianist's diploma and an absurd devotion. To old Mme. Marguet the titled bourgeoisie and the military were the joint objects of an equal hatred ; on the other hand, she had a weakness for priests and their smooth manners, although she had little religion. She was never at a loss for sarcasm on the subjects of her daughter-in-law's bigotry and of half-starved officers who made daughters for their wives as though they were wielding a sabre, and then left it to other people to support them . . . The shy and simple Lucie Marguet, the lawyer's wife, was still so innocent as to believe in her mother-in-law's good faith. In dealing with the alert-minded, alertly hating old lady, who had moreover the advantage of her eighty years, she was exposed to the strangest surprises, as she was to the most shameful reproaches. She was chiefly accused of setting the son against his mother. Not that he had ever failed to be a good son. Indeed, he was both affectionate and obedient. But when, seven years previously, old Madame Marguet had moved out of their house to a flat in the vicinity, with the object of making the friends of the family believe that her daughter-in-law's harshness had forced her to take this extreme course, she had been disappointed in her hope of being immediately begged to return. Whatever it may have cost the lawyer to keep her at a distance, he had never spoken the words she had been waiting seven years to hear, but had remained steadfast even in the face of Lucie's protests.

At the sight of his wife's unhappy face, her red nose and swollen eyelids, Maître Marguet could scarcely contain his indignation. He greeted his mother coldly, inquired after her health without waiting for an answer, and sitting down beside Lucie devoted himself entirely to her. He took her hands, comforted her with a smile which disavowed all the unkind words to which she might have had to listen, and tenderly urged her not to over-tire herself.

'If you were sensible you'd go and get some rest. You spent the whole night watching over the body in the hospital, and you scarcely got two hours' sleep this morning.'

His mother could not refrain from shrugging her shoulders at the thought of the wife of a Marguet spending a night in the morgue at the bedside of a dead servant. She saw in it nothing but an affectation of simplicity, a preposterous eagerness to seize any excuse for an orgy of prayer.

'You might have saved yourself the trouble,' she remarked to Lucie. 'Your presence wasn't going to bring her back to life.'

Maître Marguet squeezed his wife's hand and answered for her.

'You're quite right, mother. The poor child can't be brought back to life. But when her father arrived on the bus a short while ago I was able to tell him that a friend had spent the night at her side. I can assure you it was a consolation to him.'

'Did you take him to the hospital?' asked Lucie.

Maître Marguet replied at first with a nod. He seemed to reflect for a moment and then said in a quiet voice, with his eyes upon the picture of sky and garden that filled the window:

'I left him there. He wanted to be alone with her. He'll come here for dinner, and he'll sleep in the room on the ground floor. When I went to meet him at the bus stop he was trembling all over. I had to hold his arm to help him walk to the hospital. He had brought a bunch of flowers from his garden, and he told me that she could have arranged a bouquet like that with her eyes shut. He told me about a dog she loved, and about the meadows where she used to take the cows to graze . . . When he saw her on that narrow hospital bed he seemed for a moment almost comforted. The face is so calm, so childlike . . . He had brought a rosary that he wanted to put round her hands, but the fingers were twisted and the hands badly joined. He began to tremble again, and he gave the rosary to a Sister. He knelt down with his forehead against the side of the bed. Every time he breathed I heard a groan in his throat, and suddenly he began to cry, stuffing the bedclothes into his mouth. He cried . . .'

Lucie and her mother-in-law wept in silence, and Maître Marguet, whose voice had grown husky, uttered a sob that was like a cry. He went into the next room, the drawing-room, and dabbed his eyes with his handkerchief. Before returning to the dining-room it occurred to him that he might as well retrieve the two spools of photographs which he had hidden the previous evening in a small writing bureau. He had got rid of them rather hastily, in a moment of panic, hiding them in a secret drawer whose existence was, as a matter of fact, known to the entire family, and which was never used except as a joke. Last year, when they had amused themselves by writing one another literary epistles, Lucie and he had used it as a letter-box.

After pressing the button he put his hand in the drawer and was startled to find only one spool. The thing was so improbable that at first he could not believe it ; but it was a fact, none the less. Someone had opened the drawer and taken one of the spools. He considered which of the people who had had access to the drawing-room since the previous evening knew about the drawer. Neither his wife nor the cook (if, in fact, she knew of it) would have dreamed of playing any such joke on him. No one but old Mme. Marguet, taking advantage of a moment when she was alone in the drawing-room to go prying into the bureau, would have had the notion of pocketing one of the spools in order to have it developed. He recalled the quizzical look with which she had greeted him a few minutes before.

NINE

THE CAFÉ VUILLEMARD, at the corner of the Rue du Papegai and the Impasse de la Courte, was less frequented than any other in the quarter. There was no room for dancing, and its state of shabbiness kept the younger people away. It had only recently been opened by Vuillemard, who had simply knocked down the partition between two rooms without letting himself in for any further expense. The original wallpapers remained, pink in one half and yellow in the other, and the tables and chairs were of different patterns. Vuillemard based no extravagant hopes on the undertaking, but said that he was content with the modest profits achieved by his wife while he was working in the factory. A number of his fellow-workers, living in the Malleboine quarter, made a point of dropping in once or twice a week. Sunday was the best day for trade, and that afternoon had been a particularly good one. The customers had made themselves thirsty discussing the crime and the flight of Troussequin, some still believing in his innocence and others not, and they had gone from beer to aperitifs without stopping drinking. But there were far fewer customers after supper, and from nine o'clock on there was no one in the place but Pierre Artevel, the older brother of Marie-Louise, who was playing cards with Vuillemard and a couple of his friends. Trésor, who was looking for his girl Minie, had entered in passing and was standing behind Artevel. His quest had taken him from one café to another, and he was laughing to himself for no apparent reason, in the first stages of drunkenness. Suddenly he became intent and said to the players :

'Watch what I'm going to do ! '

The four heads went up together. Trésor seized Artevel's glass and distended his cheeks with a great mouthful of beer. Then, holding his lips between his thumb and forefinger, and without bending his tall figure a fraction of an inch, he squirted the liquid down to the very last drop into the furthest glass, which was Vuillemard's, in a steady stream as exact as the flight of a bolt from a crossbow. It was an incomparable feat of skill of which he was the only person in the town, perhaps in the whole world, to know the secret. He attempted it only very rarely and when inspiration came to him. Pierre Artevel and the two other men burst into friendly laughter, but Vuillemard did not take it in that spirit. Picking up his foaming glass he called Trésor a sick pig and threatened to teach him manners with his boot. Trésor seemed not to hear him. He was watching a moth and laughing at nothing. Vuillemard became furious.

'I won't have you in this place at all, d'you understand ? Why don't you pay for the two drinks you had before dinner, instead of coming in and upsetting people ? You great loafer ! At your age a young man ought to be ashamed of slouching round the streets and doing nothing with his hands ! '

Artevel and the two others uttered a conciliatory murmur containing a hint of reproof. In the idea of demanding money from Trésor there was something that troubled their sense of propriety. They found it proper that this twenty-five-year-old man should lead a life of perfect idleness. Work was not his business, the light-hearted creature that he was. At moments, while they were busy in the factory or the workshop, the thought of him occurred to them and they imagined him yawning in the Rue de la Clé-d'Or, on the bottom step of the big stairway, or kicking a pebble along the Impasse de la Sourdine. He was a friend who did their dreaming for them. Even Vuillemard felt himself to be at fault, and his anger went off at a tangent. He pointed to a big inflamed boil, dark red in colour, bleeding and suppurating, on Trésor's neck.

' Look at the dirty fellow, with that filthy thing under his chin ! It doesn't stop him drinking out of other people's glasses ! Have I got to catch all his beastly complaints ? You'd have to pay me a lot to get me to drink after him ! '

He pushed his glass away with a movement of disgust. Trésor emptied it at a gulp, without taking his eyes off the big moth flying round the table, and when it flew towards the doorway he went after it with a sudden start that made Vuillemard's chair rock. There were some moments of confusion. Trésor jumped on the tables, laughing as he did so ; he overturned chairs and bumped against the electric light, while Vuillemard threatened to throw him out in no uncertain fashion. Finally the panic-stricken moth managed to escape through the open doorway, and Trésor went after it. They heard him still laughing as he ran down the Rue du Papegai.

At about half-past nine Artevel's father came in, hand-in-hand with Marie-Louise, with whom he had been walking down by the river. He had been at work until mid-afternoon, carrying wood up into the loft of a house in the Upper Town ; but when he got home he had shaved and put on a clean white shirt with a soft collar and a tie in two colours. Despite his worn and threadbare working clothes, he looked neatly dressed. Vuillemard invited him to sit down, but he refused to take anything.

' I haven't time, the child's getting sleepy. I promised her mother I'd bring her home at nine, and it's half-past already.'

Marie-Louise drew near to her brother, who put an arm round her waist. One of the players remarked :

' Anyone can see they're brother and sister. Typical Artevels, aren't they ? '

The three Artevels were indeed strangely alike, except that the father had white hair and that his brown face was marked with countless wrinkles which deepened and spread at the smallest smile. He looked at his children and said modestly :

' As to their being like me, one can't deny it.'

' And there are eight the same ! ' said another player.

' And perhaps more to come ! ' said Vuillemard, winking.

Artevel shook his head and changed the subject. Not wishing to appear foolish, he preferred not to confess that he viewed the prospect of having one or two more children with no displeasure. They would have to be fed, of course, and his wife had some difficulty in bringing them into the world, but this never worried her. When he returned from work, in the summer evenings when he made the descent into the Malleboine, he heard the name of Artevel echoing up to him by the time he reached the top of the big stairway ; Artevels swarmed and laughed through all the streets, some on all fours, some on their two feet, some hopping on one, while the smallest made their first tottering steps. All the way home there were Artevels clustered round his legs. Sometimes he picked one up in passing, and on inspection recognised an Artevel belonging to one of his brothers or cousins. Without counting his sisters' children, there were thirty-two bearing the name in the quarter ; and there were Artevels in Lyons, in Paris, in America and Australia, to say nothing of the Flemish branch. He felt exalted and uplifted by the blond, tanned tribe, and the clamour of all those Artevels rested him after the day of labour in the factory.

'As we were coming along the Rue des Ladres,' he said to Vuillemard, 'I saw Maillard ahead of us. He turned into the Rue de l'Ourson.'

There was a momentary silence while everyone thought of Troussequin. Artevel added :

'Well, if it amuses him . . .'

The players, and even Marie-Louise, gave vent to a little murmur of satisfaction at the thought of Maillard stalking the streets like a beast of prey. His man had not waited for him, and they were glad. All his friends condemned Troussequin's crime, but there was not one who was not inclined to pity and to make some excuse for him. He was not altogether responsible. Just as a starving man flings himself upon food and tears it with hands and teeth, smearing his face and clothes, so he, the monster, the beast weary of longing for the beauty who would transform him into a man, had broken his bonds with the fury of a passion too long contained. And perhaps in some sort he had revenged himself upon life. In the depths of their hearts they were grateful to him for that act of violence, and they loved him the more for it. To the people of the Malleboine, Troussequin was not only one of themselves : his humble and terrible countenance was that of their own wretchedness : a single mask for joy and suffering, most repulsive to lawyers and the servants of lawyers. Moreover, a crime which outraged the people in good society was not deserving of their protest : vile and ignoble though it might be, for them to appear outraged would be a betrayal of themselves.

'It's a bad business for him,' said Pierre Artevel, with a sigh. 'You can't hope to hide for long with a mug like that.'

His father leaned forward with a hand on the table to give his views on the matter ; but then he gave up the attempt, and said simply :

'We'll be getting home to bed, Marie-Louise. Will you be staying long, my boy?'

'Not more than an hour,' said Pierre, kissing his sister. 'Certainly not more.'

His father seemed to hesitate, and then put a hand in his pocket.

'All the same, I'll leave you the key,' he said, laying it on the table. 'In case you should be later. Your mother doesn't like to think of the door being left open . . . Good night all.' And he went out, pushing Marie-Louise gently ahead of him.

The four men, left to themselves, began to pay more attention to their game. Vuillemard, with his sharpness of tongue, had no equal at livening up a game of cards. His rebukes, his irony, his very silences were so effective that the others played with an air of defying him. Pierre Artevel, who seldom played because he gave nearly all his pay to his mother, was less alert than the rest. Indeed, he was several times guilty of absent-mindedness. At about eleven, while he was shuffling, the door opened and the pack of cards fell from his hands.

Standing on the threshold, Troussequin gazed into the room with the species of smile with which they were all familiar, a grimace, expressing everything, which distorted the lower part of his face, throwing the ridge of his eyebrows into prominence and emphasising the sunken region about his nose.

'I'm tired out,' he said, pushing the door to behind him with his elbow.

He came heavily into the room, his head a little inclined towards the hollow of his right shoulder, moving with a lurching animal gait enhanced by his fatigue. The four men had risen to their feet and were staring at him in silence. As he passed under the light, his shadow, which had been

hovering behind, came to precede him and leapt forward to
the card table. One of the players recoiled slightly. Troussequin perceived something disturbing in his friends' attitude.
He stopped a few feet away from them, and the gaze of his
little, dark, profoundly deep-set eyes went questioningly
from one to the other. Pierre Artevel asked in an uncertain
voice :

'Where have you been since yesterday evening ? '

'I did a job for Marguet, the lawyer, yesterday, and when
I got back I took it into my head I'd go and see Klein, a
friend of mine who's got a hut in the woods between
Sexelles and Saint-Aunay. Why do you want to know ?
Were you looking for me ? '

Artevel did not know how to answer, and glanced at his
companions. Was it possible that Trousseguin should be
not only innocent but entirely ignorant of a crime committed
twenty-four hours previously, of which the whole town
knew ? Vuillemard said slowly :

'Didn't you see the paper this morning ? '

Trousseguin shook his head.

'What's happened ? Has war been declared ? '

'No, it's not that . . .'

One of them pulled a newspaper out of his pocket, but
not liking to give it to Trousseguin himself, handed it to
his neighbour. Passing from hand to hand it went the
round of the table, and it was Artevel who gave it to
Trousseguin, pointing as he did so to the story. The
monster began to read, and the card players to watch his
face, which remained expressionless. When he had finished
reading he returned the paper and uttered a feverish laugh.
But as he stood contemplating his four friends his eyes
filled with such a degree of terror that all their hands went
out to him. His mouth gaped wide and there escaped from
it a long, low moan like that of a man in his death-throes,

then a bellow of sheer fright. He strode towards the end of the room, crying :

'It wasn't me ! I didn't kill anyone ! It wasn't me ! '

He came back to the table, and going on his knees before the card players as though they were his judges he cried again :

'I swear it wasn't me ! I swear I haven't killed anyone ! I swear . . . ! '

His teeth chattered and he began to stammer. Artevel spoke some words of affectionate reassurance and put an arm round his neck. At his touch Trousequin was seized with panic. He broke roughly away and ran out through the doorway, forgetting the bicycle he had left leaning against the wall of the café. Artevel ran out after him into the Rue du Papegai, imploring him in a breathless voice to wait and listen at least for a minute. Trousequin ran on without looking round, passing from one street to another, confusedly searching for a way out to the Upper Town with its wider spaces. Artevel caught up with him finally in the Rue des Oiseaux and managed to quieten him down a little, if not to get him to see reason. He advised him to give himself up to the police and tell them his movements since the previous evening. The fact that he had returned to the quarter was in his favour, and his friends would testify that he had entered Vuillemard's café without showing any concern. But Trousequin did not grasp what he was talking about, or understand anything except his friendly intentions. He kept breaking into a run, as though he could not wait to emerge from the shadowy quarter into the bright light of the Rond-Point, and then pausing to cry out again that he was innocent. At that hour the Rue des Oiseaux was deserted, and they met no one except a party of artillerymen coming out of No. 15, Rue des Nonettes.

Lurking in the darkness of the Rue de la Clé-d'Or,

Sergeant Maillard kept a watch on their movements. A telephone call to the police station had warned him, a short time before, that Troussequin had just ridden into the town on a bicycle, and he had hurried to the spot with constables Charlasse and Guilbon. He might have caught him in the Rue des Oiseaux, at the entrance to a passage-way—there had been plenty of chances. But he had chosen the Rue de la Clé-d'Or, deliberately running the risk of letting him escape by a cross-street. The Rue des Oiseaux was dark, and he could see nothing of the two men but a vague twin shadow which at moments vanished completely. The sound of their voices and footsteps afforded a better indication of their whereabouts, but Maillard was not the less distressed. Never had he been so reluctant to carry out his duty —indeed, he was still not sure that he would arrest Troussequin at all. It was a difficult point to decide. Since the presumed criminal had returned of his own accord to the town, he might have done so with the intention of going to the police. Was it fair to rob him of the benefit of a voluntary act by arresting him on the way ? On the other hand, the sergeant knew Troussequin well enough to know that even if he was innocent he was quite capable of running away into the country to hide, thereby making his position worse. To arrest him might be to protect him from himself, to say nothing of the fact that if the gendarmes caught him skulking in the woods they would not hesitate to shoot him down at the first sign of resistance. Maillard deeply despised the gendarmes, whom he considered a crude lot. The thought that Troussequin might be left to their tender mercies was what decided him. He pushed his two men into an alleyway, and stood himself half in and half out of it.

'Above all, don't go frightening him,' he said. 'He's to be decently treated. We aren't gendarmes.'

Guilbon uttered an approving murmur, but Charlasse

said nothing. He was angry with the sergeant for having selected him to help in the arrest of a friend, when there had been two other men at the police station who would have thought nothing of the job. In his resentment he coughed loudly and with an evident purpose. Troussequin was not, in fact, near enough to hear, and he knew this perfectly well, but it was a way of showing what he felt. Maillard felt for him in the darkness, gripped him by the tunic, and dragging him close with a jerk said in his ear :

' Don't you try that game, my lad ! I'll bloody soon put a stopper on you ! '

Charlasse yielded and stood silent. Troussequin and Artevel emerged from the Rue des Oiseaux into the light of the Carrefour des Cinq. Maillard, with a sudden unhappiness, felt all his doubts return. Time was getting short. He decided that if Troussequin turned into the Rue Raulin, which was the shortest way to the police station, he would let him go on. The two men were in the middle of the small open space marking the cross-roads, and Artevel was plainly trying to head to the right, in the direction of the Rue Raulin. Troussequin followed a few steps without realising where he was going, but then, raising his head, he looked round for the big stairway, and leaving his companion hurried towards the Rue de la Clé-d'Or.

When Maillard came out of the alleyway with his two men, Troussequin started in alarm, and retreating before the sergeant stood with his back against the wall of the Rond-Point. With his lowering gaze, legs half-bent and hands gripping the stone, he looked like an animal crouched to spring.

' Where are you going ? ' asked Maillard.

The monster remained speechless, watching their movements. Artevel tried to say something, but the sergeant silenced him.

' You keep your mouth shut. You ought to be in bed.'

Artevel jerked up his head, feeling a hot flush of anger on his cheeks, but with an effort he restrained himself. Maillard turned to Troussequin and said gently :

'Come on, Marcel. Tell me where you were going.'

The monster was touched at hearing his Christian name, which few people used in these days, even those of his own age. His tense body seemed to relax, and his big head to incline forward in response to this friendliness ; but when Maillard touched him on the shoulder he misunderstood the gesture, and knocking away his hand said harshly :

'Let me pass. I want to go. Let me pass !'

His voice was threatening, his attitude even more so. Artevel realised that he would not let himself be arrested without resisting to the utmost. And suddenly he felt himself to be involved up to the hilt in this business, not only from friendship but even more from an urge to violence prompted by the unreasoning indignation which now took hold of him. If the arrest had taken place in the Upper Town he might, perhaps, have been content to remain a spectator; but here, in the Rue de la Clé-d'Or, Maillard and his men wore the aspect of intruders breaking into his stronghold to take away a friend. He felt the intrusion even more acutely when he saw Charlasse, who stood facing him, between Maillard and Guilbon, but a little behind them. Charlasse and he had grown up together in the Malleboine quarter ; for twenty years they had been so close that they had seemed like members of the same family. Only last year, after being released from their military service, they had gone out together looking for work. Artevel looked at the sergeant and said coldly :

'Send Charlasse away. He oughtn't to be here.'

'You're the one I'm sending away, back to your mother,' said Maillard. 'And with a smack on the bottom, if you aren't careful !'

118

' Send Charlasse away ! Do you hear me, you big swine ? '

Artevel took a pace forward, the hand in his pocket gripping the key his father had given him. At the same instant Guilbon dragged him back by the collar of his coat, as he might have seized a criminal. Furious at the insult, Artevel swung round and lashed out with the key still gripped in his clenched fist. The darkness was deceptive. It was Charlasse who received the blow. The key grazed his chin, causing a sharply smarting wound, and the fist fell heavily on his shoulder. Charlasse thought Artevel was deliberately trying to repay him for his treachery in being there, and he flung himself upon him.

Seeing his friend thus at grips with the two policemen, Troussequin flung himself forward and very nearly got away. Although he was ready for the attack, Maillard staggered under the impact of his head against his chest, and for a moment had the breath knocked out of him. Troussequin might have taken advantage of the surprise to escape, but his immediate impulse was to follow up his advantage over Maillard and force him to retreat. He had a far greater urge to conquer than to run, blindly feeling that he must prove his innocence by the power of his fists. Maillard did indeed retreat several paces, but then he regained his balance, and as Troussequin staggered slightly on the polished and slippery cobbles he thrust him back against the wall with a single heave. It was an error of judgment which he instantly regretted. Using the purchase of his heel against the wall, Troussequin encircled him with his powerful arms and, by far the shorter man, thrust back his chin with the top of his head. Maillard had no proper grip on him, and with his back arched had to use all his strength simply to keep his balance. He now tried to retreat, but the grip round his waist kept him motionless and he felt himself steadily giving way. His greater height and weight were of almost no advantage to him, whereas the other, crouched as he was, could bring all his strength to bear. Finally Maillard succeeded in getting his chin free, and this enabled him to thrust his shoulders forward and catch his adversary by the hips. But his grip, at full arms' length, was ineffective, and he felt himself weakening. By shaking Troussequin, however, he managed to shift him from his point of support, and swinging them both round he got his own back against the wall. The grip of the two hands clasped against the small of his back was still dangerous. He rid himself of it by rubbing his back against the rough stones of the wall. Troussequin, his knuckles skinned and bruised, was forced to let go. Maillard was now tired and anxious to get it over. He thrust his man towards the centre of the roadway, and they continued to struggle without pausing to take breath.

In the darkness of the Rue de la Clé-d'Or the two groups fought in silence, separated by only a few feet. A couple passed over the cross-roads without suspecting their presence. Artevel, with one knee on the ground, was holding Constable Guilbon locked by the neck under one arm, while with his other hand he hung on to Charlasse. While they thus mauled one another a sound of triumphal bellowing burst out above their heads. It was the town's rugby-football team, marching through the streets after arriving at the station, and proclaiming its victory of that afternoon. They passed by the Rond-Point, keeping step and shouting their chorus :

> Honour to our glorious team
> In its vests of black and green !
> However tough the match may be
> We always win the victory !

Near the head of the big stairway one of the players

hammered with his fist on the wooden shutters of Buquanant's dye-shop, and the others, following after, all did the same. Enlivened by this exercise, the team forgot the fatigues of the afternoon and charged down the Rue des Rencontres as though they were scoring a try, shouting as they went : ' Play up, the club ! Follow up ! Feet ! Feet ! Feet ! ' and then, ' Long live our noble President Fouchard ! Follow up ! Heel ! Heel ! Heel ! ' At the first sound of hammering, Buq, whose room was on the first floor, got out of bed and went to the window. He was in time to catch a glimpse of the rear view of the secretary as he strove to keep up with the glorious players.

Maillard and Troussequin, so tightly linked together that they seemed to form a single block, paid no attention to this clamour. They were fighting without subtlety, locked in an intense effort that held them motionless. For the first time Maillard felt the weight of his years, and he called upon all his reserves of strength. He succeeded finally in lifting his adversary and flinging him down in an awkward position. With his shoulders to the ground Troussequin surrendered and let the handcuffs be put on him without further resistance.

' All right,' he muttered. ' You might as well say it was me.'

Despite the heat of the combat Maillard was touched by this ingenuous despair which seemed to have expected no more of justice than an ordeal by battle. He helped his prisoner to his feet with movements that were almost friendly. The overthrow of Troussequin had brought the other struggle to an end. Artevel and Charlasse, their faces bleeding, were now regarding one another without anger, in all the friendship of the past. As he picked his cap up from the cobbles, Charlasse found the key with which he had been hit.

'It's my key,' said Artevel. 'But keep it.'

'What for?'

'You can see I'm behaving,' said Artevel, indicating Constable Guilbon, who was gripping his arm with both hands. 'Take the key back to my mother, and tell her I sent you.'

Charlasse put the key in his pocket. Maillard came towards them, pushing Troussequin in front of him. He glared at Artevel and said with a grim smile:

'So you've cooled down, have you? You're going to wish you hadn't tried to be so clever, young Artevel! Disturbing the peace! Hindering the police in the execution of their duty! Assault and battery! You won't get away with this lot in a hurry!'

Charlasse bent his head while he fiddled with his cap.

'Take the little fool by the other arm, and let's get going,' said Maillard.

Charlasse did not move. The sergeant repeated:

'Take this man by the arm!'

Charlasse looked up, twisting his cap in his hands so that the cardboard in the peak could be heard to crack. He was on the verge of flinging it in the sergeant's face when Artevel, reaching out his free hand, drew him towards himself, murmuring:

'Take my arm, Lulu. Don't let me go with them alone!'

TEN

M.ALFAN, THE EXAMINING MAGISTRATE,* was a man of youthful and happy temperament, only moderately in love with his calling, but who exercised it, none the less, with conscience and with shrewdness. He had been on terms of friendship with Maître Marguet for two years, and was in the habit of visiting him at least once a month. Their friendship was not based on any particular spiritual affinity—indeed, they differed widely in all respects—but on their common love of music. Even here, however, there was a considerable gulf between them. The magistrate was more a music-knower than a music-lover. He could never escape from the need to classify and analyse. The only real pleasure he derived from listening to a new piece of music lay in the discovery of reminiscences and analogies, and he could not always avoid the feeling of being out of his depth. The lawyer, on the other hand, while he enjoyed the qualities in a composition which made it peculiarly the work of its composer, found in all music—classics, moderns, Argentine tango or street song—the endless movement of an ocean whose least wave or surface ripple touched him no less than the swell from the depths or the thunder of the tempest. He quarrelled amicably with the magistrate for saying that he could not bear to listen to pretty or elegant trifles

*M. Alfan was a 'juge d'instruction', or investigating judge, a functionary having no equivalent under English law. The term 'examining magistrate' has been used for the sake of convenience. Translator's note.

after hearing a major work. For him it was the wholeness of music, throughout its length and breadth, which enabled him to discover Beethoven in an air sung to an accordion. He even went so far as to maintain that there was no bad music, but only music; and he dreamed of a world whose every sound would be heard as music. Listening to him talk, the magistrate was always conscious of a sense of regret: he felt the lack of something, as though he were cut off from music by music itself.

The two men were discussing the crime in the lawyer's study. M. Alfan had heard the statements of his three clerks, and was now smiling at Maître Marguet's plea in favour of Troussequin. His good-humoured scepticism irritated the lawyer.

'I know quite well what you're thinking,' he said. 'You're convinced that I'm biased in Troussequin's favour because I feel guilty at having brought him into my house.'

The magistrate shook his head and replied with a friendly gravity:

'My dear Maître Marguet, you can't be blamed for having brought him into your house, and you've no reason to feel guilty. If we were all to start weighing our personal responsibility every time we unwittingly play into the hands of misfortune, we should never know a moment's peace. But I do certainly think that you want the man to be innocent, and that this is causing you to split hairs. It's very understandable.'

The lawyer got up. He went to the window and stood gazing over the garden, and then came back and sat opposite his visitor.

'What it comes to,' he said, 'is that your case is based on the person of Troussequin himself, the monstrous head, the ape's body. In fact, you're on the way to condemning a man on account of his physical appearance.'

'No—forgive me,' said the magistrate. 'You seem to

have forgotten the weapon with which the crime was committed—the pruning-knife which came out of the shed where he had been working.'

'But did anyone see that knife in the shed before the crime was committed? The girl herself might have taken it up to her room some days before, or even that morning.'

'If she'd needed a knife she'd have been more likely to get it out of the kitchen than to go looking for one at the bottom of the garden. And then, the way he made off on a bicycle——'

'And the way he came back!' said Maître Marguet.

'Yes—at night. I find that scarcely less suspect than his running away. It's strange that he should have heard nothing about the crime in twenty-four hours! And don't forget that when he did hear his only idea was to run away again. Perhaps he had some notion that during those twenty-four hours things would have somehow turned out favourably for him, and so he came back at night to find out. There's an ingenuousness about it that seems to me to fit his rudimentary intelligence. And certainly, as you said just now, my opinion is influenced by the nature of the man. It's a factor which I'm bound to take into account. A ruffian, more than half a degenerate—a man who must be utterly repulsive to women, and has already served a sentence for attempted rape—he could hardly make a worse impression. And since neither the cook nor your office staff can have committed the murder, it can only be he.'

', All of which amounts to no positive proof,' said the lawyer. 'Not enough to get a man executed, thank God. I don't think the defending counsel will find his job too difficult. But I'd like to draw your attention to one point.' He nodded towards the garden, whose entire length was visible from where they sat. 'Has it occurred to you that in order to commit the crime Troussequin had to go twice from one end of the garden to the other? My wife was having tea in the drawing-room with a friend. The cook, who doesn't as a rule miss anything, was in the kitchen, and I was in here—all rooms looking on to the garden. Yet none of us saw him. It's at least as surprising as if someone were to cross the courtyard without being seen by my clerks, whose windows are in front.'

'You mean that someone coming from the street could have committed the crime as easily as Troussequin?'

'I'd sooner say that both theories are equally far-fetched, except that——'

Maître Marguet broke off, as though he had been struck by a sudden thought.

'Except what?'

'Well, except that it would have been much easier for anyone coming across the courtyard—that is to say, from outside. Suppose, for example, that I'm the murderer. I live somewhere in the town, and I'm planning ways and means of killing that unfortunate child. I've been out with her two or three times on a Sunday afternoon, and I've talked to her enough to get a general idea of the routine of the household. The first problem is to get into the house without being seen. At night? But that would be almost impossible. Even if I managed to climb the wall I should still have to get into the house itself. The risk would be too great. During the day, on the other hand, I might walk straight in and up to the girl's room without being stopped. But perhaps the clerks know me by sight, or even by name, and would be likely to remember seeing me cross the court-yard. So after thinking it over I have an idea. Between twelve and two the clerks are out at lunch; the lawyer and his wife are lunching in the dining-room, at the back of the house, and the servants are busy in the kitchen. So I can quite safely cross the courtyard. I go straight up to the girl's room and wait for her to come up and get ready to take the letters to the post, as she does every afternoon. When I have done the deed I lock the door to guard against the unlikely eventuality of the cook coming upstairs to find out if the girl has got back. Round about six o'clock I keep watch from the window to see the clerks leave and the lawyer go out for his stroll. Then I can cross the courtyard again without being seen—barring accidents, of course ; but I think I should have reduced the risk to a minimum. Well, how does that strike you, Monsieur Alfan ? '

The magistrate did not answer immediately, merely conceding with a somewhat reluctant nod that the theory was feasible. While he sought for objections to it he was observing the lawyer, his feelings dominated by the mingled sense of admiration and disquiet which he sometimes had when they were discussing music together. What impressed him was less the ingenuity of the argument than the assurance in Maître Marguet's voice and manner. He seemed to have the same wide and balanced understanding of the whole affair that he had of music. M. Alfan remained under the spell for several minutes : in order to recover his sense of proportion he was obliged to recall the picture of Troussequin as he had seen him that morning, the ape-like body and animal face and furtive eyes. He took a grip of himself and finally replied :

'It's a possibility I shall certainly look into—particularly if it turns out that the girl was seen with a man on her afternoons off. But I must confess it doesn't shake my conviction in the least. I believe in Troussequin's guilt because it's so perfectly obvious. If you know that a sheep has strayed under a wolf's nose you don't have to rack your brains wondering how it came to get eaten. I wish you could have seen Troussequin when I was questioning him— his sullen expression, and a kind of sly, sardonic ferocity ...

In any case, his refusal to answer almost amounts to a confession. He didn't even trouble to deny the charge, obviously because he feels the case against him is unanswerable. And then I ask you, could such a crime possibly have been premeditated? It was the act of a brute—sheer animal impulse . . .'

Maître Marguet cut him short with a movement of impatience, almost of anger.

' Do you really believe that such an orgy of studied and calculated outrages could be due to nothing more than a sudden animal impulse? I would say that it was the fulfilment of a dream, the final, meticulous consummation of an obsession that the murderer had cherished for a very long time—a sort of exorcism, perhaps the fruit of a whole lifetime. Think of the position of the body, the nature of the wounds! Can you really maintain that all those refinements were improvised, or could be the work of a clod like Troussequin? I appeal to you as a man of experience.'

' Well, I've seen a good many crimes,' said the magistrate, ' and I can assure you, perversion in a criminal is very rarely an indication of intelligence—generally the opposite. Think of the parents who ill-treat their children—they're nearly always half-wits. It is possible that among the devout bourgeoisie one may find a certain appetite for the terrors of hell, a perverted craving for ecclesiastical justice and its tortures, which might lead a few individuals, even people of distinction, to commit a crime of this sort. But even in those cases the murder is never committed entirely for its own sake : some kind of material advantage has to furnish a pretext. And in general people with that kind of obsession don't go so far as to allow it a murderous outlet. In any normally constituted family there's a poor relation or some other meek dependant who can be quietly tormented to satisfy a secret hankering after violence.'

M. Alfan noticed at this point that the lawyer had flushed and was looking rather strangely at him. He blushed himself as it occurred to him that he was being tactless, to say the least, since the Marguet family had a reputation for extreme devoutness. While he was searching for some propitiatory remark a clerk entered to say that Sergeant Maillard had arrived. The lawyer ordered him to be shown in.

'I asked him to come,' explained the magistrate. 'I thought it would be helpful to have him with me when I inspect the attic. After all, he was the first person to see the thing in cold blood, so to speak.'

Maillard appeared in a suit of sporting appearance cut in the fashion of 1925, rather tight under the armpits and short in the leg. He greeted them with a nod and remained standing by the door, his bowler hat in his hand, making no attempt to conceal the fact that he was in a thoroughly bad humour.

'I'm very sorry to have bothered you, sergeant,' said M. Alfan. 'I see this is your day off.'

'So they say,' said Maillard.

He consented to sit down at Maître Marguet's invitation, but markedly in the manner of a man who is not there for pleasure. The magistrate sought to placate him.

'You know, don't you sergeant, that Maître Marguet also believes in Troussequin's innocence?'

Maillard shrugged his shoulders as though to say that everyone could have his own views, but that he had no time to waste in fruitless discussion. However M. Alfan insisted on recapitulating the lawyer's arguments. And gradually the sergeant's face brightened until at last his enthusiasm got the better of him.

'But it's perfectly obvious! The murderer can only have come from outside!'

This was not what the magistrate had intended. He had

simply wanted to catch Maillard's interest in order to stimulate his observation and critical faculties when they went to visit the scene of the crime. He was somewhat shaken by this readiness to adopt the lawyer's theory. He tried to strengthen his own conviction by reflecting that Maillard was already prejudiced in favour of Troussequin; but then a further remark by Maître Marguet, raising a point which had already occurred to him in passing, shook him still more.

'M. Alfan considers that there can have been no premeditation,' the lawyer said. 'But in that case, how are we to explain the fact that Troussequin went straight up to the attic? Did he know that the girl went out to the post every evening, and that she went up to her room at five? Did he even know where the room was, or the whereabouts of the staircase leading to it? It's a rather out-of-the-way staircase. How could he have known? He had never been inside the house!'

Momentarily overwhelmed, M. Alfan went to the window and stood thinking, while Maillard, openly triumphant, began to hint that the case against Troussequin would have to be dropped.

'Well,' said M. Alfan at length, turning back to them, 'now I'm going to suppose that I'm the murderer—or rather, that I'm Troussequin. I leave the shed at about midday to go to lunch, and on my way back, at about one-thirty, I meet the girl, Charlotte Richon, somewhere near the house, whether on the courtyard side or the garden side doesn't matter. We get into conversation. We talk about her work and about mine, and as I'm a house-painter and handyman she asks if I could do some small job in her room—stopping up a mousehole, for instance. As it happens, there really is a mousehole in the room. Naturally I say I will. She's a country girl who isn't frightened of allowing a man in her room in broad daylight, but she hasn't time to take me up there at the moment, so she asks me to meet her in the wash-house at five, or in the ground-floor passage. Well, that's settled, and I go back to my work. But the thought of being alone with a girl in her bedroom begins to prey on my mind until finally it obsesses me. I'm not good-looking. Women aren't kind to me. It may be that at lunch-time I heard a couple laughing as I went past. I think of this, and it wounds and infuriates me. I'm tormented by the picture of the fresh, pretty servant girl. So I think to myself—we'll see! I still don't know what I'm going to do, but I'm not going to miss this chance. I've made up my mind about that. At five minutes to five I look round the shed for the things that might come in handy in stopping a mousehole—a hammer, a bit of brick, a stout gardener's knife, and so on. Then I want to make water, so I go along the path between the outer wall and the trellis, where I can't be seen from the house. In that way I get to the house without being noticed. The girl meets me at the foot of the stairs and leads the way. She doesn't want to make any secret of what she's doing, but at the same time she'd just as soon people didn't know she's asked me up to her room—perhaps partly because she's afraid of sarcastic remarks from the cook. And as I'm wearing rope sandals I go upstairs without making any noise. Well, when we get into the room I start pawing her about. I get excited and clumsy. She fights me off. Anger and pride and desire make me lose my head. I revert to type— the Troussequin who has already made one attempt at rape—and worse . . . Finally, having committed the crime, I come cautiously downstairs and get back to the shed by the same pathway, without being seen. And there you are! After that I can leave it to the examining magistrate to rack his brains!'

The sergeant uttered a grunt. He admired the plausibility

of this theory, and he was prepared to admit that, given the circumstances, Troussequin might have gone so far as to commit the crime. But he was quite sure he would never have had the presence of mind to go back to his work—he would have bolted at once, without taking the smallest precaution. However this certainty, based simply on his intimate knowledge of the man, was one which could not be proved, and so he had to keep it to himself. Maître Marguet, while seeming greatly impressed, none the less raised an objection.

'The trellis is pretty thin to have hidden Troussequin entirely, and there are several gaps in it, including a large one where a main path crosses the garden. Have a look for yourself. It would have been very easy for one of us in the house to see him.'

'Even if it didn't hide him entirely,' said M. Alfan, 'it was enough to enable him to get to and from the shed without being noticed.'

The sergeant said that he found it hard to swallow the coincidence of the meeting and the mousehole, which he thought fitted the argument a little too handily.

'Coincidences always look like miracles after the event,' said M. Alfan. 'But you can be quite sure they paved the way for Troussequin. In any case, I'm not claiming that the thing happened in just the way I've described. I simply wanted to prove to you that it is possible for Troussequin to have committed the crime. When he finally confesses we shall very likely find that the coincidences were even more improbable. But if you wouldn't mind accompanying me, sergeant, we'll think about all these matters up in the attic. I'm relying a great deal on your memory and your personal observation.'

The lawyer let them go, and remained seated alone in his study. The course the investigation was taking was beginning to cause him grave concern on Troussequin's account. It was only too clear that he had not convinced the magistrate of the wretched man's innocence, and there seemed to be little likelihood of his doing so. Nor could he count on any more help from the newspapers. Now that a man had been charged, and everything possible said about the hideous nature of the crime, the topic was dead for them until the trial came on. But Maître Marguet had another cause for anxiety. He was thinking of the roll of film his mother had stolen from him. He was afraid to ask her for it back, although he had seen it in her handbag when she opened it to get out a handkerchief. He was wondering what she meant to do with it, and whether she realised that it had to be developed. In her ignorance she might have exposed and ruined it under the impression that it only needed unrolling. Although this possibility was reassuring in one way, it caused him great alarm, because he was most anxious to preserve all the photographs he had taken in the attic.

He patted the trouser pocket in which he now carried the spool his mother had left behind. Under the pressure of his hand its metal rims pressed softly into his thigh, a little above his ulcer. He felt a return, more acute than ever, of the state of impatience which had kept him awake for a large part of the night while he lay wondering if the photographs would be a success. He was particularly worried about the light. Had the sun sunk too low by five o'clock to penetrate fully into the girl's room? Despite his efforts to remember, he was vague on this point. He was sure at least of not having made a double exposure on one negative because he had taken the precaution of counting aloud. But about other details he was less clear. His hands had shaken, for example, as he tried to fix the body in the view-finder, but whether to the point of ruining the picture he could not say. He could only wait and see.

133

He pulled the red cylinder out of his pocket and held it carefully in the hollow of his two hands, harrowed by the thought that a gleam of light on the impregnated celluloid would be enough to spoil everything. The crime was there, so to speak, in embryo; dormant within the little red cylinder, just as it had so long lain dormant in the recesses of his mind and his flesh. Maître Marguet wondered if there might be other crimes lying dormant within him, if perhaps a ray of light would efface them before they reached fruition; and he was afraid of being again tempted, of yielding to other urges. The figures of women were already stirring in his memory, the beginnings of a plan were taking shape in his mind. For a moment he felt lost; sweat started on his forehead, he was cold, his body was frozen by soft hands of death, he was death itself . . . A sombre passion seemed to thrust a tireless, meticulous knife into his hand. He closed his eyes and sought refuge with his victim. She came to him bleeding and he pitied her, soothed her with maternal murmurs, smiled fondly at her. His heart melted with tenderness, his eyes filled with healing tears. Relieved and reassured, he could face his terrors and seek for means to arm himself against temptation. There was an analogy to be discovered between crime and music. A masterpiece of crime embraced all others, and it sufficed to have committed one alone to dispose of the entire symphony. He sat gazing with a sort of gratitude at the little roll of film which would enable him to re-live his crime more completely, to recall its details in a series of images that were almost alive. He was suddenly filled with hopefulness, and no longer doubted that he would regain possession of the other spool.

But there arose the problem of developing the films. He had no dark room, and in any case no knowledge of how it was done. He had no room that would serve the purpose unless it was the attic where the crime had been committed, and he must not think of this for a long time. Besides, he would never be anything but a beginner, an amateur who would risk ruining the film.

The problem was so awkward that his optimism rapidly dwindled. And suddenly he was overtaken by panic as he recalled that his mother had spoken of having an appointment to-day with an architect in one of the houses she owned. He could not recall if she had said Monday morning or afternoon. But most probably, since she was going into the town in any case, she would take the film somewhere to be developed. Maître Marguet went out of his study by the door opening into the hall, and walked with unhurried steps across the courtyard, because the magistrate and the sergeant were still up in the attic. The house where his mother lived was at the far end of the Rue Jacques-de-Molay, about a hundred yards from his own. As he went towards this street he heard his name called in a piercing and confidential voice which for an instant sounded like that of his own conscience. In fact, however, it was his friend the organist inviting him to come down and join him in the cellar, whence he was surveying the world through his periscope. Maître Marguet at first made a gesture of annoyance, but then suddenly changed his mind and went down.

ELEVEN

WHEN THE BELL rang at a quarter to twelve, Buq, who was sitting at the bottom of the class, rushed for the door with so much impetuosity and clattering of metalled soles that his form master was annoyed.

'Buquanant! You'll leave the room last. And you'll be kept in on Thursday morning to teach you to wait until you're dismissed.'

Buq pulled up in mid-flight, damped but still quivering. The master gratified his sense of power by allowing a minute to pass, and then gave the signal to dismiss. Despite his injunction, Buq was still the first out of the door, and when Antoine came up with him he dragged him at a run out into the street. They gazed excitedly at one another. Buq had been summoned to the headmaster's study during the break to explain why he had arrived more than an hour late, and so they had not had a chance of saying a word to one another all the morning. Antoine was looking tired after a night of insomnia and nightmares; there was a feverish light in his eyes. He did not want to be the first to speak of the matter that was in both their minds.

'Well?' said Buq. 'You've heard?'

'Yes. Trousséquin was arrested last night.'

'But do you mean to say that's all you've heard?' cried Buq. 'Why, you don't know anything! Don't you know that they've arrested Pierre Artevel as well—Marie-Louise's brother? They arrested him for sticking up for Trousséquin, and he's going to be sent to prison!'

Antoine felt his breath fail him. He had not even the strength to utter a protest. He had been meaning to confide in Buq in order to get his support and advice, but this news of the arrest of another innocent man, which touched his friend so nearly, robbed him of the power of speech.

He could not bring himself to confess to a piece of cowardice that had hurt Marie-Louise, and every minute that passed made it more difficult. As he listened to Buq's account of the arrest he was again filled with a sense of unfairness at the freak of chance which had placed him in a position of such importance in this business. He tried to cheat by telling himself that the course of justice could not be affected by anything that a boy his age might say. And meanwhile Buq, enacting the battle in the Rue de la Clé-d'Or, was crying in a voice of love and pride :

' You saw what Marie-Louise was like the other day when she slapped my face ! Well, you think of her brother—a real he-man ! He had six coppers on him at once—six !— and he was knocking 'em out two at a time, and if Maillard hadn't come up behind they'd never have got him at all ! '

So much heroism in defence of the innocent wrung Antoine's heart.

' I went round to see Marie-Louise this morning,' Buq went on. ' She'd left for school already, but I saw her mother and that's why I was late.'

They had come to a stop at the end of the Rue de l'Herbe-Sèche. Buq, who had made a detour in order to accompany his friend, was starting to relate what he had seen and heard at the Artevels' ; but Antoine abruptly shook hands, and said quickly, without looking at him :

' I must go. I'm in a hurry to-day.'

Leaving him very much taken aback, he made off at a run for the Avenue Raymond-Poincaré. The sprint did him good, and falling into a walk again he could consider the position more calmly. Even if the delay had made things worse, it still remained appallingly simple. All he had to do, at the cost of a reprimand, was to make known the fact of Troussequin's innocence. Antoine made up his mind to tell his father as soon as possible. Shortly after this he saw him coming out of the Rue Belley on his way back from the office, and he turned to meet him. This astonished Rigault, who at once became mistrustful. In the ordinary way, unless they positively ran into one another, he and Antoine both took pains to avoid walking home together.

Antoine was confirming his resolution by saying over an opening sentence in his mind. As they came together Rigault stared suspiciously at him, and was struck by the fact that he was not looking well.

'You're quite pale and you're dark under the eyes,' he said. 'What's wrong with you?'

Helped by the question, Antoine tried to speak; but in his agitation he lost track of the sentence he had prepared and grew confused. Rigault raised his voice and said accusingly:

'You got a bad mark this morning, didn't you?'

To him this was the obvious explanation of his son's pallor and his unusual departure in turning to meet him. Antoine, instantly damped, was again made conscious of the gulf between them which for a moment he had thought he could ignore, and he took refuge in sullen silence.

'I asked you if you got a bad mark in class to-day,' repeated Rigault. 'I think you heard me.'

Antoine feebly denied that he had, thereby merely encouraging the wilful misgivings in his father's mind.

'You'd do far better to admit it frankly,' he said. 'But it's always the same with you. Well, we shall see!'

Neither spoke another word until they reached home. Rigault was in a bad mood. That morning there had been a rumour among the workers that the T.D.C. factory was going to close down. The report had got as far as the office, where people had merely shrugged their shoulders. It did not seem at all likely : and yet the assistant manager, when he heard it, had denied it in evasive and ambiguous terms which left some doubt behind. As for Rigault, he did not believe that a business for which he had worked for fifteen years could really disappear, and his fears were only superficial. But as he walked beside Antoine he was distorting things in his own mind so as to take the threat seriously, and for the acid pleasure of being able to tell himself that it was just like his son to get a bad mark at school on the day when the family livelihood was endangered. He deliberately overlooked the forty-seven thousand francs invested in gilt-edged securities, the house which he owned, and his wife's expectations. ' To be on the verge of being turned out on to the street ! ' he meditated. ' Overwhelmed with worry, and without even the consolation of a decent-minded child who would appreciate all one has done for him ! ' He worked himself up to such a pitch that his wife's welcoming smile, as he entered the house, came as a shock to him, and he rapped out :

' The factory's closing down. Unemployment.'

Juliette turned pale, and for a moment her voice failed her. She then burst into tears and exclaimed that troubles never came singly, because her mother's health was giving cause for alarm. Rigault was brought up short in the middle of the kitchen, rather taken aback. He felt that he had gone a bit far, and he said with an embarrassed laugh :

' Well, perhaps it isn't true.'

But as he had not accustomed his family to jests of this kind, they merely assumed that he was making heroic efforts to reassure them. Their meal dragged on in an atmosphere of consternation. Antoine was as much upset as his mother, and even forgot the crime. From his earliest childhood he had never heard his father talk about his work, the burden of his cares and the struggle it was to keep them all alive, without having a sense of guilt. At the thought of him out of work, his consciousness of sin assumed monstrous proportions, causing him to feel ashamed of eating and even of existing, as though he had somehow stolen his food and the very air he breathed.

Rigault would have liked to put their minds at rest, but since half-words did not suffice he could only do so by compelling himself to make an elaborate disavowal. He preferred to let it go. He would bring home some good news in the evening. After all, his wife and son would not die of having passed an unhappy afternoon. But as the meal drew to its close he felt the need to be very kind, and delivered himself of some moving remarks on the subject of Troussequin.

'A murderer is always a murderer,' he said. 'But still, it grieves me terribly to think that he'll be condemned to death.'

'He isn't the one who killed the maid,' said Antoine in a voice that was almost tranquil.

The mention of Troussequin's death had brought the words quite naturally to his lips, and he was astonished that he should have had any difficulty in speaking them. His parents sipped their coffee without paying any attention to what he had said. He repeated it with a slight impatience.

'Troussequin isn't the one who killed her. It was the lawyer.'

'What's that you're saying?' asked Rigault in a voice of hostile curiosity.

'I'm telling you what I saw. At five o'clock on Saturday I was on the cathedral tower with Buquanant and a girl who lives near him. While they were having a fight I was looking down, and I saw the lawyer at the attic window. I recognised him just as easily as if I'd met him in the street, and I'm quite sure he was in the attic. I couldn't be mistaken, because there's only one attic on that side.'

His mother did not at first grasp the connection between the lawyer's guilt and his presence at the attic window. Rigault saw it at once, but sensing the importance of the matter he was in no hurry to understand. His deliberate slowness upset Antoine to the point of making him feel sick. Since yesterday the word Truth had loomed large in his mind, accompanied by sensational adjectives such as 'electrifying' and 'horrifying.' He was astounded at his father's apparent indifference.

'If the lawyer was in the attic at five,' he persisted, 'it must be he who killed the maid.'

Rigault had now grasped all the implications; nor did he doubt for a moment that Antoine was telling the truth. However, he pretended to be incredulous, for no particular reason except to gain time.

'What's all this story?' he demanded. 'Where did you get it from?'

But the accusation in Antoine's eyes was too much for him, and he went on:

'Perhaps I haven't understood. Tell me the whole thing clearly.'

Antoine told the story again in greater detail, pausing from time to time to make sure that he was being followed. He answered certain of Rigault's objections, notably as to the difficulty of recognising the lawyer from the tower. The house was very near the cathedral, and in any case the lawyer's waistcoat, his black beard and his baldness would have made him recognisable at a far greater distance.

'And I can't have been wrong about the time,' he concluded, 'because the cathedral clock had just struck five.

That's what made me tell Buquanant that it was time to be going home.'

Rigault was convinced. He sought his wife's eyes, but found in them no reflection of his own disquiet. Juliette seemed to be more excited by the sensational aspect of the adventure. Rigault stayed silent for a long time, stirring the drops of coffee at the bottom of his glass. He was tempted to embarrass Antoine by professing astonishment that he had not told him before, but a sense of justice restrained him. He was already beginning to feel in himself the alarm and uncertainty which must have tormented the boy. For the moment his duty was clear to him, but he found it hard, and his first word to Antoine was one of reproach.

' Of course, you would have to go up the tower instead of staying quietly at home ! '

His wife remarked that she had been out all Saturday afternoon, and so had not been able to report the time of Antoine's return. But Rigault was thinking of other matters. After a moment he asked :

' Have you told Buquanant or anyone else about this ? '

' No, I haven't told anyone.'

' Well, see that you don't. Nor you, either, Juliette. It's better not to talk about it in case it should hinder the investigation. I'll do what is necessary.'

He got up and set off into the town, half an hour earlier than he was accustomed to do. Antoine went to the window and stood earnestly watching as he went down the garden. His father was walking with long, vigorous strides, a light of sturdy resolution seeming to enwreathe his bowler hat. When he vanished from sight Antoine was so overcome that he turned and wept in his mother's arms.

Rigault paused for a moment on the railway bridge to watch a train pass, and then continued more briskly than ever. The beat of his footsteps on the dry ground had an inexorable cadence which he found gratifying. He was vaguely sorry that the police station was not at the end of the earth, so that he might never reach it but could stride on for ever in the cause of justice. In principle he felt that nothing could be more splendid than the defence of the innocent, but he was not so pleased by the thought of Troussequin's release. No doubt the prisoner's feelings would undergo a change when he learned the identity of his rescuer, but his gratitude, which could not fail to be indiscreet, would be scarcely less embarrassing than his enmity. The newspapers would interview him, stimulated by the dramatic change in the situation, and he would certainly not be reticent on the subject of his old friend, Fabien Rigault, and the days of their intimacy in the Malleboine. There would undoubtedly be a fond reference to Rigault's father, Rigault Rigodon, and he might count himself lucky if in a moment of ecstasy and alcohol Troussequin did not enrich the hungry reporters with the shameful but picturesque episode of the piddling from the Rond-Point. It would draw a burst of laughter from the whole town, and would be an endless source of jokes and innuendoes at the office. The manager himself would be bound to hear about it. These considerations damped Rigault's proud and happy sense of being the instrument of justice, but they did not abate his zeal. When he reached the Rue Belley, along which he generally passed on his way to the factory, he did not pause but strode on with undiminished speed along the Avenue Raymond-Poincaré. But his throat was dry.

Another thing that alarmed him, no less than the prospect of Troussequin's immoderate gratitude, was the thought of testifying against a lawyer. However much he reminded himself that lawyers, too, are human and subject to human frailties, it still seemed to him preposterous that Maître Marguet should be guilty. And even if he had committed the murder, it might have been for reasons beyond the scope of the crude machinery of justice. The purposes of lawyers are impenetrable. Had he, Rigault, any right to interfere with the course of events ? It is the duty of respectable men not to call into question things that public opinion has found it convenient to accept. Moreover, there was an element of danger in this act of justice towards which his conscience was now driving him. It might well turn out that the testimony of a twelve-year-old boy would not be sufficient to overcome the lawyer, in which case Rigault would be under the stigma of having cast suspicion on a man who was not merely honourable but important. It would be said that he had done so in order to save a childhood friend.

By the time he left the Avenue Raymond-Poincaré, Rigault was beginning to have need of heroism. In the Rue de l'Herbe-Sèche he encountered Philippon, the mayor, who was talking to the prefect, the deputy-mayor, and the proprietor of the *Magasins Neufs*, who was also president of the Philharmonic Society. In reply to his greeting to Philippon, the four gentlemen, including the prefect, removed their hats and gazed civilly at him. Rigault felt tails grow on his coat, tails of good bourgeois cloth which counselled prudence and seemed to draw him back. He felt that he enjoyed the confidence of those four distinguished persons, that he shared in their vigilant watch over the well-being of the town, and he asked himself bluntly whether, as a right-thinking citizen, he would be justified in unleashing a scandal of which no one could foresee the consequences. Troussequin might be technically innocent, but he had already been convicted of one attempt at rape, and therefore might very well commit another. Viewed in this light, his condemnation would be merely a sensible precaution.

Rigault's footsteps were now flagging, but he was still

bent on doing his duty. As he emerged on to the Place de l'Hotel-de-Ville, however, he saw in the distance Artevel's father, who had come out of the police station and was standing on the steps, talking to Charlasse. The young constable said something with his head lowered, and Artevel answered without looking at him. It would be impossible for Rigault to pass through the doorway without saying a word to the man who had been his neighbour for nearly twenty years. And the thought that Artevel would call him by his Christian name, and very likely refer to his father, sufficed to undermine the last of his good intentions. He preferred to remain under the spell of the four gentlemen who had saluted him ; and so, after walking round the square, ashamed and harrowed by remorse, he went on his way to the factory.

The four gentlemen, meanwhile, had separated, and Philippon was walking with the prefect as far as his office. They were discussing their plans for the election, and the mayor was making no attempt to hide his delight.

' We've had a wonderful stroke of luck over this Troussequin business ! It's quite providential that Fouchard should be away. There's no denying his talent as an advocate, and he'd certainly be defending the man if he were here. Think of the publicity ! '

The prefect, however, seemed less overjoyed.

' It's a piece of luck, certainly,' he said, ' but I'm very much afraid that before long Fouchard will have scored a big success.'

' What success ? ' asked the mayor.

' A success against you, which is particularly annoying. I heard this morning—in fact, people have made a point of letting me know—that there's a rumour among the workers, and even in the town, that the T.D.C. factory is soon going to close down.'

' It's a false rumour.'

' Yes, a false rumour, but circulated by the management. We shall hear more of it. Have you read the report on the preliminary investigation into the crime ? It seems that on Friday afternoon Maître Marguet met Troussequin while he was visiting Monsieur Butillat, who owns the plot of land in the Rue Jouffroy. He would hardly have gone to call on that old man, who lives right on the edge of the town, unless he had some particular reason for doing so ; and when I tell you that a quarter of an hour later he paid a visit to the T.D.C. factory, you can draw your own conclusions.'

' Don't worry,' said Philippon. ' The old man will certainly have refused to sell, just as he has always done.'

The prefect smiled as he reflected that he had been much more shrewd in interpreting this matter than Philippon. He went on :

' Quite so. I don't doubt that he refused to sell any more than you do. But suppose he had accepted an offer from the T.D.C.—it would be rather tiresome, wouldn't it ? '

' Of course,' said the mayor. ' To turn the T.D.C. off the land would be extremely difficult—perhaps impossible.'

' In fact, you agree with me. You feel, as I do, that in dealing with a concern that size one has to go carefully, not because it's powerful, but because its interests are so tied up with those of the town. We shall have to discuss that matter further. But you see the connection between the T.D.C.'s failure to buy that land, and the rumour that they're closing down, which is still circulating ? '

Although Philippon did not see it at all, he preferred not to admit the fact and tried to carry it off with a sardonic laugh. The prefect was not deceived, but pretended to assume that he understood for the pleasure of witnessing his embarrassment.

' It's very annoying for you,' he said simply.

The mayor waited in vain for some further remark which might enlighten him, and finally asked :

' Well, how does it look to you ? '

' Good heavens, it looks clear enough ! They circulate a rumour that they may be closing down—if necessary, they take one or two other steps to increase the public anxiety—and having created a state of panic they sit back and wait for a telephone call from the Prefecture. And there you are ! '

' And so ? '

' And so ? . . . I ask them if it's true that they're going to turn nine hundred workmen out into the street. They say they're doing everything in their power to avert the catastrophe, but that it seems to be inevitable unless some fortunate circumstance arises to change the situation—for instance, if they should be able to acquire Butillat's land. For this to happen, the town would have to give up its idea of expropriating Butillat. In other words, the Municipal Council would have to give way to the views of Fouchard, who has always been against it.'

' But that's blackmail ! ' exclaimed the indignant Philippon. ' We aren't going to let ourselves be pushed around like that ! '

' It's probably blackmail, but one can't be quite certain. It's possible, after all, that the economic crisis, by forcing them to close down some of their smaller establishments and amalgamate them with the larger ones, may make it really necessary for them to get hold of Butillat's land. Are you prepared, by cutting the ground from under their feet, to run the risk of seeing the factory leave the town ? That is the whole question. I'm bound to say I think it's a situation that wants careful handling. Do you want it to be said that the factory was forced to close down because of the obstinacy of the Council? I don't know how you could expect to keep the mayoralty next year! The unemployed might be a bit cross about it.'

Philippon, with an anguished and apoplectic countenance, seemed to be searching wildly for a way out of the dilemma. 'It's immoral!' he groaned. 'Don't you think it's immoral?'

The prefect agreed, against his inmost conviction, because he did not wish to offend Philippon. The truth was that he saw nothing immoral in the business, and no reason to reproach the governing board of the T.D.C. He was struck, on the contrary, by the small part which management played in the matter. It was far more as though the factory were being driven by natural forces which had nothing to do with management. And there could be no denying that the purchase of the land in the Rue Jouffroy would be in the general interest.

'If only I knew how much of it was true,' stormed Philippon, 'and if the closing of the factory really does depend on whether they can get that bit of land!'

'I don't know how we're to find out,' said the prefect. 'No one knows except the manager of the factory. Or perhaps Maître Marguet knows, but as he's bound to professional secrecy he doesn't count.'

TWELVE

THE CELLAR WAS immense, but M. Crepel had built a rectangular cabin round the ventilator, made of black cloth stretched over a light wooden framework. It was almost completely dark inside, and the reflected picture from outside the house stood out clearly on the light wood of a round table. The ventilator, through which passed the upper part of the periscope, was covered by a network of fine wire which let in very little light. It was scarcely possible to distinguish the oddly designed voice-pipe hanging on the wall, which must have been specially made.

The organist and the lawyer, seated side by side at the table, could not see one another. They had beneath their eyes a landscape of the Rue Jacques-de-Molay, which was, as it happened, entirely deserted. This absence of passers-by mortified M. Crepel, who feared lest his guest should come to doubt the efficiency of his apparatus.

'It's as though they were doing it on purpose,' he said irritably. 'Generally there are so many people I hardly know where to look.'

Maître Marguet was oppressed by the emptiness of the street. He had come down to the cellar directly after lunch to watch for the passing of his mother, who, as he had now discovered, had arranged to meet her architect at four o'clock. He intended to follow her, and if she called at a photographer's to go in after her and reclaim his film.

'If you wouldn't mind keeping watch alone,' said M.

Crepel, 'I'll go outside and play you something on the organ.'

'Please, I'd rather you didn't,' said Maître Marguet, with a slight impatience.

He had no great respect for the organist's accomplishment. M. Crepel was, perhaps, too readily carried away by what he called his 'power,' which lay chiefly in his muscles. He was wont ingenuously to repeat a compliment paid him by Monseigneur Bonnet one Sunday after a choral mass: 'Your brachials and deltoids are really extraordinary!' When he had rigged up his periscope he had also installed in the cellar one of the three organs which were the pride of his establishment, and on this he played requiem masses with all the energy he possessed. He liked to pretend, while he sat at his periscope surveying the Rue Jacques-de-Molay, that he was in command of a German submarine during the war, torpedoing eight or ten ships a day, preferably British or American. Having sunk the *Lusitania* he felt that the least he could do was to play a requiem for the victims.

'You're missing something,' he said. 'You've never heard me play in this setting. There's a splendour about it——'

'Some other time,' said Maître Marguet. 'Some other time. We shall have plenty of chances.'

Something at last showed on the table, a splash of red and black. M. Crepel was the first to notice it, and he murmured:

'On the starboard bow—do you see? About a cable's length . . .'

He started to reach for his voice-pipe, but then thought better of it. He could hardly give orders to his crew in the presence of a stranger. As it turned out there was nothing lost, because it was only a little girl going down the street, and he never torpedoed children, who were vessels of insufficient tonnage. The little girl's image, which was excellently proportioned while she remained more than a certain distance away, became rapidly distorted. As she drew near to the ventilator her feet and the lower part of her body loomed enormous on the table. For some moments nothing was to be seen but a shapeless mass. Then the figure, seen now from behind, receded towards the cathedral and in doing so regained its proper proportions.

'Clear as possible, wasn't it?' said M. Crepel exultantly. 'Believe me, I see everything that goes by. I don't miss a thing—nothing!'

A small black smudge appeared at the edge of the table, very slowly growing in size. M. Crepel, who had not torpedoed anything since eleven that morning, felt a stir of heroic ardour. But unfortunately he recognised the venerable Canon Budin, walking with small gouty steps and leaning on a stout umbrella. Priests and nuns were hospital ships, and could not be torpedoed. In any case, Canon Budin went into a house and vanished from the table. This was followed by another disappointment. A numerous group —a whole convoy—appeared at the end of the street; but they were children on their way to school, and the fact had to be accepted. The street then remained empty for nearly a quarter of an hour. Finally another figure entered the field of the periscope, apparently that of a woman dressed entirely in black. It looked to Maître Marguet like his mother, and his heart leapt. M. Crepel, scarcely less excited, nudged him with his elbow to attract his attention. The black figure grew larger on the table, and they saw that it was the young Abbé Casaubon, who lived a little further on, in the Rue des Renaudes. Another hospital ship.

'Well, I don't care if it is!' stormed M. Crepel. 'After all——'

'I beg your pardon?' said Maître Marguet. 'Were you speaking to me?'

'No—nothing,' said M. Crepel, slightly embarrassed. 'By

the way, my wife asked me at lunch when the murdered girl is going to be buried, but I wasn't able to tell her.'

' Her father took her to her own village this morning. The funeral is to-morrow. My wife and I will be going.'

' A sad occasion,' said the organist with a sigh. ' I hope at least there's a harmonium in the village church ? '

' I—I think so,' stammered the lawyer.

He was suddenly overtaken by a fit of weakness. The mention of the word harmonium, in the darkness of the cellar, afflicted him with a sense of funeral awe. For a moment he closed his eyes, and when he opened them he came near to uttering a cry. Another figure had appeared on the table behind that of the Abbé Casaubon—the figure of a young girl, which he recognised instantly as that of Charlotte Richon, the murdered housemaid. He thrust a hand over the table and said in a hoarse voice :

' Behind the Abbé . . . what can you see ? '

' It's the maid,' said M. Crepel.

' The maid ? What are you saying ? Do you mean to say you recognise——? '

' Yes, of course. My wife must have sent her out on an errand. But what are you doing ? Take your hand away.'

With astonishment M. Crepel saw the lawyer's hand follow the maid's figure. It hovered like a bird, cutting off the light and casting a black and trembling shadow over the entire width of the street.

' Your hand's shaking,' M. Crepel said. ' I've never seen a hand shake so much. Your voice was shaking too. Who did you think you saw behind the Abbé ? Who did you think you saw, to make you tremble like that ? '

Maître Marguet had withdrawn his hand. He did not answer. The organist leaned towards him and said in a low voice :

' Between ourselves, you're the one who torpedoed

Charlotte Richon, aren't you?... Are you sure you wouldn't like me to play a requiem? It would be so splendid!'

'You're losing your wits, M. Crepel,' said the lawyer dryly. 'Please pull yourself together.'

'Forgive me,' said M. Crepel, genuinely apologetic. 'I get carried away in the darkness and I see things as an artist. Considered in terms of pure art that murder was so beautiful . . . I thought of you taking refuge aboard my submarine, breathing the most horrible blasphemies, revolting against Heaven; and then I thought of myself unleashing the organ and redeeming you with a requiem . . . A wonderful thought, don't you think?'

'I'm very glad to be an unconscious source of inspiration to you; but when you choose themes of that nature I'd prefer you to keep them to yourself.'

'It was stupid of me,' agreed M. Crepel. 'I'm really ashamed of myself. Why, here comes your mother!'

The figure of Mme. Marguet the elder was moving towards the centre of the table. Despite her eighty years and the rheumatism of which she constantly complained, she was walking briskly, and her son was struck by a suggestion of light-heartedness in her bearing. All his misgivings returned to him. He had still to discover whether she had sent her servant to take the film to be developed, or whether she was carrying it at that moment in the black leather bag hanging from her arm. Her figure had doubled in size on the flat surface of the table. They saw her stop and take a handkerchief out of her bag. But suddenly, as she started off again, her figure shrank to a quarter or a fifth of its original size and became strangely distorted.

'What's happening?' asked the lawyer. 'It looks as though something has gone wrong with your apparatus.'

'Not at all,' said M. Crepel. 'My apparatus has never worked better. I'm afraid Madame Marguet has fallen down.'

Maître Marguet had already realised that the poor lady must have had a fall. He had got to his feet and was feeling for the door. M. Crepel unhooked his voice-pipe and cried vigorously, ' All lights on ! ' He then turned a switch which lit a bulb in the cabin and another in the middle of the cellar. The lawyer ran out into the street and reached his mother in a few moments. She had fallen flat on her stomach, and abandoning the attempt to get up by herself was trying to crawl towards her bag, which had fallen a few feet away. At the sight of her son she made a desperate effort to cover the last few inches, because the bag was open, and the bright red of a roll of film could be plainly seen sticking out of it.

Maître Marguet at once perceived her trouble, and forgetting his own anxieties thought only of reassuring her. Before he even went to help her, he picked up the bag, ostentatiously replacing the film inside it. In doing so he was able to discover that the film had been unrolled; the cylinder was soft, and the wrapping so loose that he could have put his finger between the layers. Undoubtedly the old lady had examined it by daylight, expecting to find pictures on it, and finding nothing had carelessly rolled it up again in order to take it to a photographer. This ingenuousness melted the lawyer's heart, and he helped her to her feet so gently, and spoke to her so kindly, that she was herself touched and remorseful for her act of petty dishonesty.

' When I opened my bag just now,' she said, ' I found a photographic thing in it which belongs to you. I picked it up yesterday afternoon by mistake, with my handkerchief.'

Meanwhile M. Crepel had also come running up with the swaying motion of a sailor treading dry land after a long spell at sea. Mme. Marguet's fall had been a heavy one. Her legs were hurting her badly, and the two men had to help her home. She yielded to her son's persuasion and allowed him to send for the doctor.

THIRTEEN

BEFORE GOING INTO school, and during the short break at a quarter to three, they all talked about the crime, and all loudly proclaimed Troussequin's innocence. Buq's conviction was based on quite sensible arguments, but Antoine, with a fervour which was a little surprising, simply asserted that the truth was going to explode, and sooner than anyone thought. From the way he talked, it seemed that it would amaze everyone. In general, none of them believed in Troussequin's guilt, and they were more interested in the crime itself. Charnotey had cut a detailed account out of his father's paper, which dwelt on the disgusting nature of the murder and the mutilation of the corpse. He read it aloud, explaining its euphemisms and innuendoes in crude words and with an excited laugh, and adorning it with comments and obscene imaginative flights of his own. The others listened and joined in, flushed and a little shamefaced, disturbed by the evocation of torn and bloodied under-clothes, gashed and tortured femininity, a mystery most foully exposed.

It was towards the end of that afternoon that the history master, in the middle of a discourse on the Thirty Years War, caught big Pucelet masturbating as he sat at his desk. The offence was not proven since Pucelet had the presence of mind to argue that he had been savagely bitten by some insect that had crawled up the leg of his shorts. What was more, he had the luck to be able to produce a small beetle which he squashed to death under the master's nose with a hideous crackling and squelching sound which caused the poor man to feel, as he resumed his lecture, that his stomach might fail him at any moment, and words as well.

When they got out into the street, at a quarter to four, the tale of this episode went round, and big Pucelet, bursting with pride, extolled the virtues of his member, whose dimensions, he gave them to understand, had greatly alarmed the history master. A good many of them listened enviously and jeered at him in order to conceal their melancholy and distress at not being so well endowed, not by a long way. But Buq, shocked in his most private sense of proportion, said that he very much doubted, and for many reasons, whether Nature had really treated Pucelet so lavishly; and that, considering the filthy use he made of it, a member suited to an undersized monkey would have served him just as well; and that in any case he was just the sort of chap whose greatest pride would be situated in the region of his bottom. To which Pucelet replied with classic eloquence that when it came to bottoms his own was certainly the cleaner. Whereupon Buq said that in his eyes he was nothing but a mangy goat, only stupider, and moth-eaten and flea-bitten and lousy and shagged out and pimply and unwashed and stinking all over especially his feet.

'Ditto to you!' retorted big Pucelet to each item on the list. 'Ditto to you!'

The others took sides and joined in the argument, and the insults sped like bullets. One party rallied to the support of Buq in recognition of the service he had rendered to the self-esteem of each of them in denouncing Pucelet's exaggerations. Antoine, on his side from the first instant, but little given to insults, stayed silent. In the other camp Charnotey made his voice loudly heard and did his best to embitter the dispute. He had more than one bone to pick with Buq, and he hoped that if it came to a general brawl he might be able to get in a few useful kicks without any risk to himself.

And then Dr. Coinchot approached, on his way to examine old Mme. Marguet's legs. The invective died down as he drew near, but seeing them flushed and angry, their fists still half clenched, he realised that a battle was preparing. Some of them he recognised, having treated them for measles or mumps or scarlet fever, and so he asked in a friendly way what the trouble was about.

'It's about the crime in the Rue Jacques-de-Molay,' said Antoine, to whom the question was addressed.

'No it isn't,' said Buq. 'It's about a dirty swine who thinks he's clever because he tossed himself off in the history class!'

'Is that true?' asked Coinchot, charitably refraining from looking at Pucelet.

The offender was so ingenuous as to protest, and none of the others could prevent himself smiling.

'Well, well,' said Coinchot. 'I prefer to believe that nothing of the kind happened. It's most dangerous to the health, and once you get into bad habits there's no saying where it will end. Take Troussequin, for example. It's precisely because he did that sort of thing when he was young that he became what he is now. What's more, that's why he's so hideous. That's no fairy-tale, I can assure you.'

The doctor passed on, and the others, their anger abated, gazed at Pucelet with expressions of concern and surprise which were not entirely assumed. They seemed really to see on his face the first traces of infamy, and Charnotey said:

'You've got a very small head for anyone as tall as you are. It's about the size of a fist.'

'That's true,' said the others. 'He's scarcely got any head at all.'

' It's very unusual to have such a small head.'

' Look at him ! It's enough to make you laugh, a head that size ! '

' Sometimes you hardly notice it's there ! . . .'

Pucelet gazed about him with a look of unhappy astonishment. What was all this talk about his head ? He touched his face and felt his skull through the cloth of his cap. It seemed to him that indeed his head had lost nearly all its size ; he felt it shrink within the palm of his hand until at last he did not feel it at all, anyway not as a head. It seemed even to have lost all its shape in front, so that it was nothing more than a prolongation of his neck. Pucelet had never been so upset by anything as he was by this discovery. He realised that his head had changed into a phallus. That was what had happened to him, because of bad habits. As a matter of fact, he was not yet wholly convinced of it ; but the others were all looking at him and laughing. It was because he had suddenly become an enormous Priapus ; and at the thought he had an immense feeling of suffering and distress. Standing there in the street, with all their eyes upon him, he felt himself to be naked, pink and obscene. He might hide himself for the moment under the peak of his cap, take refuge behind his hand, but he would not be able to do so always. What would the neighbours think ? Above all, what would his father think ? In sudden terror he began to run, to escape from his father and the world, as one does after being transformed. And the others ran after him crying:

' Pucelet's head ! Look at Pucelet's head ! '

So he doubled his speed and in less than a minute had reached the Rue des Rencontres. The people on the pavement and the shopkeepers in their doorways watched him go, and a long murmur seemed to follow and surround him —' Oh, look at Pucelet's head ! . . . ' He turned into a side street, fled down the slope leading to the river, and, still running, crossed the bridge. A road bordered by small houses led to the open meadows, and he followed it. Unhappy Priapus—he, too, abandoned by his mother—he ran for consolation to gardens and the warm earth and the young shoots.

When he reached the meadows Pucelet forgot his metamorphosis, but he had still a feeling of heavy sadness. The mutter of the town was dying away behind him. He was breathless, but he still walked quickly, driven by the lingering consciousness of a threat. After walking for a quarter of an hour, he came to the bushes encircling the Morte aux Deux Boucs. There were in the meadowland a number of these deep, still water-holes, known locally as 'mortes,' which marked the former course of the river. Pucelet thrust his way between two bushes, and knelt in exhaustion at the water's edge. The bluish-green water, turning almost to black in its depths, was unstirred by any ripple. He leaned over it and saw the clear reflection of his face. A troubled memory passed through his mind, and caused the picture on the water to smile. A bird sang from a thicket, and others answered, and a warbler flew close by his head. The bushes quivered with a friendly life, the flutter of wings, the stir of leaves, and secret movements and little cries and the chirping of insects. The boy straightened himself and looked over his shoulder. The meadows were filled with a magical spring. He stretched full length on the ground, and the grassy earth was aromatic and rough and warm. He began to chew grass, and presently to sing. He sang for a long time, and then suddenly stopped in the middle of a line because of the warm moisture of the meadow and the spring flowers, which had caused the sap to rise within him. A tide of red washed over his face. Kneeling in the grass, he undid his belt and made his offering to the earth. He felt no weariness, and with his mouth open to the sun he spent himself like a god, making as he did so a soft murmur like the murmur of the sea in a shell . . .

When he arrived at the old lady's dwelling, Dr. Coinchot had found at the bedside the Marguets, the organist, and Canon Budin, who, having been informed of the accident, had called to inquire. Old Mme. Marguet was now suffering from severe pain in her legs, and she also complained of pain in her right hand, which had become very stiff. The organist listened with envy, dreaming of an accident in which he risked losing the use of both hands. He got better in the end, but only after atrocious suffering. Everybody thought music had lost him for ever, and he himself despaired more than once, and even blasphemed. But one splendid Sunday morning, restored by a miracle, inspired by the creative anguish of a long and arduous struggle, he unleashed the organ with a sublime and pitiless fervour, pulling out every single stop in a multiple, impassioned paean, a true thunder of God's wrath, which shook the whole cathedral . . . Lucie Marguet, very much upset, hovered about her mother-in-law, who was greatly vexed at not being able to blame her for the accident. The suaveness of Canon Budin perhaps accounted for the fact that there were no sharp exchanges, because the lawyer himself, despite his filial anxiety, was angry with his mother at the irreparable loss of his film, the whole length of which was exposed. While he replied absently to the remarks of the canon and the organist he clutched the other spool in his pocket, trembling at the thought that this too might be accidentally destroyed. He was now most anxious to get it developed as soon as possible.

The three men withdrew to another room while the doctor was examining his patient. The organist seemed to be in an excited state, and begged to excuse himself while he went back to his cellar for a minute. He wanted to make sure that everything was all right on board.

' A great artist,' said Canon Budin when he had departed, ' but, like all artists, a trifle eccentric.'

' Yes, a great artist,' said the lawyer. ' By the way, I wanted to ask you something. Do you still go in for photography ? '

' Scarcely at all,' said the canon. ' Now and again I take a picture of my maid . . .'

' Well, that isn't really what I meant. I was wondering if you still had the equipment for developing films.'

' But I've never had it. When I have a film to be developed, I take it to the episcopal offices. They've got a very good dark room.'

' Do you know who does the developing ? '

Maître Marguet's insistence was beginning to astonish the canon, who replied rather tersely :

' It has never occurred to me to ask.'

The lawyer realised that he had slightly ruffled the good man, but he could not restrain himself from asking, after a pause, if he would introduce him to the photographer at the episcopal offices, because he wanted to learn how it was done. The canon, growing mistrustful, firmly refused. He suspected a tale of adultery—photographs of some evil woman in her chemise, or even out of her chemise ; and so, because one couldn't have them developed in the town, one wanted to give them to a priest. It was a shrewd idea, what was more. The priest would certainly do nothing to make known the misbehaviour of a gentleman so prominent among the ranks of the faithful. The Church was too much an interested party to want to shake his credit. Maître Marguet changed the subject, but his vexation was apparent, and the canon was a little remorseful at having refused him so bluntly. After all, he supposed, one might develop his photographs without looking at them too closely. But by this time the doctor had finished his examination, and Lucie came in to fetch them.

Coinchot was able to give them an entirely reassuring report. There were fortunately no bones broken, and a few days' rest should be enough to put the old lady on her feet again. The lawyer, saying that he had urgent business, but in reality because he could not stay still, left at the same time as he did, and they walked together as far as the Rue des Rencontres. They talked about the crime; but when they were on the point of separating Coinchot asked after his ulcer and rebuked him for not having come to see him for so long. Maître Marguet, impatient to be alone, promised to call at his consulting room on Friday afternoon.

Since his conversation with the canon, which had ended in a rebuff, he had thought of nothing but ways and means of getting his film developed. With a new sense of urgency he reviewed the list of the town's photographers. So far as he knew, there were five of them, of which three could be eliminated at a glance : Pucelet, a narrow-minded, honest man ; Jurion the bookseller, said to be an adherent of the left wing ; and Vousier, whose ties, artist's hats and long clay pipes suggested an adolescent nature. There remained Michaud and Fondu. The first of these was extremely devout, as was his wife. Canopy-bearer, cross-bearer and a great kisser of rings, he would not dare imperil his conscience without consulting his spiritual director. Upon discovering the nature of the photographs he would think he had been visited by the devil, and after two or three days of delicious torment, during which he would wallow in the business, he would take the photographs to a priest. And the priest, after consulting the bishop, would simply suppress the whole thing. Maître Marguet was quite easy on that score : there was no danger. But he had to envisage a risk of another kind. The priest would in all likelihood insist that the evidence of the Church's discretion should be destroyed, which would mean the end of that lot of photographs. The lawyer was therefore inclined to address himself to Fondu, despite the very low opinion he had of the man. Although he was an excellent photographer, Fondu had the manner and the reputation of a rogue. He could probably be relied upon to start blackmailing his customer directly he set eyes on the photographs, but at least the first payment would make him an accomplice.

Walking haphazard along the Rue des Rencontres, Maître Marguet found himself—not altogether accidentally, since the thought was so much in his mind—outside Fondu's shop. He paused for a moment at the window, seeming to study some coloured enlargements while he glanced covertly inside. He could see Fondu in conversation with someone, and the look of the man was enough to confirm him in his view that he was not the sort to let slip a fruitful source of blackmail.

Meanwhile the enlargements in the window had called up a rich vision in his mind. He thought of his photographs similarly enlarged and coloured, the flesh-tints, the bright red of the wounds, the deep, dark shadows. On winter evenings, when his clerks had left, he would lock himself in his study and decorate the walls with that barbarous imagery, recalling the medical dictionary and the martyrs of the Rue Saint-Sulpice, but which for him was still a quivering reality. The passers-by, their reflections faintly visible to him in the glass, seemed to show a slight, casual astonishment at his sustained interest in the enlargements. Fondu, inside the shop, had also noticed him, and had made several attempts to catch his eye. Maître Marguet wanted to go ; but gazing at a large coloured portrait he seemed to see it replaced by the eight of his collection, one after the other, with their unlooked-for details, their monstrous perspectives. He could not turn away his head. The pictures multiplied, grew more elaborate, swept through his mind with the speed of a cinema film, seeming to bring the murdered girl to writhing, convulsive life. In a sort of terror he drew closer to the window, pressing his hands against the glass at the level of his shoulders, as though to hide the sight of that bleeding flesh from the passers-by.

Fondu, now on the threshold of the shop, was taking leave of his customer, and seeing Maître Marguet in this strange posture was certain to speak to him. The lawyer realised that once they got into conversation he would not be able to prevent himself from handing over his secret with the roll of film, and his terror increased, since he was still not sure that this was the course he wanted to pursue. He pretended not to hear the remark Fondu addressed to him, and when the photographer spoke again he succeeded in tearing himself away from the window and walking off in an almost normal fashion. Leaving the town, where he had so much to fear from himself, he went down to the river, crossed the bridge, and strode on into the meadows.

By degrees his turmoil subsided. He found himself presently on a soft and scarcely discernible path, and rounding a bush came very near to falling over Pucelet. The boy, caught in the act, hastily buckled his belt, and still kneeling gazed imploringly up at the intruder. The thunderstruck Maître Marguet stared silently down at this brother in misery—another who must tremble for his sad, secret pleasure.

'Don't tell my father!' begged Pucelet. 'Don't tell him!'

The lawyer with a tightening of his throat stayed silent, not knowing what to say.

'I promised I'd go straight home after school,' said Pucelet. 'I'm supposed to be helping him make some prints . . . Don't tell him!'

He saw a sudden light shine in Maître Marguet's eyes which so terrified him that he burst into tears. The lawyer seized his ear with a hand that trembled, and feigned indignation.

'It's infamous! I ought to report you to the police! But I shall certainly speak to your father. I shall tell him what you dared to do in front of me, and I shall advise him to send you to a reformatory!'

Pucelet sobbed more loudly while he stammered a plea for mercy. Maître Marguet wanted to run, but he tapped the roll of film in his pocket and went on:

'You mean to say your father was waiting for you to help him? And this is how you obey him! Don't you like photography?'

'Yes, Monsieur,' gasped big Pucelet.

'Do you even know how to develop a film?'

'Yes, Monsieur. My father's taught me.'

Maître Marguet asked a few more questions, repeating his threats of paternal wrath and the reformatory. He had the boy at his mercy, but found it hard to take advantage of the situation. Finally, however, he pulled the roll out of his pocket and exacted the price of his silence.

As he remained standing beside the pool, watching Pucelet's figure vanish across the meadow, the thought came to him that for the first time in his life he had done an evil thing. He felt debased by the bargain, and a desperate remorse clutched at his heart.

The boy had not gone more than two hundred yards. He could still call him back and relieve him of his shameful burden. But just as he had made up his mind to do so he heard a voice coming from the other side of the cluster of bushes which hid him from view. Round the side of the pool appeared Sergeant Maillard, in his suit and bowler hat, accompanied by his wife. The couple, on their way back to the town, followed the path Pucelet had taken and thus frustrated the lawyer's intention, since he dared not show himself.

The Maillards had only been married four years, but they had been in love with one another since 1911. Maillard was then a young constable, and Mme. Maillard had just married a man employed at the *Mairie*. One winter's evening, at a ball given by the Municipality, they had danced together at the suggestion of her husband, who had hurt his foot. Ever since, despite the changes of fashion, and until the death of her husband twenty years later, she had worn on all her winter hats a yellow and blue feather like the one she had worn that night. Maillard had passed every summer in a fever of impatience, awaiting the return of autumn and felt hats.

As they strolled across the meadow they were discussing the wallpaper of their bedroom, which they intended to replace. The sergeant, gently urging extravagance, was filled with admiration for his wife's prudence and economy.

' I saw a nice modern flower pattern at Lanois', four francs a roll,' she was saying. ' It's not expensive, and it's bright and gay . . .'

Maillard bent down and picked a buttercup, which he fixed in her hat next to the feather.

' There are two things I don't believe in skimping,' he said. ' Food and wallpaper. Your flower pattern's sure to be very nice, because you chose it, but I'd like something more—well, not showy, exactly, but—well, to give you an idea—I'd like birds.'

' Oh, I'd like birds too ! They're lovely ! But they're very dear.'

' Never mind. Let's have birds.'

' You know there's nothing I'd like better, Alexandre.'

Maillard gazed at his wife as they walked side by side, her face already wrinkled but serene and gentle, and he saw her in the spring, adorned with the meadows. He wanted to tell her that he was happy, and he took her hand.

As they reached the bridge they saw the Tetère girls on the other side of the river. They were coming out of a café and laughing at the remarks that were flung at them from inside. Marion was no longer feeling her wound, and if she was walking a little unsteadily it was because she had had too much to drink. Crossing the embankment, the sisters came and sat on the parapet of the bridge. Maillard's heart was so light that he forgot his resentment at the quarrel with Dr. Coinchot to which they had given rise. But the Tetère girls watched their coming with ironical comments, and as they passed Marion cried hoarsely, jerking her chin towards Mme. Maillard's hat :

' Oh, look at the pretty feather ! I must get one for my grandmother ! '

They burst into loud laughter, and Minie in her excitement capped the remark.

' A great, big husband, and a pretty feather ! '

Maillard had gone purple in the face. He strode on raging with his head averted, already meditating reprisals.

FOURTEEN

COMING OUT OF the Impasse de la Sourdine, Trésor
paused in front of a shrunken and fragile old man who
sat sunning himself on a chair, and said as he bent towards
him :

'Watch what I'm going to do.'

With his forefinger he pushed his long nose to the left,
so far that its point touched his cheek. Then he took his
finger away, and his nose stayed bent as though the cartilage
were broken. The old man stayed motionless and silent,
but his eyes brightened as a gleam of gaiety appeared in
their depths. Trésor stuck out his tongue, which was
marvellously long, and curled it upwards in an evident
attempt to lick the end of his nose. This was when the
old man began to quiver, but restrainedly and still without
a sound. The tongue was surprised at not finding the nose
it was looking for. It waved about feeling for it, reached out
and drew back, seeming at moments timid and mistrustful,
rather alarmed too, and at moments impatient and angry.
Finally, after searching vainly to the right, it found the nose
over on the left, and did a little dance of happiness. The
old man was now visibly shaking ; his breath was coming
faster, and he laid a feeble hand on his stomach in case
anything should break. Trésor withdrew his tongue, while
his nose stayed miraculously bent, and said :

'Now watch this.'

He took the lobe of his right ear between his thumb and

forefinger, and gave a sharp jerk. There was a little sound like the ringing of a bell, and the nose, suddenly released as though it were india-rubber, snapped back into place. The old man sat writhing, allowing a small and almost inaudible sound of laughter to escape from his lips. When this was over he said in a piping voice :

' I could do tricks, too, when I was young.'

' Of course you could,' said Trésor. ' Everybody has his tricks. Well, I just showed you in passing, because I happened to be passing and I thought I'd show you.'

The old man looked at him enviously and half-angrily, and said, thrusting up his chin :

' I knew a thing or two, I did ! '

' That's right, of course you did ! Well, enjoy the sun, old skin-and-bones ! '

Trésor strolled casually along the Rue des Oiseaux, passing through conversations, talking with his hands and with his feet and even with his tongue, laughing at good news and at bad news and at nothing at all. When he reached the Carrefour des Cinq he was singing the *Marseillaise*. A voice from behind interrupted him :

' Do you think you're funny with your *Marseillaise* ? Shut your mouth ! '

He turned and saw, dragging himself along, a man with a face of *papier mâché*, a man wounded and suffocated by war, burnt by gas, his eyes darkened with a long fury. War was still in his guts and his lungs, and both were wasting away.

' Can't you find anything better to sing than that bloody song ? ' he demanded, between spitting and a burst of coughing.

' A bloody song ? ' said Trésor. ' But why ? It's a pretty song.'

The man cursed him, and when his breath failed Trésor shrugged his shoulders and left him to cough out the remains of his life into his handkerchief. Why should the chap want to stop him singing?

On that early afternoon the Rue de la Clé-d'Or was warm and bathed in sunshine. Trésor sat down at the foot of the big flight of steps, with his back against the wall of the Rond-Point, and slept for a little over an hour. He was awakened by a kick in the ribs, and half-opening one eye recognised the large boot of Sergeant Maillard.

'You great mule, can't you look where you're going?' he exclaimed, turning his back and not condescending to look at him.

The sergeant uttered a grunt of fury and satisfaction. Taking him by the collar, he lifted him without apparent effort to his feet.

'So I'm a mule, am I? You don't care what you say any more, is that it? The family can do what they like! They can insult the police, or——'

'You mustn't be cross with an old friend,' said Trésor, rubbing his eyes. 'I didn't see it was your boot. Naturally, if I had . . . I'm much too well brought up to call a sergeant a mule.'

Before letting him go Maillard relieved his feelings by shaking him severely. Trésor laughed as though it were all a game, and seeing faces appear at windows in the Rue de la Clé-d'Or he put right any possible misapprehension by saying in a loud voice:

'Attention everyone, please! . . .'

These words alone brought smiles to the faces of the listeners. The Malleboine people delighted to hear him when he was in the mood, although there was nothing out of the way, or even picturesque, in the language he used. Nor was there anything forced in his intonation. His originality consisted simply in making appropriate use of words and phrases which had never been current in the quarter, and which were invested, in consequence, with an extraordinary virtuosity. Few people resident in the Upper Town would have been capable of appreciating the peculiar flavour of audacity and irresistible humour which the words ' Attention everyone, please ! ' acquired when spoken in the normal accent of the Malleboine. Certain juxtapositions produced a similar effect. But it called for a very special feeling for the language of the quarter to avoid carrying the thing to excess. No one possessed this feeling like Trésor, who had, moreover, a trick of pronunciation which laid especial stress upon the alien flavour of these borrowed words.

' Attention everyone, please ! . . . Just now I was having a nap at the bottom of the steps, when all of a sudden I was woken up by a great kick in the ribs. It was a shock to me, naturally, and so I shouted out, " Great mule ! " And who do you think I saw standing over me ? It was Monsieur Maillard ! I had called Monsieur Maillard a great mule ! Imagine my embarrassment ! But it's all right. I've apologised, and I told him he was quite right to kick me in the ribs.'

A woman's voice cried :

' Being a sergeant he can do what he likes to anyone in these parts ! '

' He's taking the chance while he can ! ' said another. ' He won't dare to-morrow, when the factory's closed and the men are all on the streets.'

' Don't you believe it ! He's too sure of himself ! And the proof is that he didn't mind attacking Pierre Artevel ! '

More faces appeared at the windows. All the houses in the street seemed to be bristling with hostility towards Maillard. For a moment he was disconcerted. The anger of these people was greater than the kick in the ribs warranted ; there was a vehemence in their fury, hinting at bad faith, which perturbed him. He admitted to himself that he had chosen a bad moment to come walking through the streets of the Malleboine with his boots itching. It seemed indeed that the closing down of the T.D.C. factory, which had been rumoured since Monday, was rather probable. It was said that the manager had been to call on the prefect that morning. Moreover, Pierre Artevel was due to come before the magistrates to-morrow, Thursday, and this was causing excitement.

Yes, Maillard had undoubtedly made a mistake ; but on reflection he was disposed to hold Dr. Coinchot responsible, and the mayor, and the police commissioner, and all the other notables. The previous evening, after following them up for an hour, he had managed to catch the Tetère girls soliciting in a corner of the Upper Town at the hour when the cinemas closed, in defiance of regulations, and he had promptly pulled them in. The arrest had been perfectly in order, and the normal consequences should have followed. But the next morning—that was to say, to-day, Wednesday —the commissioner, after ringing up the mayor, had calmly let them go. And on top of that Philippon had dropped in at the police station on his way home to lunch, simply to give Maillard a dressing down and ask him whether he was paid by the T.D.C. factory to act as an *agent provocateur*. The sergeant had turned his back on him without replying, but he had made up his mind to arrest the Tetère girls every chance he got. One of these days he'd get them sent up the river, with a cast-iron case. And on that day, when he came to give his evidence in Court, he'd see to it that everybody knew who'd been taking care of them. The town should learn about the nice people who were running its affairs.

With the heavy and measured gait which he was accustomed to adopt when he went on night patrol through the Malleboine quarter, Maillard withdrew, followed by the hoots of the onlookers. He went to prowl round the entrance to the Impasse de la Sourdine, while he planned his revenge.

Having no hope of getting to sleep again, Trésor left the steps and followed him a short way. But at the Carrefour des Cinq he turned into the Rue du Sire-de-Roulans and entered the shop of Oudard, the carpenter. He stayed there an hour, during which time the two men did not exchange a single word. Trésor was as much at home in the carpenter's shop as in his own dwelling, and his entrance had not even caused Oudard to raise his head. Physical presence was all their friendship called for, they had no need of speech. The visitor made himself comfortable on a pile of planks, and sat watching his friend's skill with an expert eye. The fact was that his knowledge of the work was entirely superficial, because he had never attempted it himself. He had been paying a daily visit to the shop for twenty years, and in that time had learnt a great deal, but it had never entered his head to try to use a plane or to hammer in a nail. Yet Trésor had no prejudice against work, and greatly admired the efforts and the perseverance of others. The thought of it was in no way repugnant to him. He would have been quite ready to work had he not suspected that it was a great waste of time.

Before leaving the shop he helped himself to a cigarette from the jacket hanging on the wall and put it behind his ear. And in passing, by way of good-bye, he laid a finger on the carpenter's shoulder as he bent over his bench. Oudard straightened up and with his hands on his hips stood watching his departing figure against the light. He wiped the sweat from his forehead with a bare forearm, and picking up a mallet went out after him. He stepped into the street, and hammering furiously with the mallet on a hand-cart, which he smashed to bits, he began to shout :

' He's innocent ! I swear Troussequin never killed anyone ! They ought to let him out of prison ! He's innocent, Troussequin is—innocent ! I swear he never killed the lawyer's maid ! '

The veins on his forehead swelled to the point of bursting, his eyes grew bloodshot, his face scarlet. After delivering a last ponderous blow at the hand-cart, he went back into the shop and resumed his work. The people in the street, old men sunning themselves, women in their doorways keeping an eye on their children, and a few unemployed as well, had drawn near and formed a circle round the wrecked hand-cart. Not one of them doubted the truth of what the carpenter had said. One could see it in his eyes and in the great blows he had struck ; one could tell from the sound of his voice that he knew it for certain. To the passers-by who asked what had happened they replied, ' Troussequin's innocent. Oudard has just said so,' and they pointed to the hand-cart. But then the *patron* of No. 15, Rue des Nonettes, happened to come by. He heard the tale, saw the wreckage, and was not impressed. When Trésor stopped him, in order to light his cigarette from his cigar, he saw fit to tell him what he thought.

' All that's just silliness and nothing else.'

' Why is it silly ? ' asked Trésor.

' Because it's not so,' said the *patron*. ' It's no use you trying to tell me that Troussequin's innocent. My answer is, no, not on your life ! And you want to know why ? I'll tell you. For the very good reason that it was bound to happen to Troussequin sooner or later. Anyone who knows what's what could see that Troussequin's the vicious type, and there's no getting away from it.'

' Vicious ? ' said Trésor.

' That's right—vicious and capable of anything. I've seen it for myself when he's come to our house. You know the way he insulted me two years ago, when he tried to jump on my wife. I admit I was a newcomer to the town and only just started in business, still that's no reason why he shouldn't have treated my feelings with respect. You'll say he didn't manage to do it anyway, and I agree, but you can't say he didn't try. The wish is as good as the deed, and he who steals an egg steals a hen.'

'So you think——?'

'Now you wait a minute. I'm going to tell you something that'll give you a shock. He came pretty near to trying the same trick over again last Thursday night. He was sitting there in the bar, with his ugly monkey-face, and he started looking at my wife——'

'I shouldn't think he looked at her very long,' said Trésor in a tone scarcely flattering to the lady's attractions.

The *patron* (his name was Léonard) was hurt and said aggrievedly :

'You're all on Troussequin's side without even thinking about it, and then you're surprised because they say people in this quarter haven't got any morals . . .'

They had arrived at the red lamp outside Number Fifteen. The *patron* entered the doorway of the establishment and concluded his remarks before ringing the bell :

'It's just like I was saying this morning when I was having an aperitif with the Captain of Gendarmerie—it's a waste of time being sorry for you, because you aren't interesting. There are people who'd like to talk to me by the book-full about all the misery and wretchedness in the Malleboine, but what I say is—you tell that to someone else ! That's what I say, and the reason is that the man I'm interested in is the honest, respectable workman. And this is what you've got to get into your head—the respectable workman doesn't live in the Malleboine any more. When the boom was on the respectable workman put a bit of money aside and got himself a cottage in the suburbs with a garden, and now he doesn't want to mix with you people. Well, for instance, what happens on a Sunday ? The way

175

he's dressed when he goes out with his family, he might be a clerk in an office. And that's the sort of workmen I like, the ones that are trying to better themselves. We get them here in the house now and again, when they're out with a few men friends, or after a trade union meeting. And never the slightest trouble, never. You couldn't have a better behaved set of men. You can take it from me, they aren't the sort to go sticking up for a murderer. Troussequin ? Never heard of him ! Good luck to the law, that's what I say, and let justice take its course ! '

The *patron* pressed the bell, and the opening of the door allowed a ruddy light to escape, and the pounding of a mechanical piano. Trésor turned sadly away thinking of those residents in the suburbs, former neighbours in the Malleboine, who nowadays had cottages and gardens, and conducted themselves in Léonard's establishment like men of the world. But he thought still more of the families remaining in the quarter, who perhaps dreamed of emigrating to the other end of the town, only continuing to inhabit the sombre streets of the Malleboine because necessity compelled them to do so. Trésor felt less happy. When a cluster of little girls with a skipping-rope asked him to swing it for them, he said he was busy, and passing along the Ruelle des Soeurs-Mignot, which was a prolongation of the Rue des Nonettes on the other side of the Rue des Oiseaux, he went and sat on a footbridge over the Sourdine. He sat facing the mouth of the stream, watching the water flow beneath his hanging legs. The escarpment of the Upper Town separated from the stream at that point, running off at an oblique angle. The first houses of the right bank, their foundations lapped by water, stood with their backs to the rocks, and the lowest steps of the narrow stone stairway leading to the plateau almost touched the footbridge. Trésor dozed to the murmur of the water trickling over the

sluice-gate which diverted the Sourdine for the benefit of a
wash-house on the left bank. And presently he heard the
sound of boys' voices behind him.

Buq and Antoine, coming from the Rue des Oiseaux,
had reached the stream after passing through a maze of
passage-ways. They were trying to make their way along it
by clinging to the rugged edges, to gutters and cornices.
Buq, caught on a narrow ledge, could go neither forward
nor back, and Antoine was scarcely more comfortable.
Trésor left the bridge and reached them by way of the network of passages along which they had come. The task of
rescuing them was made more difficult by Buq's insistence
that he did not need help.

'If I was there, it was because I wanted to be there,' he
said, after they had been helped to safety. 'I know what I'm
doing.'

'Don't be pig-headed, Buquanant,' said Trésor. 'If I'd
known you wanted to see where the Sourdine comes up
I'd have taken you to my house right away. You wouldn't
have been able to see anything from where you were even
if you'd managed to get twenty yards further. There's more
than one bend. The stream makes a turn directly it comes
up out of its hole. You come with me and I'll show you.'

Buq gave Antoine several hefty digs with his elbow as
they went along, because he did not seem to realise how
signally he was being favoured by fortune, which at a single
stroke was leading him, not merely to the subterranean
stream but to the dwelling of two daughters of ill-fame.

'What's your friend's name?' asked Trésor.

'Rigault.'

Trésor paused to look closely at Antoine, and tried the
name over several times. He did not much care for it.

'What's your other name?'

'Antoine,' said Antoine.

This time Trésor was delighted. Antoine was the name he would have chosen for himself if he had had the choice. He raised his arms in the air and looked up at his hands as though he were gazing at them from the bottom of a well, and this was his way of saying that no doubt Antoine lived in the Upper Town.

'The Paris road,' said Buq. 'A bit beyond the railway bridge.'

'And I expect you've got a house of your own, with a garden?'

Antoine nodded and blushed as he seemed to catch a hint of irony in the question. Trésor perceived the blush, and sought to put him at his ease.

'Everybody can't live in the same place,' he said. 'There are statues in the Upper Town. That's nice, too.'

Tetère's daughters were both at home. Minie was washing her chemise in a basin, and Marion was telling fortunes with the cards spread out beside a bottle of *vin rouge*. At the sight of the two clean, respectably-dressed small boys, they both stood up, blushing at the thought of their reputation. They stood side by side, greeting them with little nods and greatly concerned on account of the bottle of wine, the unmade beds and the filthy walls. Buq and Antoine, themselves no less overwhelmed by the occasion, saw nothing but the two women. The room was dark, and in the half-light of the late afternoon, which prevented them from seeing their faces clearly, they found them strangely small, almost like two little girls. What also struck them was the smell of the room—a stench of dirty crockery and chilly gloom, paraffin, cigarette ends and dead rats. The sisters sensed their repulsion, and were themselves conscious of it for the first time.

Trésor opened the glass-paned door giving on to the Sourdine, and a damp and chilly draught of air blew in.

Buq and Antoine went with him on to a small wooden platform giving on to the water by a few slippery and probably
rotting steps which looked as though it would be dangerous
to tread on them. At the end of a stretch overshadowed by a
half-circle of rocky walls, they could see in deep shadow the
mouth of the subterranean stream, which was covered by a
stout wire grill. The water was clear, and it seemed very
cold. In its depths, in the dark crevices, it was almost black,
with vivid metallic gleams. Antoine gazed in rapture.
The wooden stage, the iron grill, the secret and shining
pathway at the foot of the escarpment of the Upper Town,
were an enchantment beyond his dreams.

Marion and Minie had plucked up courage to draw near
to them. They stared at the boys, talking to one another
in low voices and stifling their laughter like shy little girls.
They said that the boys were both like Trésor when he was
young.

'What's that noise one hears?' asked Antoine. 'A sort
of regular noise.'

'He wants to know what the noise is,' Minie murmured
in Marion's ear.

'Yes, you can hear something,' said Buq. 'Not exactly
a noise—a sort of shaking.'

'It's the mill,' said Marion, advancing a step forward.

'It's the mill,' said Minie, and she too advanced a step.

'I see,' said Antoine, taking off his cap. 'The mill.
Thank you, Madame.' And he explained to Buq: 'It's
the mill.'

In reply to their questions Trésor said that he had never
been along the stream where it ran underground, nor did he
remember having ever known anyone do so. As for
oubliettes, caves, catacombs and skeletons, it was very
possible that all these things were to be found there. They
would scarcely have put up such a solid grill simply in

order to keep the draught out. He agreed at once with Buq and Antoine that a voyage of discovery should be attempted, and was, indeed, rather astonished that he himself had never thought of it. It was too late to do anything that afternoon, but the boys had only to come to-morrow afternoon in good time. And to-morrow, as it happened, was Thursday, their free day from school.

At about five o'clock Sergeant Maillard, strolling along the Rue des Oiseaux, glanced round and saw Buq and Antoine walking down the Impasse de la Sourdine. Tetère's daughters were standing on their doorstep watching them go, and it seemed to Maillard that Antoine exchanged a smile with them over his shoulder. Tempted though he was, he passed on without turning his head; but after going a few steps further he stopped to roll a cigarette, and casually surveyed the mouth of the blind alley. The boys were talking in low voices, and he could not hear what they were saying. As they entered the Rue des Oiseaux, they stopped and turned round to wave. Maillard was able to have a good look at them. One was unknown to him, but the other was Buquanant, the son of the woman who had a dyer's shop at the top of the big stairway. Maillard lit his cigarette and went slowly towards the river . . .

At supper that evening Antoine had some difficulty in restraining his unusual exuberance, and several times burst out laughing for no apparent reason. His father glanced at him covertly and reprovingly, but dared not question or reprimand him. Since burdening his conscience with a guilty silence, he had become afraid of his son. Every glance Antoine gave him seemed a reproach, an urgent question to which he could make no reply. He wanted to be able to explain why it was so difficult and dangerous to tell the truth, to make Antoine understand that he was not free, that no one was free; but he knew that the boy would never accept these old man's excuses. What pained him most of all was to feel that he had lost his authority as the head of the household. Antoine had, as a matter of fact, no notion of defying the parental discipline, and if he took advantage of the situation he did so quite innocently. When his mother asked him what he intended to do on Thursday, he said without any afterthought :

'I shan't be in all day except for lunch. In the morning I'm going to the Artevel trial, and in the afternoon I'm going to see Buquanant.'

But his father's look of misery at these words afforded him some inkling of the extent of the revolution that had taken place.

FIFTEEN

PIERRE ARTEVEL GAZED curiously and not unamiably at
the gentlemen in black robes who were observing him
over their white ruffs. He had no particular mistrust of them,
because he had no illusions. To him this whole apparatus
of justice, the words exchanged, the smiles, the eloquent
gestures, was nothing but a display. No doubt the judges
meant well, but they were so remote from him, and so
strange, that their proceedings had a touching quality in
his eyes. They strove honestly and ponderously to set aside
the instinctive feelings of hostility and repulsion which
his social status aroused in them ; but without realising it
one was protecting his daughter, another his country house
or his stamp collection, against the rabble from the Malleboine, who were pressed, devoted and vehement, against
the barrier at the end of the courtroom. In short, the case
was settled before it came up for trial. Such was the opinion
of Artevel, and also of Maître Marguet, seated among the
more privileged spectators at the side of M. Alfan, the
examining magistrate, who had invited him to be present.
The lawyer was almost sorry for those irreproachable
citizens, bowed, black and taloned, over their papers,
their faces lined with deep wrinkles of anxiety, their eyes
dimmed by a lifetime of probity and honour. He reflected
that justice is a passion which has almost nothing in common with goodness.

In appearance, however, the trial was a lively one. The

presiding judge, the prosecutor and the counsel for the defence, wishing to make what profit they could out of the connection between this minor affair and the murder, sought to enhance its importance by bringing to it all the portentousness at their command. The presiding judge was by turns sarcastic, insinuating and gracious, and the prosecutor fervent, solemn and funereal. Counsel for the defence was all these and more : plaintive, compassionate, noble, supple, pointed, jocular and torrential. When the sergeant appeared in the witness box a threatening murmur arose from the back of the Court. The presiding judge called the public to order in a stern voice, but without result. Maillard, his hands resting quietly on the edge of the box, looked searchingly over his shoulder as though he were trying to recognise the murmurers, and the tumult died down at once. Buq, Antoine and Marie-Louise, scarcely visible in the front row of the crowd, felt their indignant mutterings die in their throats beneath that weighty gaze. Maillard turned back to the dais to respond to the ritual question.

' I swear,' he said, raising his hand.

' Will you now tell us, not what you think you know about this business, but what you actually saw ? '

' I was at the police station when I received a telephone message informing me that Troussequin had just entered the town. I took Charlasse and Guilbon with me and went down to the Malleboine quarter. I saw my man coming along the Rue des Oiseaux with Artevel, and I waited in the Rue de la Clé-d'Or, at the foot of the big stairway. Before arresting Troussequin I asked him where he was going, and the man, Artevel, butted in and tried to answer for him. I told him to mind his own business and turned back to Troussequin.'

Thus far Maillard had spoken in a calm and level voice, but now he looked at the accused and grew suddenly wrathful.

' And that's when he chose to interfere ! He had the impertinence to give me orders—me ! He ordered me to send Constable Charlasse away ! What's more, he repeated it, and he called me a swine ! '

He made a movement of his shoulders, and even stamped his foot, as though to crush Artevel where he stood.

' That's what he had the cheek to say to me, a guttersnipe I could have handled with one arm behind my back if I hadn't had Troussequin to deal with. But he knew that, of course, and that's what made him think he could get away with it. And then I saw him strike Constable Charlasse, and he fought the two constables while I was busy with Troussequin. I wish to state that if that man hadn't been present there would have been no struggle and the arrest would have been carried out perfectly quietly. I also wish to state that he struck the constables with a key, and struck them savagely, which is proved by the wounds he gave them.'

The sincerity of his manner impressed the Court. The public behind the barrier gazed with a fervent hatred at the huge back and shoulders.

' How do you account for Artevel's conduct ? ' asked the presiding judge. ' And to what extent, in your opinion, was it calculated to help the murderer ? '

' I said nothing about a murderer,' replied the sergeant loftily. ' I don't know of any murderer.'

The presiding judge, greatly vexed, nevertheless corrected himself and repeated the question.

' His conduct was simply due to imbecility,' said Maillard. ' It could only harm Troussequin—that's all his conduct could do ! '

As he spoke these last words, which were in a sense favourable to the accused, he turned towards him with a look of ironical disdain which he knew would mean more to Artevel than the opinion of the Court. Counsel for the defence put a few questions to him—among others, whether he had heard anything of what Artevel and Troussequin were saying as they approached the Rue de la Clé-d'Or.

'No,' said Maillard.

'But perhaps you got some idea of the sense from Troussequin's attitude and the tone of his replies?'

The question was important, because Artevel claimed that he had advised Troussequin to give himself up. Maillard bowed his head and stared at the hairy backs of his big hands as they rested on the edge of the witness box. He remembered Troussequin's attitude perfectly well, and had no real doubt as to what Artevel's intention had been at that moment. He was simply asking himself whether, in plain justice, he could refrain from testifying to this effect. His back curved slightly with the effort of thought, and one seemed to see the muscles of his conscience stirring under his tunic. At length he replied:

'I've sworn to speak nothing but the truth, and I shall say nothing of which I'm not perfectly sure. After all, I'm not his lawyer.'

'Very well,' said the defending counsel. 'The Court will note that your testimony is influenced by your fear that Pierre Artevel may be acquitted.'

Maillard at once protested against this, and there was a lively exchange between the prosecution and the defence, apparently to the advantage of the latter. Seated among the spectators, Philippon and Dr. Coinchot were siding fervently with the defence. They had come far less out of interest in the trial than for the pleasure of beholding the gloomy countenance of Fouchard, the barrister, who had returned from his trip to Italy the previous evening. He was sitting almost directly in front of them, listening with melancholy to his colleague and thinking what he might have made out of Artevel's case, and, later on, out of Troussequin's.

Because for once he had happened to go away, he had missed the biggest chance of his whole career!

When Maillard's testimony was concluded, Constables Guilbon and Charlasse were heard. Guilbon was even more bitter than his sergeant. He went so far as to say that Artevel seemed to him to be acting in concert with Troussequin.

'Constable Guilbon is to be congratulated,' said the defending counsel. 'His exceptional zeal apparently enabled him to see more than his chief, who was merely guided by the dictates of his professional conscience!'

'Does the defence question the good faith of this witness?' inquired the prosecutor.

The judges and other more knowledgeable persons smiled to show that they had seen the point. It seemed unwise of the defence, which had not hesitated to cite Troussequin as a witness on their side, to be over-punctilious. Maître Fouchard turned towards Philippon and Coinchot, who had been loud in their praise of Artevel's defender, and said in an undertone:

'Did you ever know anything so ham-handed? He'll get the boy condemned. You'll see!'

'Not on your life!' murmured Coinchot. 'I'll eat my hat if he doesn't get off!'

Things seemed, indeed, to be going pretty well for Artevel. Guilbon stuck to what he had said with an angry, aggressive air that displeased even the judges. But the testimony of Constable Charlasse was to be even more helpful to the accused. He told the Court how, before he joined the police force, he had been Artevel's friend.

'. . . And I can say that I went on being his friend—and still am, at this moment. That's why when he saw me being ordered to do that particular job he asked the sergeant to send me away. He was upset on my account, and as a matter of fact I wasn't very proud of myself either . . .'

Charlasse spoke without assurance, in a flat, unhappy voice in which there was a note of shamed sincerity. The judges, their hearts melted by this tale of conflict between duty and friendship, were moved to search at the back of their minds for literary parallels. Contemplating the two decent and generous young men, the presiding judge felt Virgilian shivers pass over him, somewhere between his skin and his robes. Maître Marguet, although he perceived a certain softening on the faces of the upholders of correct living, was not deceived. In his opinion, as he remarked to M. Alfan, they were merely clutching at a sentimental diversion in order to delude themselves for a moment into believing that the outcome of the trial was still in doubt.

For some minutes there was a feeling of relief and hopefulness among the public beyond the barrier. The testimony of Vuillemard and the two other men who had been playing cards with Artevel on the night of the arrest was not important, but such as it was it favoured the accused.

At length, escorted by two gendarmes, Troussequin was brought handcuffed into the witness box. The public at once forgot Pierre Artevel and transferred all their sympathy to him. But in the whole courtroom there was no one, not even Maître Marguet, whose feelings were comparable to those of Antoine. At the sight of the innocent man between the two gendarmes Antoine squeezed Marie-Louise's hand very tightly and burst into tears. Feeling suddenly overwhelmed by the weight of the crowd around him, he made a movement as though to break out. He wanted to be free, so that he might join Troussequin. Not even in the first warm moments of his friendship with Buq had he felt the great wave of tenderness that now filled his heart.

Between his two keepers, rigid in their blue uniforms and

both a good head taller than himself, Trousseuin had the aspect of a ponderous and clumsy animal born in darkness and servitude. As he came before the tribunal he raised his head and looked up at the judges on their dais. His sunken, knotted face expressed nothing but the most simple curiosity, that of an animal briefly observing the place where its masters have brought it. As the presiding judge began to speak he turned his back on him, obliging the gendarmes to execute a half-turn, and continued his survey. His eyes became lively at the sight of Maillard, seated among the other witnesses. He gave Artevel a friendly nod, and paused for a moment in his inspection as he encountered the gaze of Maître Marguet. Finally he perceived the Malleboine people at the end of the room, who greeted him with an affectionate murmur. His face twisted in a grimace, and he raised his manacled hands in the air as though to show them to his friends. A clamour of sympathy, in which the voices of women were predominant, rose up from the crowd. The presiding judge, who had thus far been indulgent in his treatment of this notable witness, now called him to order in a good-humoured voice. But when Trousseuin seemed not to hear he repeated the injunction, this time with some impatience. It was then that Trousseuin turned to him and with the utmost coarseness referred him to a certain unmentionable part of his body.

By order of the judge, who turned scarlet with embarrassment, he was instantly removed from the witness box by his escort. And then a huge burst of simple, candid laughter rose up from among the witnesses. With his head flung back and his fingers thrust into the collar of his tunic to relieve the pressure, Sergeant Maillard was laughing without restraint, forgetting his solemn surroundings, forgetful even of his stripes. He was the only one of all that company to be amused by Trousseuin's obscene outburst. To most of them it seemed tragic—the expression of an ultimate contempt, and of something like a desire to be rid once and for all of certain forms of behaviour which they still sought to impose on him. The presiding judge's anger, and the indignation of the other judges, was no consolation for Troussequin's despair.

Maillard himself was not sure why he had laughed, although the mortification of the presiding judge and his colleagues was undoubtedly pleasing to him. Since the intervention of Coinchot and Philippon in favour of the Tetère girls he had begun to feel an urge to revolution. Only the previous night he had dreamed of being a dictator and riding through the town in a palanquin carried by Coinchot, Philippon and their two protégées. But perhaps his happiness had arisen chiefly from the fact that he was now finally assured of Troussequin's innocence. The forthrightness of that retort, the self-certainty that it implied, meant as much to Maillard as any alibi.

His great explosion of laughter had caused the judges to glare and the audience to tremble. The Malleboine people were uncertain what to make of it, finding it hard to believe that the man who only a few minutes before had seemed bent on Artevel's destruction should now be so sensationally approving the attitude of Troussequin. The presiding judge peremptorily requested Maillard to control himself. For some moments he succeeded in doing so, but then his laughter broke out again, louder than ever.

'We aren't going to suspend the proceedings on your account!' shouted the presiding judge. 'Kindly leave the Court at once!'

This restored Maillard to complete sobriety. As he was rising to leave the presiding judge added:

'I was not aware that it was a part of the functions of a police sergeant to aid and abet disorder!'

Maillard's face grew dark. As he passed in front of the dais he said:

' Now that I know how an honest man speaks to a judge I'd sooner leave!'

Coming from an ordinary police sergeant to the presiding judge of a Court of Law, this was an unparalleled effrontery. Such was the stupefaction of the Court, that Maillard was able to reach the door before anything more could be said. In a state of great agitation he went to await the verdict in the courtyard of the Palais de Justice. Here he strode up and down, repeating to himself with a gloomy pleasure that the Court had chucked him out, and thereby maintaining himself in a state of enjoyable fury. Recalling his dream of the night before, he pictured himself in the exercise of full dictatorial powers, sacking judges, whores, commissioners and municipal counsellors. He sent Coinchot and Philippon to rot in an underground dungeon, and installed Marion and Minie in their official functions, just to show what he thought of them. Things would be a bit different with him in power! And then he had another idea, which could at least be put into execution—it was to buy a subversive newspaper and ostentatiously read it when the people were coming out of the courtroom. There was a newspaper kiosk almost opposite the Palais. Maillard asked for the communist paper, *l'Humanité*, but the vendor had none left. He was rather at a loss. Politics were not his strong point, and he was only familiar with a small number of newspapers. He picked up several, looked at them, and finally hesitated between *l'Ere Nouvelle* and *Le Temps*. The title of the first looked promising, but he remembered having seen a copy in the hands of the president of the Philharmonic Society. The other attracted him by its typography and its spidery title. So he finally bought *Le Temps* and returned to the courtyard. Presently Constables Guilbon and Charlasse came out of the chamber. The verdict had just been announced.

'Six months without remission,' said Guilbon. 'He's going to appeal.'

'It's disgraceful!' said Maillard. 'It makes me sick!'

The two policemen went off, and he spread out his paper so as to display the title. People drifted out of the building, talking with animation. Buq and Antoine were exchanging views with a group of Artevels. Maillard saw Philippon, Coinchot and the barrister, Fouchard, pause in the doorway. He bent over his paper to make sure that the title would be noticed, and waited anxiously . . .

Buq and Antoine were in a state of great excitement. For two pins they would have gone to a café. Buq, who had been witnessing a trial for the first time in his life, said that he had never seen a more disgusting lot of judges. What was more, not one of them could have stood up to Pierre Artevel in a fair fight. Even if they'd all gone for him at once, he'd have knocked the whole lot out without the slightest trouble.

Antoine, although less vocal in his indignation, was filled with shame and remorse. He was shocked by his father's weakness and felt himself to blame for not having done more for the innocent Troussequin. Tears pricked his eyes at the thought of him displaying his fettered wrists to his friends from the Malleboine. Seeing Maître Marguet cross the courtyard in company with M. Alfan, he went impulsively towards him and blurted out:

'It wasn't Troussequin! He wasn't the murderer!'

His voice weakened as he spoke the words. The lawyer looked at him with a mild surprise and said gently:

'No, my boy, Troussequin wasn't the murderer. That's what I think, too.'

His serene and tranquil gaze put Antoine out of countenance, and he dropped back to let the two men pass. But

Buq was greatly impressed by his audacity and zeal in the cause of justice. A few minutes later, as the boys were passing the photographer's shop, big Pucelet came out and put his hands on their shoulders. He had taken no interest in the trial, but despite this his eyes were as troubled as their own, and there was an unaccustomed gravity in his whole manner. Antoine nudged Buq to get him to cut the conversation short ; but Buq said aloud :

'How about taking him with us this afternoon—for you know what ? He's sure to have things like magnesium flares. He could take pictures, if we find anything.'

Antoine frowned, feeling that this addition to the party would rob their expedition of something of its mystery. But without knowing where they were going, big Pucelet begged to be allowed to come, and with so much distress in his voice that they were moved to sympathy. Leaving Buq to arrange matters, for it was nearly midday, Antoine started for home. He arrived to find his father already seated at the lunch-table.

'The trial didn't end till late,' he said as he sat down. 'Artevel was sentenced to six months in prison.'

Rigault gave him a look of despair, but Antoine met his eyes without flinching and said in a hard, accusing voice :

'Six months without remission. But if it had been proved that Troussequin was innocent they'd have acquitted him, or anyway he'd have got a remission.'

The meal, although they got through it as quickly as possible, was the most painful Rigault had yet endured. His son's silences seemed to him more marked than ever, more filled with unspoken reproaches. Juliette, who had no great sense of justice, understood nothing of the drama that had been enacted at meal-times during the past two days. She was, on the other hand, very conscious of the fact that the centre of authority had changed, and all her attentions were now reserved for Antoine. Rigault was not unaware of the fact, and nothing was more hurtful to him than this witness to his decline. Towards the end of the meal Antoine looked at his father with blazing eyes, and said :

'I saw Troussequin in Court. He was between two gendarmes, and he lifted up his wrists to let us see the handcuffs.'

Rigault uttered a sigh of protest. His lunch had consisted of radishes, grilled pork, a dish of beans, a salad and a piece of Camembert. He was not pleased with himself, his conscience was troubling him ; but still, there was a time for everything, and he would have liked to be allowed to drink his coffee in peace. What good did it do to rub salt into the wound ? But Antoine kept his eyes upon him. He thrust his straw napkin-ring over his wrist and held it in the air, as Troussequin had done.

'He was between two gendarmes ! . . .'

It was too much for Rigault. He got up, resolved to rid his conscience of its burden, and left the house without waiting for coffee. And by the time he had gone a hundred yards his ardour had already begun to diminish. There was nothing irrevocable in his decision. He set out every day with the idea of telling his story. He had made for the police station three times already, and each time had felt his courage fail him at the last minute. Indeed, even at the moment of leaving the house he had been remotely conscious of the fact that he would weaken in the end ; but the half-hour's walk had been soothing to his conscience, besides being good for his figure.

So he went unobtrusively on his way, in a manner designed not to attract the notice of the gods : and then, when he least expected it, he had a sudden inspiration. Instead of continuing in the direction of the police station, he turned to the left, along a street which led to Philippon's house.

The mayor was lunching with his wife on a piece of roast veal which for two hours had been gently simmering in an earthenware casserole in company with some onions, some carrots, some turnips and a sprig of thyme. However he seemed delighted to see Rigault, and asked him what he thought of the situation in general. Rigault replied that he didn't think much of it, but that he knew who the murderer of Charlotte Richon really was.

'On Saturday afternoon, after my son had come out of school, he . . .'

The mayor listened to the whole story without once interrupting, and his wife, who had been left alone in the dining-room, also listened from behind the door . . .

'Monsieur Rigault,' said Philippon, when he had finished, 'you were very wise to come to me. The testimony of a twelve-year-old boy, if it isn't carefully handled, may do considerable harm to his parents. But don't worry, I'll take charge of the matter. I hope that for your part you will be careful not to say a word to anyone.'

Philippon was too honest a man to be able to make up his mind to suppress the story without some preliminary qualms of conscience. It was only after Rigault's departure that he finally decided to keep silent. His first reason was one of expediency. It would be dangerous to expose the lawyer, because it would give Fouchard a chance of defending him and thereby acquiring fresh laurels. The other reason, although it was perhaps conclusive, was one which the mayor scarcely mentioned to himself : but he did not fail to see how many respectable houses in the town, whether they supported the left or the right, were interested in sustaining the honour of Maître Marguet.

SIXTEEN

MARION AND MINIE had swept and dusted everywhere, scrubbed the floor, spread out the bedding in the sun, and left the room with doors open all the morning. The stench of the previous day had given way to a smell of furniture polish. They had pinned a coloured portrait of Marshal Joffre on the wall, and a photograph, also coloured, of an American film star with bare legs, eating a grapefruit while seated on the back of a dromedary. The room, in short, had been brightened up, and a fragment of spring had crept into it. The marshal looked particularly splendid.

Big Pucelet had been long and carefully warned that he must behave properly, no matter what happened. Just because he was being taken to call on two women of the town, said Buq, was no reason for behaving like a sod and a person of no breeding. Anyway, if he so much as breathed a word about his—well, anyway, he'd be out on his ear, and he couldn't say he hadn't been warned. Merely to hear them talk brought Pucelet's eyes popping out of his head and his tongue sticking out of the corner of his mouth. But just the same, he was as good as gold, and throughout the afternoon gave no cause for complaint. The Tetère girls, who had not been expecting him, were somewhat startled by the sight of this tall boy with a small head and a camera slung round him.

'He's our camera-man,' said Buq.

'It's Pucelet,' added Trésor. 'You know Pucelet, the photographer.'

The Tetère girls said they were delighted to make his acquaintance. They had been to his father to have their photographs taken in 1924. Pucelet was pink with rapture and amazed at the good manners of loose women. He resolved when he reached the status of long trousers to be a regular customer at red-lamp houses.

Leaving the sisters in the room, the boys went out on to the little wooden platform, and Trésor told them of the soundings he had taken that morning. The Sourdine was deeper than the clarity of its water led one to suppose. Moreover, it was so cold that it would be madness to put so much as a toe in it. The expedition thus encountered serious difficulties at the start, and there was an interval of unhappy silence.

'What's that noise?' asked Pucelet, opening his mouth for the first time.

'It's the mill,' answered Antoine.

'What it comes to,' said Buq, 'is that we've got to find some way of getting as far as the grill. If we had a boat . . .'

Antoine made a gesture of scorn. In the first place, they hadn't a boat. And supposing they had? All really great and heroic adventures were carried out by the means which chance provided.

'And can you swim?' asked Buq coldly. 'No? Well, then...'

'I've got an idea,' said Pucelet.

But Buq and Antoine believed so little in Pucelet's ideas that they went on bickering without listening to him.

'I'm a realist,' said Buq.

'You're afraid of taking a chance,' said Antoine.

Behind them the Tetère girls coughed to try and divert them from their ill-humour, and when the argument grew heated Marion fetched a mouth organ out of a drawer and blew it in their ears. They turned and laughed, out of politeness.

' Just now Pucelet said he had an idea,' remarked Trésor.

' An idea ? ' said Pucelet. ' I don't remember.'

' If any of you are thirsty,' said Minie, ' you've only got to say so.'

' Thank you, Madame.'

' If only we had a rope . . .'

' But what would you do with it ? '

' Well, nothing. But at least we'd have a rope.'

Antoine stood at the edge of the platform, gazing at the mouth of the underground stream with a despairing ardour, like a conqueror prevented from putting to sea by contrary winds. Pucelet suddenly uttered an exclamation and rapped his fist against his skull.

' I've remembered my idea! Why couldn't we use a tub ? '

Buq and Antoine gazed respectfully at his small head, which now seemed to glow with the light of genius. Trésor found a good-sized tub in the Impasse de la Sourdine, and put it on the water. It would only comfortably hold one person. The passage encountered great difficulties, and raised many awkward problems. When, after countless adventures, Antoine finally reached the iron grill, it suddenly dawned upon them that the tub could not come back by itself. Antoine had to return to the others. At the suggestion of Pucelet, who throughout displayed an admirable resourcefulness, a length of stout string was attached to it. All this did not take place without many hitches and delays, and it was nearly five o'clock by the time the four adventurers found themselves clustered together on a narrow ledge of rock. The wire network covering the mouth of the underground waterway was strongly secured, and the thickness of its strands left them with little hope of being able to break through. Buq said it could only be done with a large pair of wire-cutters. Antoine thought of cutting it with a nail file. But all they could do for the present was to shine their electric torches into the darkness, lighting up a passage about the height of a man, which curved after fifteen yards. At the point where it turned they could see a round, polished object which might be a knob of rock, or possibly a skull.

The Tetère girls, still standing on the platform, waved their arms to them. They were a little apprehensive at seeing them so far away, at the end of that narrow creek where it was already growing dark. They could scarcely hear their voices and wanted them to come back.

The return was noisy and glorious. Even Pucelet felt the splendour of the vision they brought with them. Antoine nearly fell out of the tub several times trying to catch his heart, which was constantly leaping out of his breast. Thinking it over, he was inclined to believe that the skull they had seen was a relic of *pithecanthropus erectus*, and Marion said she wasn't surprised.

During the explorers' absence the girls had spread the table with a white cloth borrowed from a neighbour. They had bought a tin of salmon, a pound of biscuits and a half-bottle of Pernod. Travel and much talk had made everyone thirsty. The Pernod was greatly appreciated. Buq and Antoine each had two glasses, and Pucelet went so far as to have three. Their projects for the morrow achieved an undreamed-of scope and audacity, by which, however, no one was at all dismayed. Big Pucelet laughed the whole time.

' What did you say that noise was ? '

' It's the mill ! ' cried Buq, and he went on singing.

By the time the three boys left Trésor had had so much to drink that he did not even notice their departure. Marion and Minie stood on their doorstep watching them go arm-in-arm along the Impasse de la Sourdine. Sergeant Maillard, who was chatting to the *patron* of No. 15, Rue des Nonettes, saw them turn tumultuously into the Rue des Oiseaux, and heard the manly voice of big Pucelet raised in a drinking song.

SEVENTEEN

MAITRE MARGUET FOUND in his morning mail a letter addressed in an elegant but somewhat shaky feminine hand. He opened it with a slight feeling of apprehension, and turned pale at the first line.

' Darling murderer—Don't be frightened, I shan't give you away to the police. I have read all Marcel Proust, and I'd like to slit the stomachs of all my family and wallow in their entrails. But when one occupies a certain social position one has to give up certain things. But you weren't afraid, were you ? If only you knew how I envy you, and how I should adore to be a vile beast smothered in blood . . . etc.'

There were four pages, all similar to the foregoing, except that the last two were filled with unspeakably crude language and violent obscenities. It was the most ordinary sort of anonymous letter, its author probably some timid virgin. The lawyer was none the less extremely alarmed as he wondered where and how he had happened, by his words or his aspect, to give this person the idea that he was guilty of the crime. But he very quickly set his mind at rest. The only time he had shown any sign of disturbance was when he had stood outside the photographer's shop : but his mother had just met with an accident, and this was a sufficient explanation.

Three days previously young Pucelet had returned him his photographs, all except one of them excellently developed and printed. The lawyer thought of them now, locked in a drawer of his desk, but he had no desire to look at them. Despite all his reasons for not being perturbed, this anonymous letter, whose writer could only have been guessing, had had a most painful effect on him. His crime had given rise to an unworthy echo, a discord reflecting all its vileness. He had a glimpse of his own frenzy in the squalid frenzy of those four pages, where there was even to be found an echo of the lyricism with which he had complacently adorned his deed. In each case it was no more than a dreary outburst of animalism, mean and calculating—a blow struck in silence. He seemed suddenly to see that butchery in the attic with the eyes of a stranger. He was tempted to take the photographs out of the drawer and tear them into tiny fragments—to do anything which might to some extent obliterate his memory of the crime.

And then he was informed that M. Philippon had called and wished to speak to him. He kept him waiting several minutes. Before putting the letter in his pocket he glanced again at the last page, which contained the coarsest expressions, and thought how foolish he had been. He, too, might have found relief in the writing of anonymous letters, instead of burdening his conscience as he had done.

Philippon seemed embarrassed, and there was a strange look in his eyes. Maître Marguet was on the alert at once. In any case, the mayor's visit was a little surprising. They had never been particularly friendly, and Philippon had no professional relations with him. They talked a little about the weather, and about the chances of a European war, without making much progress. Finally Philippon seemed to have nothing more to say, and fell silent. He gazed to right and to left, not knowing where to look. Maître Marguet began to suspect the truth.

'It was very good of you to call on me,' he said in a cool voice which invited him to state his business.

Philippon looked at him, and his eyes so clearly expressed his thought that the lawyer was on the verge of showing him the door without listening to what he had to say. However, he said instead :

' Is there anything I can do for you ? '

But Philippon had turned red, and was at once so filled with shame and anxiety to get it over that his throat tightened and he could not speak. Maître Marguet shrugged his shoulders. The mayor broke into an unpleasing, catarrhal giggle which lasted for some time.

' I know everything,' he said at length.

' Monsieur Philippon, I don't want to play guessing games. Please speak plainly. What do you know ? '

Maître Marguet was contemplating his caller with a disdain which was in no way assumed. Stung by his attitude, the mayor said sharply :

' You'd better change your tone. What I know is that the murderer of your maidservant was not Troussequin. You yourself were the murderer, and I have a witness to the fact whom I can produce at any time. On Saturday afternoon, just as it was striking five, someone saw you close the window of the attic.'

' Well ? '

Philippon was not greatly impressed by the lawyer's calm. Nevertheless, for a moment he hesitated. He had not supposed that so simple a piece of blackmail could be so difficult in practice. As a respectable man, he did not want his victim to think badly of him, and he looked round for a formula.

' You mustn't think I'm trying to make any personal profit out of this. In fact, I've really come to see you more in my capacity as mayor—for the good of the town. You are the murderer, are you not ? Well, on my side I need some information. I know the T.D.C. company has been trying to get hold of Butillat's land. Apparently they're regrouping their various units. I thought you would probably be able to tell me whether they——'

'In other words,' said Maître Marguet, 'I am to disclose a professional confidence in return for your silence?'

'Well, that's just a way of putting it. If the conversation had been started on the right lines, we could have understood one another without seeming to touch on it at all, and without saying anything to offend anyone. It's partly my fault. I—I was thinking, and I was a bit upset . . .'

The lawyer went to the door of his study and called in one of his clerks.

'Now, Monsieur le Maire, would you be kind enough to repeat what you have just said?'

Philippon, now purple in the face, gazed furiously at the clerk, who was standing in front of him in an attitude of respectful indifference. He felt sure the lawyer was bluffing. But still, there was the possibility that Rigault's son had been mistaken. It was fragile evidence, now that he came to think of it. In any case, he was now doubly interested in sustaining Maître Marguet's innocence, since if he were ever brought to trial he would be hardly likely to overlook this little matter of attempted blackmail. He could not help admiring his audacity.

'Show this gentleman out,' said Maître Marguet . . .

When he was alone again he racked his brains in a vain effort to determine how the mayor had come to be so sure of his guilt. There must certainly have been a witness. Someone must have seen him close the attic window, as Philippon said. Could it have been the author of the anonymous letter? The sense of danger restored to him a little of his respect for his crime. After telephoning the examining magistrate to say that he was coming to see him, he went upstairs to tell his wife that he would be out until lunch-time and would probably have no time to call on his mother.

Lucie was knitting a jersey for an apostolic charitable organisation. In the hands of Lady Visitors to the poor, it would become a simple and potent argument for the conversion of the godless. Maître Marguet admired his wife for devoting a part of her time to tedious labours which might well have reminded her of a petty humiliation in the past. She, too, had once been a Lady Visitor, but had been reduced in rank by the committee because on her first visit to a poor family she had tied a coarse linen apron round her waist, had washed up dishes and changed the children's nappies, and had gone on doing these things for a whole week, until the sick mother was well enough to resume work.

Lucie said she would take her knitting round to her mother-in-law's, and as her husband turned to go she said :

' Is anything wrong ? You're looking worried.'

' No nothing at all. Don't be disturbed.'

She looked fondly at him, and a warm and simple smile illumined her still-youthful face, whose softness and purity caused one to forget her heavy limbs and ungainly walk. The lawyer felt suddenly comforted. If in the end he should be discovered and sent for trial, Lucie, in her innocence, would be able to stand the shock. She would not faint or blush, but as she had done on her first mission as a Lady Visitor, she would tie a coarse linen apron round her waist and simply be a murderer's wife. He saw the great depth of love in her clear eyes and marvelled, almost with a feeling of exasperation.

The examining magistrate received him with an air of discomfort, and cut short the usual expressions of politeness.

' I've come to see you,' said Maître Marguet, ' because I myself have just had a rather curious visit.'

M. Alfan listened with lowered eyes, and without at first

showing the slightest interest. The lawyer was very struck by this.

'My visitor, who is a person of some importance in the town, wanted some information which he thought I could give him if I broke my pledge of professional secrecy. This is roughly the bargain he proposed to me—"You are the murderer of your maidservant, and I can produce a witness who saw you shut the attic window at five o'clock. But if you'll tell me what I want to know, I'll keep quiet about it."'

'And what did you do?' asked M. Alfan, whose interest seemed to have grown as he listened.

'I had him shown out.'

'And you don't intend to say who he was?'

'No, I've decided not to—in the first place, for professional reasons, because one never knows . . . And besides, I'm like everyone else, I don't like mentioning names, particularly in an affair of this sort. But I still haven't told you everything. I should really have begun by showing you this letter.'

Maître Marguet produced the anonymous letter from his pocket. After reading it, the examining magistrate handed it back to him without a word, and looked curiously at him.

'I was very astonished when I read it,' said the lawyer. 'Unpleasantly astonished. But when the gentleman I've been speaking of came into my study, when he flatly accused me, and talked of being able to produce a witness, I must confess that I was really frightened—panic-stricken. You must bear in mind that he's not a nobody. Anything he says carries considerable weight.'

He looked steadily at the magistrate, seemed to hesitate, and then said in a lower voice:

'There's something else I've just discovered . . . You're not

204

treating me as you normally do. I felt it directly I entered the room.'

M. Alfan smiled for the first time, but his smile was reassuring.

' That's true,' he said. ' I'm afraid I'm a bad examining magistrate—I don't know how to hide my feelings. You're perfectly right in saying that I haven't been behaving to you as I generally do. In fact, I was not feeling very friendly towards you, and I'm glad you came. The thing's more clear to me now. I was angry with you because of the rumour that was circulating yesterday that you were guilty of the crime. I was at the house of some friends, and a young woman who can't have realised who I was talked in front of me about this mysterious witness who is supposed to have seen you shut the attic window at five. According to her it was a boy of twelve who happened to be on the cathedral tower on Saturday afternoon. I got the impression that the story was not so much going round the streets as going round the better houses in the town. But I gather you hadn't heard it ? '

' No,' said Maître Marguet, looking disturbed. ' I must confess that until I read this anonymous letter I had no idea at all . . . and indeed, even afterwards . . .'

' Well, don't let it worry you. Of course, it's very annoying. The people who started the rumour are certainly no friends of yours.'

Maître Marguet shrugged his shoulders. He seemed at once puzzled, grieved and angry. M. Alfan did his best to comfort him.

' It's very possible that it originated simply in a mistake of some kind. And even if it did cause a bit of a sensation at first, one only has to think twice to see how absurd it is. How much value can one attach to the testimony of a boy that age ? Even if he's convinced he's telling the truth, how likely is it that he would have remembered everything so clearly a week later? To say nothing of the very extraordinary chance that a child should have recognised you at that distance, and should have known which was the attic window. No, really, there's no need to take it seriously.'

'Perhaps not,' said Maître Marguet. 'But it seems to have been enough to convince my anonymous correspondent and my blackmailer.'

'One had reasons for wanting to believe you guilty, and the other's a maniac who used it as an outlet.'

'But even you yourself . . .'

'But I never believed a word of it! I assure you, not a word! . . . It simply led me to examine the theoretical possibility of your being guilty, which until then I'd scarcely considered. And I don't mind admitting that my conclusions weren't altogether favourable to you. I can see now that it was absurd, but until you called . . . Well, I started by having to admit that the thing was materially possible. It would have been easy enough for you to get away for ten minutes, without your staff knowing, and go up to the attic.'

'I should have been running a considerable risk,' said Maître Marguet. 'My clerks are liable to come into my room at any moment. Supposing a client had happened to call, or someone had rung up? They'd have found that I wasn't there.'

'Yes, I thought of all that. But I've got an account of your movements that afternoon. You gave it to me yourself. At about a quarter past four you went upstairs to the drawing-room and had a cup of tea with your wife and her friend Mme. Berton. After leaving them you could quite easily have slipped up into the attic before coming down again.'

Maître Marguet smiled amusedly and nodded his head in approval.

' So you see it was physically possible,' M. Alfan went on. ' But I really can't explain to you, now, how I came to think of it as psychologically possible. There was a sort of picture of you in my mind—a mixture of vague impressions, intimations, the recollection of small incidents—which began to dissolve the moment you entered this room. For example, I seemed to see in you a certain simplicity of heart which would have enabled you to put aside the sentimental scruples and other intellectual concepts that trouble the conscience of the ordinary murderer. I had, as it were, drawn a blueprint of your soul—a series of superimposed levels, all of which you yourself see clearly, but which have very little vertical communication between them . . . But all that is nonsense that doesn't explain anything. Really I don't understand how the idea ever entered my head ! Naturally there was no danger, because I should never have been able to convict you, but I'm embarrassed all the same. And when I think of the way I greeted you when you came in ! . . .'

The lawyer said that it was nothing. Then he said in a tactful voice, as though he feared to vex the magistrate :

' I don't attempt to explain how you came to suspect me. But I do know one thing—that you needed to suspect someone.'

' Why—what do you mean ? '

' Simply that you're no longer at all satisfied with the theory that Troussequin committed the murder.'

' To say that I'm not at all satisfied is to put it too strongly,' said M. Alfan. ' But I'm certainly less convinced of it than I was. And yet, no new fact has come to light to make me change my mind . . . You mustn't think that nerves or atmosphere have anything to do with it. It's simply that after a week's interval the facts look different. Take Troussequin's flight, for example. At the time that seemed to be the most significant thing of all—even more so than the look of the man, and his police record. Two days later, after his arrest, it already carried less weight because of his return, but I still had no difficulty in using it as an argument against him . . . But to-day—well, I'm afraid to do so. If one assumes Troussequin to be innocent, the fact of his going off on a bicycle, on a Saturday evening after finishing a day's work, becomes the most natural thing in the world. You may be surprised to hear it, but even his appearance weighs with me far less than it did. It would be much easier to suspect a good-looking, glossy-haired young man, because one would understand how he got up to the attic.'

'What it amounts to,' said the lawyer, ' is that you have no more case against Troussequin than you have against me.'

'Well, don't let us go too far. There is always Troussequin's police record. And then there's a fundamental difference which I should like to make you understand. If I felt angry with you, sitting here alone in this room, it was partly due to a sort of mental gymnastics—self-protection on the part of an examining magistrate. Why shouldn't I admit it ? Perhaps it was a kind of revenge.' M. Alfan smiled at the lawyer's look of astonishment. ' You see, I've been following in your footsteps. I have found myself inclining more and more towards your own theory of a murderer from outside. As a professional, it was slightly mortifying to me to feel that I was being put right by a layman, and now and then I've had a sort of defensive reaction, as I had just now. But in any case, I haven't waited until to-day to follow up that line of inquiry. I learned on Monday evening that Charlotte Richon was in the habit of going out with a young man on Sunday afternoons. Unfortunately he has a cast-iron alibi, and there seems to be nothing——'

But here the magistrate abruptly broke off and flung himself back in his chair. He was suddenly so excited that for a moment the lawyer feared the heat was affecting him, or that he was on the verge of an attack of apoplexy.

'No, it's nothing,' said M. Alfan. 'Forgive me . . . But I believe I've hit on the real murderer!—a sudden inspiration—I don't merely believe it, I'm certain of it! . . . I can't tell you anything at the moment—I mustn't—but——'

'Be careful!' stammered Maître Marguet, horrified by this sudden conviction. 'One can't be too careful in a case of this sort.'

'This time it isn't a matter of psychology,' said the magistrate in triumph. 'You'll see!'

He calmed down and apologised for his outburst of uncontrollable delight. The business had given him so much trouble that it was an immense relief to feel that he had reached the truth at last. Maître Marguet warned him again against jumping to conclusions, and reminded him of how convinced he had been of Troussequin's guilt. But then he began to be irked by his role of moderator, and to feel that he was being injudicious. There was a brief pause while M. Alfan seemed to be exploring his new idea.

'In spite of all that,' said the lawyer finally, 'I'm still in an unhappy position. I hoped you would be able to advise me——'

'You can enter a charge of defamation against some person unknown. Of course, its only effect will be to prove to your fellow-citizens that your conscience is clear. But if you care to wait until to-morrow, when the murderer will be arrested, you'll be able to triumph over all your ill-wishers without having condescended to answer them.'

Maître Marguet hastened his departure. The situation was making his friend, the magistrate, look so foolish that it exasperated him. At that moment he would have taken the same perverse pleasure in confessing his guilt that he felt on election days, when he secretly voted for the communist candidate. When he got out into the street it struck him that certain people looked rather fixedly at him. The thought that the rumour had spread to a large section of the public did not, however, cause him to be troubled by any sense of danger. There was, in any case, nothing hostile in the eyes that met his, nor did they show any alarm. Just before reaching Dr. Coinchot's surgery he was held up by one of his clients, who, although he had obviously heard the story, consulted him about a mortgage investment. The worthy man seemed at first slightly apprehensive, but the lawyer's quick grasp of the facts, the incisiveness of his comments, gradually dissipated the hint of misgiving in his eyes.

Dr. Coinchot had the same expression of embarrassment and hostility that Maître Marguet had seen on the face of M. Alfan, and he was deeply grieved by it, because he had always had a fondness for the doctor, and even a certain admiration for him. Coinchot was the first to hold out his hand. He gazed at him for some moments in silence, shrugging his shoulders.

'My poor old boy ! ' he said at length.

'What ? ' stammered the lawyer. ' So you've heard ! . . . And you—you really believe it ? '

'Believe it ? ' exclaimed Coinchot. ' But of course I do ! '

Being confronted by a murderer he adopted something of his hospital manner, as though he were dealing with one of the poor. Maître Marguet, shocked by his off-hand familiarity, turned his back on him and began to let down his trousers.

'In fact, it didn't really surprise me in the least,' the doctor went on. ' Last Saturday, when I heard the kind of crime that had been committed in your house, I thought at once that only you could have committed it. After that, of course, I let myself believe the same thing as everyone else, but now I rather wonder whether I ever really believed it.'

The lawyer made no comment, but stayed with his back to him, holding up his trousers.

'I warned you last year, if you remember, when your wife was ill. I asked you how it was that after twelve years of marriage . . . You gave me a lot of high-falutin' arguments; but reverence and adoration and all that sort of thing are no reason why . . . remember? . . . And I warned you that one could pay dearly for that sort of nonsense. But you paid no attention to me, did you?—and now you've done for yourself! There's nothing left for you to do but to give yourself up—in the first place, to save Troussequin, and secondly to make sure that you don't do it again!'

Maître Marguet looked round with a laugh, and said calmly:

'An excellent plan, my dear fellow; but the fact is that I haven't killed anyone. It seems that you'd be only too delighted to hand me over to the executioner, just for the pleasure of being right. I'd better say it plainly, even at the risk of disappointing you: not only did I not kill that girl, but the thought of doing so never entered my head. And even if I had the tendencies you credit me with, my courage would certainly have failed me at the crucial moment. I'm too afraid of my own death.'

He spoke with so much assurance that the doctor regretted what he had said and began to feel that he had been too hasty in jumping to conclusions. The story had come to him from his sister, who had heard it from the mayor's wife. Perhaps, after all, it had been nothing but a bit of garbled tea-time gossip.

'However,' said Maître Marguet, 'I'm rather glad you said it. In a way it's a comfort to me. So far I have seen no hint of reproach or indignation in the faces of the people who presumably have heard this story. The fact is that they look at me in the street with the same sort of indulgence that they might have for a charming but very naughty child. I was half-tempted to start skipping a little while ago. Doesn't it seem to you strange that the rumour of my infamous conduct should be received with so much tolerance ? I know, of course, that a lawyer, in a little town such as ours, is a large shareholder in the machinery of justice who has to be tactfully handled ; but still, I should have expected a hint of disapproval. Think of the reactions of the crowd at the end of the courtroom during the Artevel trial—those people had a passion for justice ! But I can discover no such enthusiasm in the people on a certain social level, the ones who take a pride in only working with one hand. I'm almost sorry not to be the criminal, for the sheer pleasure of occupying the position. Half my fellow-citizens would be my accomplices.'

'Don't flatter yourself ! ' growled Coinchot.

'I'll go even further. If I were convicted of murder all the doctors in this town would be unanimous in declaring that I was not responsible for my actions. I should be put in a mental home, and my honour would be unstained.'

Coinchot made no answer, but signed to him to let down his trousers.

'It hasn't healed yet,' he said, examining the ulcer on Maître Marguet's thigh, ' and yet I think it has improved a little. In fact, I'd say it was getting better. If only you'd let me treat you regularly I'd have got rid of it long ago. Incidentally, did you have it before you were married ? '

'I think so,' said the lawyer, blushing slightly. 'I think I had it already.'

EIGHTEEN

MAILLARD STOOD IN front of the mayor's desk, awaiting that gentleman's pleasure. Philippon was writing a letter which he extended unnecessarily to four pages, simply for the pleasure of making him wait, while he thought happily of the dressing down he was going to give him. For his part, Maillard was getting what revenge he could by telling himself that Philippon, although he might be the mayor of the town and a man of means and intelligence and all the rest of it, had a face like a calf's head, or like a man three days drowned, or like an English pig, or—not to be too hard on him—like a pair of boiled buttocks. Finally the mayor signed his letter, put it in an envelope and looked up.

' Oh, it's you, is it ? ' he said.

' Yes, it's me, Monsieur le Maire,' said the sergeant in a bright, affable voice which he thought charged with searing irony.

' Ah, yes ! And it seems that you're a great detective, and that you've just picked up a new scent ! '

It was Philippon's turn to be ironical, and Maillard could not keep it up. With knitted brows, he thrust his thumbs into his belt and rolled his shoulders, the better to contain himself. Philippon was delighted. He reflected that progress and civilisation were not meaningless words, after all. There he sat, faced by a colossus who would like nothing better than to eat him alive, but whose sense of order and human values kept him at a distance.

'So you've picked up a scent! You thought you'd be clever, and listen to the tittle-tattle in the Malleboine! You swallowed it whole, didn't you?—this story of a twelve-year-old boy who saw the murderer from the cathedral tower! . . . A superb detective!'

The sergeant's face was now scarlet, his eyes reddening, his breath coming faster. After a pause the mayor said softly:

'Tell me, Maillard, how much longer are you going to go on annoying me?'

'I beg your pardon, Monsieur le Maire?' said Maillard with a smile of disdain which came off admirably.

At this Philippon abandoned irony, and giving rein to his fury shouted at the top of his voice:

'I asked you if you're going on much longer! I don't like people to try and be clever with me, understand? You're a policeman, that's all you are, an ordinary policeman, and your job is to carry out orders, not to start being clever! I forbid you to have anything more to do with that affair. But, by God, I'd like to know what put it into your head to start holding forth at the police station about Maître Marguet being guilty!'

'But I never said anything of the kind,' protested Maillard. 'I simply repeated what I'd heard other people saying. I thought it my duty to do so.'

'Your duty! Your duty! I don't give a damn for your duty, understand?—all you've got to do is to shut your mouth! Even if you know the name of the murderer ten times over, kindly keep it to yourself, because I only know one murderer, and that's Troussequin! I don't want any others. Do you understand me? I don't want any other murderers!'

'I'm afraid I *don't* quite understand,' said Maillard. 'It's like the case of your relations . . .'

'What relations?'

'I mean the two trollops you're protecting.'

Maillard felt a glow of pure rapture, because it seemed that Philippon was on the verge of choking. Bereft of speech, he was opening and closing his mouth like a carp coming up for air. But although he racked his brains, the sergeant could not find the words to finish him off.

'Get out!' gasped Philippon. 'You'll be hearing from me!'

He pressed a bell on his desk, and repeated the order when an office boy appeared, although Maillard was already leaving the room.

'Get out, and be quick about it! Go on—get out!'

This savage dismissal, in the presence of a third party who had not heard the rest of the interview, was particularly humiliating. Maillard was so deflated by it that he left without being able to think of a reply, without even looking round. Once he was outside he bitterly regretted his lack of presence of mind. 'I ought to have punched him in the eye,' was his first thought. But he was soothed as he recalled the job he now had to attend to. The time was half-past three. He strolled for a little while along the Rue des Rencontres, and then went slowly in the direction of the school.

Only the previous afternoon, at a quarter to four, Buq, Antoine and Pucelet had left the others when they came out of school and gone off by themselves. From certain remarks they had exchanged in class it appeared that they had also spent Thursday afternoon together. It was a strange association, and one which no one would have thought possible three days earlier. When the others tried to question him, expecting to get the better of his simplicity, big Pucelet had merely replied, 'It's something terrific!' This was all they were able to get out of him. What was more, there

seemed to be a change in Pucelet. One no longer saw him
seated in class with his hands hidden under the table.
He used them sensibly for writing, or for playing
noughts and crosses at the back of his exercise book. He
had stopped making smutty jokes, and when he went to the
lavatory it was for the proper purpose. And finally, heroism
and friendship seemed to have lent his eyes an especial
glow, golden in the daylight, sea-blue in the shade. Buq and
Antoine were very fond of him.

The three friends passed Sergeant Maillard without
paying him any attention, and the sergeant heard Buq ask :

' You've got the camera, haven't you ? '

' Of course,' said Pucelet, pressing his hand against his
satchel. ' Can't you see the lump it makes ? '

The sergeant noted that one of the compartments of the
satchel was distended. ' A camera ! ' he thought. ' Better
and better ! ' . . . He let them get fifty yards ahead and
then followed them into the Rue Petit-Clairon. It was not
difficult to follow them because they were walking briskly,
never looking round. Maillard was a little ashamed to be
thus spying on three youngsters. He was tempted to go
ahead and wait for them down in the Malleboine, but he
was afraid that his presence there might arouse misgivings.

At the Rond-Point he had a shock. Instead of going down
the stairway, the three boys went into Buquanant's shop.
Maillard sat on a bench, half-hidden behind the trunk of a
lime tree, and kept unhopeful watch. But his spirits rose
when ten minutes later he saw them come out again, each
with a large slice of bread and butter. They had got rid of
their satchels, and Pucelet now carried his camera slung from
his shoulder. Mme. Buquanant stood in the doorway watching them go with a smile that touched the sergeant's heart.
Leaving the bench, he went and sat on the wall of the Rond-
Point. Down in the Rue de la Clé-d'Or he could see the

boys walking fast; they crossed the Carrefour des Cinq and entered the Rue des Oiseaux. Maillard went down the big stairway and saw them turn into the Impasse de la Sourdine. His suspicions confirmed, he took time to roll a cigarette, which he placed behind his ear.

Then, without hurrying, he strolled down the blind alley. The house had no window on that side, so no one could see him coming. Before knocking he stood listening at the door, and heard sounds of talk and laughter. It was Marion who called to him to come in.

His first feeling was one of surprise at the tidiness and cleanness of the room, but he was in no mood to pay compliments. Buq and Antoine were out on the platform finishing their bread and butter and looking at three tubs floating on the water at their feet, one of which was adorned with a skull and crossbones. They were waiting for the return of Trésor, who had heard of a fourth tub that he could borrow. Pucelet was still in the room, in the act of putting his camera on a chair while he asked the sisters whether Trésor had managed to attend to certain details of great moment to the expedition. The sergeant at once sent him to join his friends on the platform, and closed the glass-paned door behind them.

'Now,' he said to the sisters, who were regarding him with startled eyes, 'if you want my advice you'll confess at once.'

'Confess what?' asked Minie, although she already understood.

'Don't let's have any nonsense. Come on—I'm in a hurry! . . . No? You aren't going to? So much the worse for you!'

Despite their protests and abuse he turned them out on to the platform and brought in the three boys. He stood with his back against the door to prevent the sisters returning.

Buq, in a furious rage, was glaring in a way which showed that he was not afraid. He had no idea what Maillard suspected. But Antoine had a presentiment. He knew very well that his father would never have allowed him to visit Tetère's daughters, and he supposed that in this matter, as in so many others, his views were those of the police. In spite of this, however, he looked innocent enough. But Maillard at once noted signs of alarm in Pucelet, whose hands were trembling slightly, and it was he whom he sought to intimidate.

'Well, they've told me everything!' he said. 'A fine story! What do you think your families would say? The question is—have I got to tell them?'

There was no reply. Buq glanced at Antoine, shrugging his shoulders to say that he did not understand.

'I'd much sooner not say anything to your parents,' said Maillard, 'and I hope I can arrange matters with the police commissioner so as to prevent the story getting into the newspapers. But only on one condition—that you tell me exactly what has happened.'

He made a gesture inviting Pucelet to begin, but the terrified boy merely rolled his eyes without speaking. He tried to help him.

'Well, now, let's see—when did you first come here?'

'On Wednesday after school,' said Antoine.

'Never before? You're sure? Well, if you say so I believe you, because I can see you're telling the truth. And that first time, how long did you stay? . . . Only a quarter of an hour? That wasn't very long . . . But perhaps you don't exactly remember . . . Well, and what did they do to you?'

The three boys looked in bewilderment at one another, and then Buq suddenly grasped the meaning of the question. It seemed to him so comical that he burst out laughing and took a whole minute to recover. Then he bent towards his friends and explained matters in a whisper. Pucelet seemed at once to forget his alarm and grinned broadly. They were all looking amiably at Maillard, flattered that he should have thought them worthy of such suspicions. It began to dawn on the sergeant that he had gone astray.

'You don't understand,' said Buq. 'You don't understand a bit ! . . .' He was again convulsed with laughter, and then said : 'We come here because the platform's handy for going to the underground passage.'

'The underground passage ? ' murmured Maillard.

They explained what they were doing, but without saying anything about their plans for penetrating the wire grill.

Looking through the glass pane of the door, Maillard could see the ships at anchor. The truth of what they said could hardly be doubted. He stared glumly down, past the angry faces of Minie and Marion, at the clear waters of the Sourdine bathing the foot of the Upper Town. He was having a bad day. He had been so happy in the prospect of pinching Philippon's protégées on a squalid charge of corrupting minors that it was hard to have to give it up. But then, as he turned back to the boys, it struck him that Pucelet was trying to edge close to his camera without being noticed. He pretended to look elsewhere. Standing motionless, with his eyes half closed, he seemed to be listening.

'It's the mill,' Buq said to him.

'Oh, I see—the mill,' murmured the sergeant.

Pucelet had drawn a step nearer to his camera. Without taking his eyes off Maillard, he reached out his arm and grasped the strap. When he had it in his hand Maillard looked round and said :

'That must be very interesting, what you've got there. I'd like to have a look. May I ? '

He held out his hand, still with his back against the door,

looking fixedly at the unhappy Pucelet, who had turned pale.

' It's his camera,' said Buq. ' He can do what he likes with it.'

Pucelet clutched the leather case to him, and seemed on the verge of flight.

' If you don't mind ! . . .' said Maillard, his voice growing sharper.

' There are things in it that aren't mine,' stammered Pucelet. ' I can't . . .'

Maillard snapped his fingers, bent forward and caught the hanging strap. Pucelet let it go, and turning to his friends began to sob. Buq and Antoine, not knowing the reason for his despair, were at a loss to console him. Maillard pulled the camera out of its case and found nothing remarkable about it, except that it was an old model in very bad condition. But when he held the case upside down he brought to light an unsealed envelope from which a photograph emerged.

' Ah—just what I thought ! ' he said at a first glance.

But then, when he looked at it more closely, he started and began to swear. Buq and Antoine looked curiously at him, while Pucelet turned his back on him, still sobbing. Leaving the glass-paned door, Maillard went and sat on a chair. Minie and Marion at once came into the room, exclaiming loudly at the way they had been treated. Trésor came in by the front door at the same moment, rolling a wash-tub. They started to tell him what had happened, but the sergeant shouted to everyone to shut up. He was flushed and excited. The envelope he was examining was stamped and addressed to Maître Marguet, 11 Rue Jacques-de-Molay. He made no bones about reading the accompanying letter. It bore that day's date, Pucelet having written it at lunch-time while his father was taking a wedding group at the town's principal restaurant.

'Dear Sir,

'You remember I said one of the photographs was completely blacked out. I must have been mistaken because I have found this negative and I am sending it to you with three prints. I did not keep it on purpose, and I hope you will not beleive . . .'

'Why didn't you finish this letter?'

'Because I wasn't sure how to spell "believe",' said Pucelet blushing.

Maillard raised his eyes to gaze with respect at a boy who could be so meticulous.

'So you've been developing photographs for Maître Marguet?'

'It's the only time.'

'And when did he give them to you, and where? Come on—let's have it!'

Pucelet blushed again, wept, sniffed, cleared his throat and described how, when he had been out in the meadows doing nothing in particular, Maître Marguet had asked him to develop a roll of films in return for payment.

'He said the examining magistrate asked him to take them because he wanted them for his collection.'

Putting the letter and photographs in his pocket, Maillard left the Impasse de la Sourdine and hurried to the examining magistrate. He was thinking with enjoyment of Philippon's countenance when he heard the news of an arrest which he seemed to fear more than anything else in the world. M. Alfan, when he first mentioned the name of Maître Marguet, did not even want to listen. The sergeant laid the prints before him, then the letter, and finally the envelope bearing the lawyer's name and address.

'Well, yes . . .' said the examining magistrate with a sigh. 'This photograph could only have been taken by the criminal. There was no possibility after the crime was discovered, and besides, the body was removed at ten that evening. What a pity ! I was on the track of a most promising suspect. I should probably have had him arrested later to-day.'

' So Maître Marguet was right when he said Trousseequin was innocent,' observed the sergeant.

' Yes . . . He was certainly in a position to know. One must admit that it was a clever move.'

' But it was decent of him, all the same.'

The magistrate asked Maillard to go back to the Malleboine and fetch young Pucelet, so that he and the lawyer might be confronted. Then he picked up the telephone receiver.

' Hullo ! . . . I should like to speak to Maître Marguet . . . Maître Marguet ? I have a question to ask you. If I have been correctly informed, you were out in the meadows at five o'clock on Monday afternoon ? '

' Yes, I was.'

' And you gave a boy called Pucelet a roll of film to develop ? '

The lawyer did not reply.

' We have found one of the eight exposures in the boy's possession—the one which he told you was blacked out. He seems to have made a mistake. It has come out admirably, and the three prints he made from it are perfectly clear. It's a full-length picture of the body.'

There was a silence. When at length Maître Marguet spoke his voice was a little husky.

' I shall not deny anything,' he said. ' I'm very grateful to you for ringing me up—although, to be frank, I've no wish to commit suicide, none at all . . . But you mustn't think, on the other hand, that I'm one of those poor creatures who cling to life like the animals. I love life only when it's good, and I have great hopes of the future life that awaits me. Since you are being so kind as to listen, perhaps you would be good enough to inform Dr. Coinchot and to ask him to break the news to my wife and mother. I shouldn't have the strength to do it myself—in particular, not to my mother. My wife is with her at this moment, if you would be so good as to make that clear to Dr. Coinchot. I shall not venture to thank you any more, in case I should seem indiscreet. Good-bye, Monsieur.'

M. Alfan hung up, and sat for five minutes with his chin on his hand thinking about the criminal. Not all his efforts could make Maître Marguet appear a monster in his eyes. Indeed, he was not finally repelled even by the thought that he still felt friendly towards him—rather the opposite. Unfortunately a friendship that cannot be avowed is without value, and M. Alfan could not see himself publicly proclaiming, 'I have a dear friend who committed a revolting crime and is in prison for twenty years.' He was rather ashamed of this weakness. He tried not to think of it any more, and thought instead of poor Troussequin's rapture at his release, but without much enthusiasm . . .

Maillard felt wonderfully light as he went down the big stairway. He had many reasons for happiness, but at that moment he could think of only one—Philippon's fury when he heard the news, and his possible alarm, because his attitude had been more than doubtful. But suddenly he forgot Philippon and the joys of revenge. As he passed the spot where he and Troussequin had fought together, in the Rue de la Clé-d'Or, he thought affectionately of the prisoner, seeming still to feel on his face the gusts of his despairing breath. He felt a lump in his throat, and his heart swelled beneath his tunic.

'You know,' he said to a group of people in the street, 'Troussequin will be free before to-morrow.'

The news spread quickly, and brought the women down into the street.

'They're going to let Troussequin go! Maillard says so! . . .'

And Maillard, he went quietly along the streets of the Malleboine, with his hands hanging idle and friendly at his sides. He thought that he loved no one in the world as he loved Troussequin. He nodded his head to the people as he passed, and his eyes seemed to be saying, 'If ever you go to prison, don't worry, I shall be there.' The children ran up to touch the buttons of his uniform, and a friendly murmur sounded behind him—'Maillard! Maillard! . . .' And the people of the Malleboine, leaning out of their windows, or standing on tip-toe, or running to look a little longer, saw the sergeant's heart swelling the stuff of his tunic.

'Where are you going, good sergeant?' asked the people passing by. 'Where are you going with your shoulders?'

'I'm going,' said Maillard's eye, 'I'm going to see my two friends on the Sourdine.'

'But, sergeant—sergeant—what about Artevel's son?'

'I have all the keys, so don't be frightened.'

He found Minie and Marion on the wooden platform, and leaned over them to smile at each in turn. On the waters of the Sourdine was a flotilla of four stout tubs, beflagged and boldly manned, proceeding to the end of the creek. Maillard waved to Pucelet to tell him that all was well and that he need not worry. The magistrate could wait. As if he was going to disturb him at such a moment! . . .

Trésor was at the head of the flotilla, with Buq and Antoine behind him. Half-way to the subterranean passage he paused and said, turning to the others:

'Watch what I'm going to do!'

And he did such wonderful things with his tongue, his nose and his ears that Maillard's great laugh echoed late into the evening.